Room to Grow

Room to Grow

Elizabeth Dale's 1963 Journal

By Vera Halls

Copyright © 2022 Vera Halls

The moral right of the author has been asserted.

Apart from any fair dealing for the purposes of research or private study, or criticism or review, as permitted under the Copyright, Designs and Patents Act 1988, this publication may only be reproduced, stored or transmitted, in any form or by any means, with the prior permission in writing of the publishers, or in the case of reprographic reproduction in accordance with the terms of licences issued by the Copyright Licensing Agency. Enquiries concerning reproduction outside those terms should be sent to the publishers.

This is a work of fiction. Names, characters, businesses, places, events and incidents are either the products of the author's imagination or used in a fictitious manner. Any resemblance to actual persons, living or dead, or actual events is purely coincidental.

Matador
Unit E2 Airfield Business Park,
Harrison Road, Market Harborough,
Leicestershire. LE16 7UL
Tel: 0116 2792299
Email: books@troubador.co.uk
Web: www.troubador.co.uk/matador
Twitter: @matadorbooks

ISBN 978 1803132 884

British Library Cataloguing in Publication Data.
A catalogue record for this book is available from the British Library.

Printed and bound in the UK by TJ Books LTD, Padstow, Cornwall
Typeset in 11pt Adobe Jenson Pro by Troubador Publishing Ltd, Leicester, UK

Matador is an imprint of Troubador Publishing Ltd

To my sister Maria

INTRODUCTION

This is the story of Lizzie Dale at seventeen, then eighteen years old, covering the calendar year of 1963. Leaving the parental home she believes she will have the time of her life. Despite the privations of early sixties bedsitter squalor her expectations are optimistic and she resolves to record an exciting new life. Lizzie never completely breaks with her family who later face a trauma.

In Part One we see Lizzie working in low paid employment in a North of England food factory. The coldest winter since 1948 strains her meagre budget, but she copes by devious means. Nor does the overbearing landlady, 'The Dragon', dampen her spirit at first. Fellow bedsitter tenants provide rewarding friendships. Each have surprising stories.

But things begin to change. Her friends are making opposite sex partnerships leaving her lonely. She longs for love but it is not forthcoming. The beginnings of a more liberal era of sexuality leaves her feeling behind the times as she waits, and waits.

Until in April. In Part Two, she meets her man at last; Colin, ten years older, smart, good looking and attentive. She is truly smitten as he offers love and many enjoyable experiences. But there are undercurrents of serious future outcomes that she must learn about, manage and sadly accept. He is not what he seems and although Lizzie is committed she is floundering into danger.

In Part Three, Lizzie has come to terms with her situation realising her only escape is to become emotionally and financially independent. She takes progressive steps towards this aim despite a duality of feelings for this man who has hurt her. She has learned how to look after number one, and it has changed her into a stronger person. She has had room to grow.

This story is set in the 'Sixties,' usually remembered for showy psychodelics. But 1963 wasn't quite there yet. It was before the Beatles had long hair, Afghan coats and Gurus, before trousers flared to fanciful angles and youth looked as if it was going to a fancy dress ball. Post war greyness was still clinging on as Lizzie's story begins.

PART ONE
INDEPENDENCE

SATURDAY 5TH JAN

Why, oh why are they so…so….last generational fuddy duddies! Why so strict about nothing? Just because I stayed out all New Year's Eve night with a boy they didn't like in his parents' cellar! What do they think happened! I am not a child anymore. I didn't nearly set the bedroom alight with a cigarette; it was only a small burn on the bedside table so why all the fuss? Everyone smokes now. And the unrealistic curfew time! Time I left.

Suddenly, at seventeen, with two brown paper carrier bags of belongings, a good dose of teenage optimism and naiveté, I'd left home with £2.2.6d to my name! I'd looked all week at unaffordable pricey bedsitters. Then this one turned up.

MONDAY. 7TH JAN

Single bedsit to let.
£2.2.6d per week plus gas and electricity.
No pets. No children.
Apply within for address.

This would be such great fun! Oh the freedom and independence!
I do hope I get it, and if I do – I'm going to journal my whole new
life.

TUESDAY 8TH JAN

Found the house, secured the room – all in twenty-four hours!
The landlady is fat with a crumpled face like my old headmistress.
The bedsitter? Dark and scruffy but I can move in tomorrow if
I like. I'm so excited.

It was a large, three-storey Victorian house, probably last
painted by Victorians by the look of it too. Drab, tired, with a
broken-down fire escape leaning at an odd angle from the top
floor, one hand-rail dangling uselessly, a definite fire trap. You
could be stuck on that with nothing substantial to hold, just a
slanting little grid to stand on. I rang the bell.

'Yes?' A skinny middle-aged man, yellowed teeth, Brylcreamed
hair opens the door, cigarette between fingers. His tweed jacket
with patched elbows and brown cord trousers looked like they
were someone else's, too short for his arms and legs. His eyes

travel from my face to my feet, and up and down again. 'Yes?' he repeats.

'Er,... I've come about the bedsitter. The one in the newagent's window.'

'Yes?' The eyes travel down again stopping a few seconds at knee level, then back up again.

'Are you looking for something, on your own... just for you?' he asks. He looks surprised, ill at ease – as if it was unexpected.

'Yes. It was a single room wasn't it?'

'Yeah but...I don't know...Wait a mo. I'll have to get the wife.' He smiles showing his uneven teeth, looks me up and down again and disappears. Is there something wrong with me? Ladders in my stockings? Seams not straight? Shoes dirty? Or do I look too young to rent a room?

A solid looking woman appears, large, with a grumpy flushed face and hair squashed into a hair net. She eyes me suspiciously, arms folded.

'How old are you?' she demands loudly.

'Eighteen.' I lie.

'Hmmph. Are you now.' She scowls. 'Well you don't look it. You're after the bedsitter I believe...well...I don't know if you'd be suitable, I wanted someone a bit older really, but I suppose I could show it you. No-one else has applied.'

I can tell she's not a bag of sunbeams, more dragon like, and nineteen sixty-three is the Chinese 'Year of the Dragon.' I imagine a flaming tongue forking from her mouth, grabbing tenants by the neck and dashing their heads against the wall. She's solid, a formidable combination of my ex headmistress and Ena Sharples – from that programme, Coronation Street. The hair flattening hair net doesn't improve her features either – and that frown!

She's paused. Oh dear; perhaps she's changing her mind. I do hope not. I'm desparate. I want this room. No…no… I think she's thinking it over.

'Umm, not sure about her,' she's thinking. 'She does look a bit young. We've had problems with young ones before…. like that last one. Men visiting at all hours – then disappearing off without telling anyone… police thinking we had something to do with it too. But …on the other hand perhaps no-one else will want it – it really needs decorating but I really need to let it. We need the rent.'

'So, I'm Mrs Bryson,' she suddenly continues. 'I'm the landlady here. Me and me husband, Mr Bryson own this house. We live on the premises so we can take care of things. Know what I mean? You'll be quite safe here. What's your name?'

'Elizabeth. Elizabeth Dale.'

'Are you sure you're eighteen?' she looks searchingly at me.

'Yes,' I lie again.

'Well I don't want no trouble. Know what I mean?'

I don't really. 'Trouble' for girls usually means pregnancy, but I nod in agreement.

'Well, I suppose I could show you. Won't harm. Come in. Follow me. I'll show you the flat – and wipe yer feet.' She called it a flat which makes it sound bigger. It wasn't.

So, I followed her across a dingy linoleum floor, up some stairs and past one, two, bedsitters crudely numbered in white paint. There was another flight of stairs but she'd stopped at the third

INDEPENDENCE

door, sorting through a large bunch of keys. A nice looking fair haired lad appeared, nodded at her, smiled at me and went downstairs and out.

'This is the one,' she announces opening the door. Inside it's brown, everything dark brown, furniture, carpet, brown plaited light flexes and door. More fifties than sixties. Faded floral curtains hang at a window; a hook missing at one end. It smells of gas and previous occupants. Those shabby rooms in Sheila Delaney's 'A Taste of Honey?' Yes just like that. Could I live in it? Well... if I wanted independence. I'd have to. It's all I could afford.

A bed, with grubby looking bedding, a rickety chest of drawers and a wardrobe took up the 'bedroom' end with a two-ringed gas cooker perched on a cupboard at the 'kitchen' end. A tall, pale green, kitchen cupboard with a pull down door you could use as a table had been modern some years ago. The worn coconut matting in the kitchen area looked shiny with grease.

'It's fully furnished and there's hot and cold 'ere' she continues as if it's a luxury, and pointing to a square, porcelain sink with a wooden drainer.

'And you can keep your food in this cupboard. Don't leave any out though. We've had mice in 'ere. And you'll have to pay regular like,' she continues. 'Every Friday on the dot... and two weeks in advance for the first payment. If you want to move in tomorrow you can start paying from Friday, then Friday every week, no exceptions or late payments. Are you working?' she suddenly asks. 'I don't want no-one on National Assistance or the dole. Lazing in bed all day while everyone else is working, then they can't pay the rent. That's what they do y'know!'

'Oh yes, yes, I'm working… at a bakery…a cake factory in Old Trafford.' I hoped I could afford it on my paltry wages. They were to rise when I was eighteen… but that was months away. I'd have to be extremely frugal.

'Yer electric meter's 'ere.'

She points to a chunky black metal box bracketed to the wall.

'And 'ere's the gas meter for the cooker. Make sure you turn the gas off when you go out. The last tenant nearly blew the house up. And I don't want none of them foreign coins neither. All this holidaying in Spain and fancy places these days, bringing back all that funny money. Only English shillings.'

'I'll only use English ones,' I promise. Foreign holidays? I'll be lucky to afford food.

'What about the bathroom?'

'Shared with two others, further down this landing. There's a gas geyser. Take your turn with baths mind and don't use anyone elses hot water.'

'How would I know which is someone else's hot water?' I'm not trying to be funny.

'Just use your common sense.'

I don't want to look as if I haven't any, so I say nothing.

'Yes..well …I'll take it then… please. It's fine for me, if that's OK with you.' She nods in assent.

'And there's a pay phone in the hall – but don't be talking on it after ten o'clock.'

She takes five, single green patterned pound notes from me, hands me a ten shilling note and five shillings in change and a Yale key.

'And mind you don't go losin' it. Keys is expensive. Oh – and me husband'll see to you if anything goes wrong.'

What? That thin staring man who'd stood in the hall. I hoped nothing ever would. I wouldn't want to be seen to by him.

The Landlady is looking thoughtful again.

'Maybe I shouldn't have,' she thinks. 'I shouldn't have youngsters here but he's not bringing in much money now he's on the sick. At least she's working…. in a proper job. The trouble I had with that unemployed one. Lazy sod. Then he gets into arrears! Well I'm not being that soft again with anyone never again.'

WEDNESDAY 9TH JAN

Moved in! I'm a bit wary of the landlady. She appeared from the door of her ground floor flat as I was carrying things through the front door. She'd heard it open and noticed my bags.

'You've not got one of them gramophones …record players whatever they call them now?' she asks eyeing the carrier bags.

'No. No. Just my clothes and things. I'll be very quiet.'

I don't mention the transistor radio beginning to poke its aerial through the paper carrier bag. It's a treasured possession.

'Good because I don't allow no loud noise.'

She's not going to stop me listening to it, but I'd better tune in quietly.

So, I dumped my belongings onto the bed, found a whistling top kettle and tried to fathom out how to work the two-ringed gas cooker that's perched on top of a cupboard. Hardly a cooker. The gas rings hissed and emitted an unpleasant smell when I clunked in a shilling so I turned off the taps and fed the electric meter. Both glowing red elements of an electric fire came on. I switched on a light, a bare bulb over the tiny kitchen area.

I sat warming my hands on the fire enjoying the heat and trying to warm up the chilled room. I found a tea caddy containing damp tea and a cracked brown teapot but had no milk so I couldn't even make a cup of tea. But it was evening. I'd do the shopping tomorrow and go to the pub tonight with my friend Janet, both of us under age with hardly any money.

The Kings' was crowded with men and local boys. 'Please Please Me,' played from a speaker. The Beatles are on their way up now with mop cut Beatle look-alikes everywhere. Janet has a new hair do, short layers combed forward like last year's fashion of trying to look like Helen Shapiro.

'Hey Janet. Love your hair.' I pat her head. 'Suits you short.'

'Yeah. Good isn't it. Dead easy. Wash it, let it it dry, go out the same evening!'

'Wow…takes the whole evening to do mine.'

'Like that advert – 'Friday night is Amami night,' she mimics. All night just to wash your hair! No thanks. Get yours done like mine. Joan from our school did it. She's qualified now and she'll do yours too if you want.'

'Yes, yes, maybe, but listen, I've got loads to tell you.'

I tell her about the bedsit, the leaving home, the freedom. She's impressed and agog with possibilities.

'Oh Lizzie! You've done it! What's it like? Where is it? How much is the rent?'

I don't get chance to answer. She continues, 'Oh my God – won't we have some fun in your flat! Think of the parties. We could invite everyone. I could bring my boyfriend and we could stay overnight and he could bring his guitar and…'

'Wait! It's not exactly a flat,' I interrupt. 'It's just one room with a sort of kitchen end. I don't think many could fit in, but maybe, sometimes, just a very small few of us.'

'Yes, we could buy drinks… play records.' Her imagination riots on; painting the room in bright colours, sewing up nice curtains, putting up posters up of Liverpool bands, listening to Radio Luxembourg …

A few others we know join our table and conversation. They offer round cigarettes and we sit in a haze of smoke.

'What were you saying? Where did you say this house was?' asks Noel, a jokey lad we'd gone to school with. He grins broadly as he delivers some salacious information.

'That's where that girl lived – the one who was y'know – on the game. The sixteen-year-old with her older pimp. She ran off from him – had everyone looking for her – police and everything.'

What girl? What's he talking about? I look blankly at him.

'Everyone knew about it. It was in the paper,' he continues. 'She lived in one of the attic rooms.'

Phew, I think. Not my room. I wouldn't want to sleep there if it had been.

'My cousin had a flat there once,' another buts in. 'The landlady's bonkers and her husband's a bit of a lech. Watch yourself going upstairs. He'll be looking up your skirt!' Everyone laughs except me.

'And the electric meter's set at about a pound a minute and they lock the door at half eleven. You ring the bell and she starts shouting,' he says enjoying the effect. 'And there's mice in ….'

'Oh just shut-up.' Janet orders. Don't take any notice of them, Lizzie. They're just trying to put you off – and that girl… it was ages ago. It won't be like that now.'

I try not to to be put off, but I think about the girl. I think about the bedsitter. I know it's a dump but it's the best I can do for now. I could always change my mind. Was it so bad at home? But no, NO! I'm going to do it. I need independence. I don't want parents governing my life. They're good people but they've no idea how it is now! When they were teenagers there was a war on. There wasn't even a word for teenagers then. They didn't even dress differently. My generation is going to be so different.

Janet's boyfriend arrives greeted by Noel.

'Hey Andy! That team of yours was bloody rubbish on Saturday.'

'Oh yeah, what about yours! Your goalie couldn't catch a cold – and has your referee gone to the opticians yet?'

The banter continues. I join in and we girls giggle over our Babychams, one each to last us all night. I'd not had anything to eat so we bought chips on the way home. It had snowed while we were in the pub – like it had done every day since December.

I walked home alone and crept up the front steps at 10.55 clutching them. Net curtains moved as I arrived. Who is it? Is it her? Or him? Who cares, I can come and go whenever I like and I'm being quiet so they can't complain. I creep into my first floor room and press the light switch. Nothing. No electric and I only have tomorrow's bus fare in my purse.

I ate the chips in the dark and got into bed fully clothed. I'll be sleeping alone now. I think about my sister and the bedroom we shared. We used to swing a long corded light switch with a hard blob on the end to and fro when we were in our side by side beds, hitting the wall sometimes, click clack, click clack until we got yelled at. We argued sometimes but had a sisterly bond and I miss her. But that's the past and tomorrow's pay day.

FRIDAY 11TH JAN

Its great living alone but I've got to make these wages last the whole week! I'm buying my cigs in fives and trying to make them last.

Evening: Stayed in. Unpacked a few things. They look strange, as if they don't belong in this room. I'd worried I'd not wake this morning but the alarm clock worked fine. I woke up confused.

What? ...Where am I? The feeble tinny rattle of my wind-up alarm clock rang out from its biscuit tin amplifier. I'd wound its little wing nut as tight as possible the previous night, and hoped for the best. It had an annoyingly, rhythmic 'tick-tock' and its cheap little face was illuminated by a shiny sort of paint making it shine reasurringly in the night. Someone told me the paint was radioactive but I'm don't know what that means.

But such a rush. I get up quickly. No time to wait for the whistling kettle, and damn it; someone's beaten me to the bathroom. I'm bursting. Surely they're coming out now. What are they doing in there? Did I hear the toilet just flush? Wasn't that water gurgling down the drain? I peer round my door to see someone else there. A queue! Quick – to the upper floor, there's another bathroom there – someone else's. I leap up the stairs. Yes. No-one in it thankfully! Then quick – back to my room for a cold water wash.

I look round once more at the tatty floral curtains, the worn brown carpet and notice the chill of the room, but no time to think now. I need to get to the factory. Outside there's snow on the ground – again! It's either snowing, has been snowing or going to snow these days.

SATURDAY 12TH JAN

My first Saturday of independence! Did a Saturday morning overtime packing batches of Cherry Genoa. Time and a half – so good money next week! My supervisor said I looked tired and winked at me. He thinks I have a better social life than I do and have a boyfriend keeping me warm at night. I should be so lucky! I need to clean this bedsitter to get rid of the previous tenant's smell. It's like having a chain smoking ghost living with you.

Evening: went to the Gaumont with Janet and her boyfriend, Andy, to see *The Brides of Dracula*. Glad to have him walk us both home in the dark! God it's so cold! The weather is bleak. So is my love life. I haven't got one. Janet has one. All my friends have one. I badly need one. I'm going to be on the shelf at this rate.

INDEPENDENCE

It was the raison d'etre for us girls. It was 1963 and I was a virgin. No-one else I knew was! I wasn't keeping up with things and beginning to feel like a freak. How come everyone is in a relationship except me? I'm a wallflower, a gooseberry, a shy loner. I vow to lose my virginity before I am eighteen, but I've no idea how to go about it. Finger wagging from another generation warns, 'Don't be too easy, don't get into trouble,' only applicable to females of course. Males can be as easy as they like and don't get pregnant.

It's a yes, no, yes, no wobbling ambivalence, but the yes bit is winning and I want to be part of it. With someone special. All my friends are doing it. Their boyfriends don't seem to mind if they're generous with their favours and there've been no pregnancies so far. It's just older generation sour grapes.

SUNDAY 13TH JAN

Slept in until 11.30. It snowed a lot this week. In fact it's hardly stopped this year. Shops close on Sundays but plenty of eggs and baked beans in. Walked round to Janet's but guess what, Andy, her boyfriend was there. He's always there. Felt a gooseberry so left and went for a walk on my own. Well a trudge in about six inches of snow!
Chaos when I got back! A tenant had not paid his rent or been seen for a fortnight causing Mrs Bryson to enter his room abuzz and humming with bluebottles. They must be feeding on his body she thinks! It may have been there weeks!
'Call the police!' she shouts slamming the door shut in panic leaving the keys inside so Mr Bryson cannot be of any use.

He heaves his scrawny body against the door to no avail. Mrs Bryson is dialing 999 with trembly fingers. 'POLICE,' she shouts breathlessly. Mr Bryson tries to grab the phone which drops and dangles from its cord. She grabs it back and gabbles the address to a calm operator trying to understand the situation.

Two constables in a dual-coloured Ford Cortina police car quickly arrive. It's white top and bottom with a red middle like a jam sandwich. Another key turns up so one of them tentatively enters and finds bowls of cereal in congealed milk, remains of mouldering food floating in greasy water and some maggot infected meat. Some kitchen equipment and a lamp is missing, but there is no rotting corpse. He asks questions about this habitual flitter already known to them who rents and runs, and sells anything he's pinched in local pubs. Well he wouldn't get much for his booty from here.

MONDAY 14TH JAN

France's President, Charles De Galle, has vetoed our entry into the Commonmarket. It keeps coming on my radio news and everyone is talking about it, even some of my workmates. I don't know much about it or why it matters, so I haven't taken much notice, but a lot of people seem very upset by it.

TUESDAY 15THJAN

Work: Extremely busy. Extra orders so overtime workers needed until eight o'clock. I volunteered as it's time and a half. Tired.

Had a luke warm bath. Someone had used my hot water and left a tidemark round the bath! Went to bed early. I wish I had a TV like the woman upstairs. She must like Westerns as I sometimes hear cowboy gunfights – but I don't mind. She's a very quiet person really. She reads a lot too and has lent me a book called *Cold Comfort Farm*, which I don't like.

I read this book on a simple level featuring miserable grumpy people being horrid to the main character, Flora, and feeling sorry for her and wondering why anyone would want to write such rubbish. Irony, or satirising of style or people hasn't entered my reading experience yet. Everything is literal, I am seventeen, everything is black or white and, if I ever read one at all, I choose a tabloid newspaper which has nice unnuanced phraseology and dramatic stories.

But I enjoy reading – even on this level. It's my substitute love life although I'd give it up in a heartbeat for a lover. Next comes Ian Fleming's *Dr No* – a best seller, to be a film success soon. It'll be my Saturday night companion as there won't be any better offers.

SATURDAY 19TH JAN

The Brysons didn't waste time letting that bloke's room out! Lots of cleaning noises all day and a heap of dirty curtains dumped by the dustbin. A girl moved into it yesterday called Brenda. She's eighteen. I've not to tell anyone she's here. I don't know why and didn't like to ask. It's about some ex boyfriend. She wears stiletto heels, has her hair in a chignon and smokes menthol cigarettes. She works at 'Television House.'

Brenda became a friend. 'Television House' suggested TV or recording studios, or if she was part of a production team – or something more interesting than a shorthand typist in a company no one had heard of, but was the name of a building. She had an air of sophistication but was warm and friendly and and we soon bonded. Before long I'd copied her menthol cigarette habit and started to grow my hair so I could have a trendy chignon like hers. So chic, so French.

MONDAY 21ST JAN

Chatted to Brenda today. We left for work at the same time and walked to our bus-stops. You can tell Manchester office workers from those going to Trafford Park by their clothes. They're smarter and start a bit later but Brenda doesn't. She can start and finish late as long as she gets the work done and when she takes off her thick coat she looks the very efficient secretary in her navy blue two piece and clean white blouse. She left school at fifteen then did a shorthand typist course but I didn't like to ask about the bloke she's avoiding. I'll get to know her a bit first.

'Well if you're not going out much this week come up one evening,' she says as our paths divert and she joins the city workers. 'We can play some records – I've got a record player.'

That's a good idea I think. Not going out much? I'm not going out at all! She waves to me as she makes her way onto the Manchester bus. She'll go to the top deck to have one of her menthol cigarettes I expect.

INDEPENDENCE

WEDNESDAY 23ʳᵈ JAN

I met the lad I'd first seen here. Bobby his name is, but he doesn't mind Bob either. We met at the front door by the payphone. He is slim with fair wispy hair and he invited me for a cup of tea and a chat which was so nice of him. I learned about some of the other tenants here, but Janet rang just as it was getting interesting, damn her!

'Thanks,' Bobby says as I help him pick up pennies he'd dropped by the payphone. 'I'm Bobby by the way. You're in the next room to me. I've seen you around.'

'Oh hi. I'm Lizzie. I've seen you too. I've heard your music. That's not a complaint,' I hurriedly add. 'I like it. Tell me…Is the landlady always so …' I can't think of a suitable word. 'Bossy?'

'Fraid so,' he answers. 'Very nosey too. Be careful. But don't let her bother you. And have you met Frank, the bloke upstairs yet?'

'No. I thought he'd run off without paying the rent.'

'No. That was another one. There are three rooms up there. He was in the one at the back. And there was a young girl in there before that. Tell you what. Give me a knock in a minute or two and I'll tell you about them. I'll make you a cup of tea too if you like.'

'Oh yes. Yes please. I'd like that. Thanks. See you soon.'

I left him looking through the post. Minutes later we were chatting about other tenants over mugs of tea. We laughed at his anecdotes about the landlady, Mrs Bryson. We'll probably always call her 'The Dragon' and it felt good to have an ally.

'Yeah she's a bit much,' he says. Have you met the woman upstairs with a TV yet? Doris? She's nice. She sometimes lets me watch *That was the Week that Was*. She has a budgie called Jacky.'

'I thought you weren't allowed pets?'

ROOM TO GROW

'Yeah well… they've allowed that one. Don't know why. Doris is a bit neurotic. She had some sort of bad experience in the war. When they test out the warning siren she hides under the table.' I grin at the image.

'Yeah. A shame for her though. Her house was bombed. It must have been awful.'

'And that young girl you mentioned, who lived here once? I've heard some scandal about her. Is it true?'

'Yes, she was in the room before the moonlighter. Jenny her name was. It was in the local papers. Some man took her away from a Children's home and acted as her pimp. In the paper they made out she was a crafty little slut. But Doris said she was nice – cheerful and pretty. She was only sixteen.'

'But what about the man! What about what he did. Did he get into trouble?'

'Don't think so, probably because she wasn't underage – just, by about two weeks, so not much was made about him. Too busy shredding the girl's character. When she disappeared from here, they thought the landlord had something to do with it and the police came and interviewed him. She wasn't dead or anything – she'd just cleared off somewhere. It was all before I came so I don't know much more.'

'She'd only just turned sixteen and a grown adult corrupted her, made money out of her and the press went for her!'

'Yes, well that's today's double standards for you Lizzie. She was a little temptress, luring weak men into sin poor things. One day people may see it differently but we're nowhere near there yet.'

The phone rings downstairs. 'Phone!' Someone calls up the stairs to me.

'I'd better go,' I say reluctantly.

'I'll tell you more some other time.'

I leave. It's only Janet on the phone wanting us to meet up.

'I was having a really interesting chat then with the guy in the next room.' She doesn't catch the resentful tone.

THURSDAY 24TH JAN

Got to know Brenda a bit. I went to her room tonight like she'd said and we had a long chat. She told me why she's avoiding her ex boyfriend, Colin. He's very good looking, she says, but very possessive, won't accept they are finished as an item and pesters her. She's worried that he'll find out where she is. He wouldn't let her go anywhere without him and used to hit her if he thought she'd looked at anyone else. Why did she put up with that! She's so beautiful she could have anyone.

'What! He'd hit you! And …well, did you look at anyone else?'

'No. Well, not really. But you know I'm a friendly sort of person. I'll talk to anyone, men or women and I have friends of both. He made such a scene when I spoke to an old school friend once, accused me of going with him and allsorts…and slapped me really hard in front of people!'

'So why didn't you chuck him then – straight away – after that?'

'I don't know. I thought I loved him. I had such good times with him; holidays, night clubs, theatre. Not like the local lads I'd been out with. He had this hold over me. …and I thought he loved me. I thought he was scared of losing me … so I kept on forgiving him.'

'Even though he ill treated you?'

'Each time it happened he'd be really sorry, there'd be flowers and promises. But he was jealous of everything! I ended up losing all my friends – and even contact with my parents… for a while.'

'Good heavens! Well rid of him then aren't you! Didn't anyone help you? Did anyone know what was going on? What about your parents?'

'They suspected something, so he made me move away from them as well, to his flat. He was older than me and had his own place. Then things got worse. He stopped me wearing make up, told me what to wear, didn't like me going anywhere without him… He wouldn't let me end it ….so I had to get away from him.'

'That sounds awful! He doesn't know where you are now does he? What about your work? Would they tell him?'

'No. They won't say anything. They all know about it. He kept pestering them on the phone so they said I've left the company. Mrs Bryson knows too. She was really nice about it.'

'Was she?' I'm surprised. But she let's lonely Doris keep a budgie, so she may have another side. Pity she doesn't show it more.

FRIDAY 25TH JAN

Spoke to Mrs Bryson today. She said not to say Brenda lives here if **he** ever comes. We have to say: 'Who? Brenda who? No. Never heard of her. No-one of that name here.'

Evening: The things you have to do to look after yourself! Washed the sheets and pillowcases Mrs B provided in the bath and cleaned the room, then met Janet at The King's Arms. Forgot to have something to eat so had peanuts and two packets of crisps. I dropped the little blue screw of salt and this guy Denis picked it up for me. He's so gorgeous!

SATURDAY 26TH JAN

Bobby called in to see if I had any shillings for the meter. I made him some Maxwell House coffee – expensive, but nice to give to people. He told me more about the tenants (quite surprising and a bit scarey) and I told him about my work. He was so interested in what I said, and so easy to talk to I felt I had known him ages.

Bobby is a university drop out. His parents don't know he's dropped out and pay him an allowance expecting him to become a lawyer. We continue our chat from the other day sitting on the single bed that pretends to be a settee with a daytime cover on. He sits at a narrow end against a wall, knees bent looking at me as I wriggle into a comfortable position.

'I was going to tell you about Frank upstairs. He's just out of prison,' Bobby begins. He slurps some coffee and wipes his face. I look at him slightly alarmed.

'What was he in prison for?'

'GBH.'

'What's that?'

'It's short for Grievious Bodily Harm. I think he may have done some robberies too.'

'Oh my God! Does Mrs Bryson know?'

'No I don't think so. I only found out myself by chance. He doesn't advertise it you know.'

ROOM TO GROW

'So, there's some dangerous criminal living above me! That's really scared me! What if I meet him on the stairs!'

'Oh he's Ok. Unless you want to fight him of course. He's really friendly. Just smile and say "hello." He's nice with women. He'll be fine – honestly he won't bother you. He's got a job as a security guard so he's trying to keep his head down and keep out of trouble. I went out with him for a drink once. Intelligent guy. A pity about his temper though. And there's Olive and Stan too. Married couple at the front. I think she's pregnant. But…anyway, what brings you here – to this place?' he asks, 'it's cheap isn't it? Are you a student?'

'No. I'm not a student. I only left home a few weeks ago. I work at a cake factory…a bakery, but I don't get full money till I'm eighteen so I'm usually skint. But, yes it's cheap.'

I can't think of anything else to say. I'm conscious it won't sound very interesting so I deflect it.

'What about you?'

'I'm a university drop out I'm afraid. My parents would go mad if they knew. I guess I'll have to tell them some day but I haven't had the guts yet.' He looks slightly embarrassed. 'I still get an allowance from them, but I need some extra cash now, so I'm going to start at that new store, Finefare, on Monday,' he says looking a bit more chirpy. 'It's a supermarket,' he adds. 'You know, self service. It's really catching on now isn't it. They've been doing it in America for ages and it's going to be the future of shopping here too. Great idea don't you think? Just help yourself to what you want and pay at the end. Anyway, you?' he asks. 'A cake factory you say? That's different. Interesting. I've never known anyone who worked in a factory. What's it like? Can you sample the cakes?'

'Only the damaged ones. But after a while you don't want to.

I can buy them really cheap though. Because I'm under eighteen I can buy a whole slab cake for about threpence.'

'So – is that what you live on? Slab cake?'

Is he serious? I smile at the teasing tone.

'No silly. It's a food factory, so all the canteen food is subsidised, so it's really cheap to eat a meal there. And the fellas there – in the store rooms, they give me little bags of coffee, or raisins, things they put in the cakes. It's not allowed, but they like to look after me.'

He looks interested. I guess he'd only known middle-class people before.

'Ok, but tell me about the work. Doesn't it get a bit…well, boring?'

I think for a moment.

'Yes, it can be, but they change us round to do different things. There's lines of us working along these moving belts – and we swap jobs regularly. Yesterday I had to stamp numbers on labels on these fruit cakes as they went past. Then I changed to spreading jam onto swiss rolls. Lots of these flat sponges come streaming down the belt. A set of taps squirts jam onto them as they pass and I have to spread it – quickly! If I miss any I have to chase them down the belt with a trowel.'

He smiles. 'That sounds fun.'

'Yes it makes them laugh too, but you should see my workmate Terasa roll them up after I've spread them. Fingers like lightning.'

'Reminds me of that joke,' he says. 'How do you make a Swiss roll…?' he waits.

'Push him down a mountain,' he says. I laugh but don't say I've heard it before.

SUN 27TH JAN

It's snowing outside. Has been for weeks and it's cold in here. Met Olive from the double flat today. It's the biggest one. It has a small separate kitchen but the main room is big. She's pregnant so where they'll put a baby in one room I don't know. I've not met husband Stan yet. He'd gone to a pub. He goes there a lot. I saw him once – staggering home dragging his coat along the ground. I think he likes a drink!

Yes he did. We're hanging out washing in the garden when she tells me about the lovely house they had in the leafy suburbs and I wonder why, if they'd had this nice house, do they now live in a bedsitter? Stan never answers the phone, or does much else except drink their income and roll home. I can't see him helping with a baby either. He seems pointless, but Olive loves him.

MONDAY 28TH JAN

I've seen most of the tenants now but not spoken to them all. Frank would be interesting to talk to, though I'd be a bit scared to even though Bobby says he's OK.

TUES 29TH JAN

Spent the evening with Brenda after going up to see if she could change a ten shilling note but I stayed there all evening so didn't need the shillings. We'll use my room another time to save money. She'd been given a bottle of Pieseporte for her eighteenth birthday some time ago and we had quite a lot of it! I'd never had it before and wasn't that keen but it's better than beer. Brenda has taken to use a cigarette holder for her menthol cigarettes. It stops her getting nictine stained fingers and looks sophisticated.

We talked about everything including the girl who'd lived here who had disappeared from a children's home when she'd reached sixteen with a 'sugar daddy' who promptly put her on the game. Not such a sweet daddy. Then she'd disappeared from this address too. We ended up making up silly things and laughing.

'You'd think the Brysons would have thought it funny wouldn't you,' Brenda says.

'What, her being so young?'

'Yes, and turning up with a man old enough to be her Dad and renting a room.'

'I've heard people say Mr Bryson was involved. The police interviewed him you know when she disappeared.'

I'm enjoying peddling this third-hand gossip. Brenda looks interested.

'Maybe they thought he'd murdered her,' she suggests.

'And buried her body in the cellar,' I add mischieviously, knowing full well she'd turned up safely. 'And her ghost walks the house at night waiting to avenge her killer,' I continue in mock seriousness. She takes my cue for fun.

'Yes, and that's why Mr Bryson always has that furtive look. He's anxious you might sneak down the cellar and find out his guilty secret.' We giggle at the image.

'That's why there's a large padlock on it.'

'Yes, he's trying to lock her in.'

'Or us out! But it's your room she'll haunt first you know,' I tell her.

'Why's that? Why my room?'

'Oh haven't I mentioned it? It was your room she had. She lived in this room!'

She doesn't know whether to believe me. Her face straightens – then relaxes into a grin.

'Lizzie you're joking!' She laughs and throws a pillow at me which makes me spill my wine.

'It's a wonder you haven't seen her in here. With her head tucked under her arm…. No really…No kidding. She lived here…. in this room. Bobby told me.'

She realises I'm not joking, but the mood soon lightens again and we're laughing. By the end of the evening we'd composed a farcical murder story, complete with Mrs Bryson as a fat accomplice – and consumed most of the wine. I wouldn't recommend it. It gives you a headache the next day.

WED 30TH JAN

Went to 'The Horse and Jockey' this evening. Sat with Janet and Andy and several others we know so I didn't feel such a gooseberry. Someone brought in their younger brother and swore he was eighteen. He looked about twelve and only drank coke so the landlord ignored him.

Quite a few are underage but the pub owner doesn't question it. Seventeen and eighteen blurs in appearance and good liars are believed. We drink Babycham which was supposed to be like champagne but was like sweet fizzy pop. A cute 'Bambi' deer featured on special glasses with the slogan, 'I'd love a Babysham' was supposed to appeal to young girls. The shape of the glass and the bubbles gave it unwarranted sophistication. We could only afford them at weekends unless boys, fuelled by hormones and egos, bought them for us.

FRIDAY 1ST FEB

Tonight Brenda spent the evening in my room to save her shillings this time. I thought it would be nice to invite her to join Janet and I to the Bodega tomorrow. She's been hiding herself for weeks and it's about time she went out. She'd be safe with us two. But she surprised me. She's going out with a bloke from work – such quick work, but I'm pleased for her. She can't hide for ever and I'm pleased she's getting over the last one.

'So who is this new guy? What's he like?'

'He's Alan. He's one of the sales reps. I used to see him before sometimes but we kept it quiet in case Colin found out.'

'That would have been tricky! You were lucky to get away with after you told me what he was like. His jealousy and all that!'

'Oh but this one isn't serious, Lizzie. We're sort of friends, well friends with, you know…"extras" sometimes. You can do that these days. Things are different now, we're freer aren't we… so we can enjoy ourselves without all that last generation guilt.'

'But what about…you know…contraception? Aren't you scared you'll get caught?'

'No. I'll be fine. He takes care of all that.'

She doesn't say how, and I'm about to ask when the last record drops to the turntable and she's up dancing and 'Feeling Glad all Over' with the Dave Clark Five. A modern girl is Brenda.

SATURDAY 2ND FEB

Morning – Food shopping. Tonight – Bodega! Too busy to write about it. Will do tomorrow.

SUNDAY 3RD FEB

So, 'The Bodega' on Brazonose Street in Manchester last night. Very trendy, smokey and crowded. Smoked two cigarette and danced until midnight. Shared a taxi home with two very drunk girls who slumped over Janet, dropping their money as they paid the driver, then fell out of the taxi. The driver was grateful they hadn't been sick as he'd have to clean it up. I was too!

The Bodega, a club in a dimly lit basement, is the place to go in Sixties Manchester for trad jazz. Trendy and dingy, parents can object to its bohemian image, late night finish, city location or even the fact that it was licenced. Young people travel miles to it, usually on public transport to soak up the experience.

INDEPENDENCE

Inside it's like a Manchester smog, but warmer and noisier, with shady undercurrents, as if police could raid any minute adding to the atmosphere, and everyone seems to wear black – but could be dim lighting. There's a special kind of slow, jazzy, style of jive there, but you can also dance alone, sort of writhing with the rhythm, waving arms artistically above your head.

MONDAY 4ᵀᴴ FEB

Bus was late for work. Snow stuck last night again so deeper, crunchier. It wets your shoes making your feet cold and numb. I need boots. Watching people at the bus stop was fascinating. Cold and huddled, they stamp their feet to keep warm before heading for Trafford Park which my dad says is the industrial power house of the North because of its important heavy industry. I bet it's warm working with furnaces and those huge engines and machines.

I study them as I wait in a sub zero temperature. Women, waiting like me, turn from the biting wind, legs bare except for fifteen denier stockings, not a trouser in sight. Headscarves preserve hairstyles in the damp atmosphere, fastened under the chin, like the Queen's when she's out riding. They've stiffened their hair with 'laquer' and probably slept in monster sized prickly rollers which give you a sore scalp the next day. They'll do a full day's work before returning home to cook, clean and care for children, and anyone else who happens to live there.

I strike up a conversation with one. I've spoken to her before. She cleans offices but she's late today because her child-care arrangements had fallen through.

'So who's looking after your baby and toddler then?'

'Me mam. I had to go and wake her up and dump them on her. My husband was on nights – he'd just got in, but I couldn't ask him to take her could I? Push a pram!' he'd say. I'd look a right fool pushing a pram wouldn't I? Not likely.'

She's a multi-roled mother, wife, cleaner, cook, exercising post war frugality to keep her family fed and clothed and receiving fractional earnings compared to her night-shift working man.

'Stay at home?' she says when I ask her why she works with such a young baby.

'I couldn't manage – his wages only cover basics like food and rent.'

Many women don't work though. Earlier nineteen-fifties child development theories say mother and baby attachment and bonding should come first. Fine for those who can afford it.

I'm stamping my feet to keep warm but still minutes to go, so I look at the men. They all have jobs to go to. It's northern England, blue collar full employment. They're better dressed for the cold than the women, although they still stoop from the wind and clap arms to sides. They wear dark coloured donkey jackets or beige belted gaberdines and warm caps. Many smoke and cough out visible breath in the cold. On a passing bus I see clothcapped heads through the steamy, grimey windows; men sitting in pairs, or standing, swaying, arms raised, to clasp overhead leather handstraps. They aren't expected to share domestic chores but they are a hard working lot.

The early morning 'Metropolitan and Vickers' siren in Trafford Park wails as I take a last look before boarding a crowded bus ushered by a cheerful conductor.

'Lovely mornin' luv,' he says ironically. 'Mind you don't slip now.'

TUESDAY 5TH FEB

Worked late. Brought home a damaged dundee cake. I met Bobby coming in and offered him half as I don't like it that much. Had a 'Vesta curry' for tea. Quite spicy but OK. So easy, you just boil it in its bag. I'm going to have to learn to cook.

THURSDAY 7TH FEB

Worked until seven o'clock on time and a quarter. Saturday morning available too if orders keep up.

Saw this man leaning by next door's hedge tonight. Or was it a lad? Or a man? Man, lad, man? I think he must be a man. Not sure how old he was. I only noticed because it was a funny place to stand in the shadows. Probably just having a smoke – but why would you do it in the cold?

He was so still he looked part of the hedge, but I wanted to get in and warm and didn't take much notice. He didn't seem sinister or anything – just there.

FRIDAY 8TH FEB

Snowed again. Overtime! Nothing much has happened. Met Olive's husband, Stan, from the front flat for the first time. He was at the dustbins dumping lots of Newcastle Brown bottles at the side of the bin. Doesn't he know you can get money back on those! I'd take them myself but I'd be embarrassed seen taking things from the rubbish.

After dark I sneak back and recover two shillings' worth, enough for a packet of cigarettes which I'm trying to quit. I clank self consciously to the off licence and buy ten menthol cigarettes. Menthol is refreshing for your breathing so must be good for your lungs.

SATURDAY 9TH FEB

Worked until 12.30. Met Brenda on her way to the shops so we stayed together. Had coffee and toast and cigs in 'Teds' coffee bar. It's got a jukebox. Brilliant! All the hits at sixpence a go. We played Gerry and the Pacemakers: 'Ferry Across the Mersey' over and over. Two old schoolfriends came in. Joan's a hairdresser now and Carole, a typist in the Refuge building in Manchester. We take turns to hand round cigarettes and talk football. United played and didn't win on Saturday. Never been the same since that plane crash six years ago.

Evening: Janet went out with Andy so stayed in on my own and read a book. A book!! On my own on a Saturday night!! All my friends are with their boyfriends but I'm on my own. Is this the rest of my life?

INDEPENDENCE

SUNDAY 10TH FEB

Mrs B asked me if I would clear the snow from the path for her. I couldn't think of a reason not to! Why didn't she ask Frank or one of the men! It was hard work! I'd tried to get past her but she'd cornered me as I was going out before I could escape! 'Oh Lizzie. Glad I've caught you love. I was going to ask you a favour.'

I wonder what she has in mind but she presents me with a large shovel before I can think.

'Could you just clear some of the snow from the path for me,' she asks, 'I'd be so grateful. It's too much for me, and Mr Bryson has a bad back y'know so he can't. Its going to get slippy again and dangerous.'

'Er ...yes. Ok,' I say weakly taking the heavy shovel. It takes nearly an hour! Then there's salt to put down and – could I just move a bit more from the pavement, oh, and some from the back path.

'Thank you love. You're a good girl,' she says as I finish, face flushed and sweating. I'm flabbergasted. She called me 'love' and said something nice but my visit home is delayed and my hands and feet are freezing.

TUESDAY 12TH FEB

I sent a Valentine to Bobby as a joke. I've never had one except when Janet once played a trick on me. Took my library book back and had to pay a fine! Noticed the lad/man I'd seen outside the house the other night. He was walking towards the house. He must live round here. He must be in his twenties? He's actually very good looking now I've seen him again. Don't think he saw me.

THURSDAY 14TH FEB

I don't think I'll ever get a Valentine card. Does Bob know his was from me. He gave me a knowing smile. Ms B watched me go out to buy milk. She knows when tenants come and go. She has an arm chair with cushions by her front room window and sits there as if it's a viewing platform. It's a wonder she doesn't use binoculars! I sometimes wave to her in a mocking sort of way but she pretends she's not looking.

Brenda of course has two Valentine cards and waves them in my face. One has a large, red velvet heart and the other, roses and a soppy verse. A bit insensitive of her but I pretend to admire them.

FRIDAY 15TH FEB

Hooray. I got paid – with extra for the overtime!! I'll spend it tomorrow but I'm NOT going to buy cigarettes. Much too expensive! (One and three a packet of ten.) I'm going to give it up tomorrow. The bus journey to work this morning has put me off!

Not for long though, young, nicotine addicted and immortal, I enjoy the smoker's image despite the cost. But these journeys were unpleasant even for a smoker! It was like being squashed and hurried in a kipper factory. I'd squeeze onto a bus where a conductor would compress passengers up the aisle, ignoring maximum numbers and people would pile on as if it was the last bus on earth. There'd be that damp day, wet, woollen clothing smell mixed with the fetid breath of smokers.

'Move along the bus now', shouts the conductor. Then, louder, 'top deck only.' He blocks my way to the overcrowded lower deck so I am forced to go 'upstairs'. I emerge into a damp, grey choking haze of smoking rituals; lighting up, inhaling, flicking ash, blowing out noxious breath, grinding dimps into the floor or placing behind ears for later. Nicotine stained fingers strike matches on purposely provided rough plaques built into the back of seats above brimming ashtrays. NO SPITTING says a notice. Spitting! Not a pleasant thing but is it worse than smoking?

I sit next to a chatty workman bound for Turners,' an asbestos manufacturers in Trafford Park, who tells me about his work which he seems to enjoy.

'What is asbestos anyway?' I ask innocently.

'It's the most versatile and effective insulating material ever,' he tells me. 'Cheap too, an absolute wonder product. It's a good firm to work for too.'

'Are there any jobs for girls there?'

'Just turn up at the office and ask,' he tells me. That's how he got his job there. I might do that.

SATURDAY NIGHT 16TH FEB

Is this the worst winter ever? Snowing every day. Overtime every day! At least its warm in the bakery. Got some overtime money yesterday! Bought food: tins of beans, spaghetti, tea, instant coffee, bread, packets of 'Vesta Curry,' milk and eggs. Treated myself to nail varnish from Woolworths. Gone up to one and threepence! I'd like 'The Night has a Thousand eyes' by Bobby Darrren but nothing to play it on. I also want some knee-length boots like Janet's but wellies will have to do. I'll have to collect them from 'home.'

Evening: I asked Brenda in as she was on her own like me ON A SATURDAY NIGHT! I made Maxwell House and she brought custard creams. I know more about Colin now, but I think Brenda exaggerates sometimes. She says he has strange ideas. I used to write strange stories as a child so I can understand that.

'He's nuts,' she says. 'He hears people that aren't there! He thinks there are these invisible people he can hear talking …but most of the time he's very intelligent.'

I've never heard of anything like that before but it sounds harmless, like having a dream I think. A dream isn't real, so how could it harm anyone. You could become a good writer or make exciting films or something if you thought like that. 'Doesn't that make him more …sort of artistic? I suggest. 'He must have a good imagination. I always liked writing stuff at school,' I continue. 'You know, with people I'd invented. They seemed almost real when I wrote about them. Teachers thought I was being creative.'

'No Lizzie. It isn't that sort of thing… It is a sort of story he thinks he's in – but I don't think its being creative. I never knew if he was putting it on or not…using it as an excuse for things.'

'Um… maybe,' I say. 'But I do sound a bit like him. I like to imagine that…'

INDEPENDENCE

'Lizzie you are not a bit like him!' she interrupts emphatically. 'Anyway it doesn't matter now. He's history.'

We change topics as the nine o'clock news comes on the radio. Something about the Beeching Report and railways. I turn it off. So boring. Who cares?

SUNDAY 17TH FEB

Went 'home.' Or is home my bedsitter 'home' now? I'm homesick sometimes but not enough to go back. They've got used to the idea of me living away now and probably glad to be rid of me! I don't think I was an asset!

But I'm greeted with hugs and given visitor status.

'What have you got there?' asks my dad.

'It's my radio. It's not working.'

'I knew you'd want something,' he teases. 'Give it here.'

He can mend anything: lawn mowers, watches, dolls with dismembered limbs, anything failing through neglect or ill treatment. His toolbox takes up half the width of the understairs cupboard. Handy Andy they call him.

My sister, Ruth, shows me her school photo, taken with closed eyes and looking awkward.

'I'm going to tear it up!' she threatens. There's rising sap in my thirteen-year-old sister. They could have another challenge soon.

'Don't,' says Mum. 'You look just fine.'

'Have you come back?' asks my little brother. He doesn't understand independence and thinks I'm here to stay. I start to explain.

'Only for today. You see ....' but he's pulling my arm.

'Come and see my new hamster.' Attention span of a gnat – but he's only six.

Mum asks if there's anything I need and gives me towels and candy striped flannelette sheets.

'Yes, here, take some pillow cases too,' she says thrusting a folded pair at me. 'These match the sheets – and these tea towels. You can never have enough tea towels.'

I accept them gratefully. Mrs Bryson can have her faded, tatty ones back. She also slipped a ten shilling note into my bag which I found later.

Mum's thinking:

'I'm so relieved Lizzie is coping on her own. She's quite young to live alone. I miss her... even the wilfulness but.... she was out of our control and I can't cope with her. She angers her father with her behaviour; staying out all night with that boy with a den in his parents' cellar ...and ...the arguing, answering back and not listening. It is more peaceful here now, and mustn't risk my health with any more stress. She doesn't know how ill I feel... I don't want to alarm her ...but she looks well – which is more than I do.'

MONDAY 18TH FEB

Work: Overslept. Clocked on at 8.35. A supervisor (Ivy) gave me a dirty look as she'd had to get someone else on the team. I don't care. It's the first time I've been late and I've always done the overtime when she's asked. Silly cow. She has bad breath too.

INDEPENDENCE

Evening: Brenda came in with another bloke from work called Brian! They brought beer but I only had one pint beer tanker someone had pinched from a pub which I gave to Brian, so Brenda and I drank from bottles. I still don't like beer but it's what you do. We sat on Brenda's bed with a cover on it like mine. Somebody nudged Brian's arm which spilt his whole pint all over her bed!

'Brian, you fool,' she berates. 'Be careful. Look! It's gone all over the bed.'

'Sorry, but it's not my fault. You nudged me. Don't shout at me like that!

'I didn't shout!' she shouts. 'I've got to sleep on that tonight. It's soaking!'

The three of us get up, yank off the cover and fuss about with cloths. Brenda ignores his repeated apologies and maintains a sour look. I don't hold out for that relationship.

Later, when he's gone I help her remove the sheet. How can one pint of beer cause so much wetness? It's gone down to the mattress and Brenda is not happy.

'It's still wet!' she complains.

'Its only a bit now. You won't feel it, fusspot. Who are you? The Princess and the Pea!'

She smiles at last.

'Help me turn the mattress over. At least that side will be dry.' It reveals a grubby history as we tip it onto its narrow end where it hits a low hanging light bulb which swings and threatens to extinguish itself.

'Why didn't we shove it wide side up. It would have been easier!' We're in a ridiculous position balancing a tipped up mattress and trying to turn it.

41

Then, as we're about to wrestle it to its dry side I spot something on the base of the bed.

'What's that?'

'What?' she says. 'I can't hold it like this much longer, Lizzie! What is it?'

'There's a little book and an envelope, look there.'

'Well I can't reach it and you can't, so just let's leave it there and put this down before I have to let go!'

'Just lean it against the wall for a minute while I get it.' She reluctantly complies and I scoop up the objects, place them on the table and return to mattress turning.

'Right what are they?' I've helped her remake her bed and she's picked up the little book and opened it.

'It's a diary…I think, with addresses.'

'A diary? Let me see.' I'm hoping to find a well-kept diary, but disappointment; no narrative or personal entries, just addresses, a few dry notes and figures; nothing to portray a person at all. A diary in name only.

'It was probably that girl's. The one who had this room before the flitting guy.' I tell her. 'The one we made a story about a couple of weeks ago. Remember?'

'So this mattress hasn't been turned …for ages.' She pulls a disgusted face. 'But I never asked you before, how did you know about that girl? You weren't here then were you?'

'Bobby told me about her. He'd heard from someone else – and I'd heard about it in the pub too, so it might be a bit distorted.'

I don't remind her about the personal services the girl was offering. After the mattress turning, probably best not!

'Let's see what's in the envelope,' I suggest, taking and opening it.

'Bloody hell!' I take out several five pound notes. 'There's fifty pounds here!'

'Brilliant!' she beams. 'Twenty five each. We can have some good nights out with that.'

'Yeah. That's nearly a months' wages for each of us…and it would be great …but… it's hers isn't it? Shouldn't we try and get it to her.'

'We don't know her name or address or anyone who knows her, so how can we?'

'Listen, if you'll agree I'll put it in my Post Office account to keep it safe. We can't just leave it here. It's a lot of money. But if we can't trace her in one month, I'll take it out – then we'll share it. You do trust me don't you? You know I'm not trying to keep it don't you?'

'Of course I trust you, Lizzie. It's just …well, wouldn't it be so nice to have some extra money for a change. She's probably forgotten about it anyway…and I doubt we'll be able to find her.'

'We already have her name. It's Jennifer Freeman – it's at the front of the book.' I'm flicking through the pages. 'It's as if she'd like it returned if found, but gives this address – here.'

'Not much use to us then.'

'No, but let's put the money in my post office account …for safety. Can I keep the diary for now? I'll see if there's anything else that would help.'

My Post Office balance is one pound, ten shillings and sixpence. Maybe it would be a good thing if Jennifer can't be found.

TUESDAY 19TH FEB

Went through the diary to see if I could find a contact for Jennifer. All Jennifers calls themselves Jenny so I'll call her Jenny. There are several addresses, but not hers. She went to the hairdresser's regularly but doesn't say which one. She took taxis a lot so she must have been earning much more than me! There are men's names which I think are 'clients' and someone called Harold who could be the 'sugar daddy' Bob told me about.

I peruse the little book and wonder about the people, mainly men, and about neatly set out sums like this:

'Total cash: £180.0.0 Harold £65.10.0 + Earnest £65.10.0. £149.0.0 for me.'

It's repeated sometimes with different figures. Who are Harold and Ernest? There are also dates and addresses, just parts of addresses as if full ones are not necessary.

'Taxi to Beechways 7.00.' 'Harold 7.00pm – to 13 Crawley Avenue.' 'Harold – pick up at 3.00pm. To Hairdressers 5.30pm,' reads another.

She goes to the hairdressers most weeks and has manicures and beauty treatments. Harold seemed to be her transport when she doesn't get a taxi.

She's booked appointments with various men, often the same ones, sometimes different. Sometimes weeks are left bare of dates and notes as if she's fed up with organising them, then starts again. I know the feeling; it's hard writing every day. It's a sparse and irregular record and I'm no wiser how to contact her.

INDEPENDENCE

I'll ask Mrs B. tomorrow.

WEDNESDAY 20TH FEB

I asked Mrs B if the young girl had left a forwarding address. She was in Dragon persona, not loud, just evasive and didn't like me asking. I didn't mention the money; only the diary. That's clever of me. She's not getting it if Jenny doesn't!

She's sifting out mail for previous tenants and tossing them into a bin followed by ash tapped from her cigarette. She's a fire hazard – like what my dad used to say about me. Amongst those letters could be life changing communications; invitations from long lost relatives, legacies or family member deaths, poignant scenarios, fractured relationships, postal proposals but – no point, she's binning them all. I ask her about Jenny though. 'How do you know about her?' she asks suspiciously. 'She caused some trouble here and I don't want to hear any more about her…and no, I haven't got her address… Why do you want to contact her anyway?'

'Bob told me about her. It's just that …I found her diary and I thought she might want it. I wouldn't want to lose mine… I'd be glad if someone returned it.'

'Good God, it's nearly a year ago when she left. Get rid of it. What good is a last year's diary?'

'There are some addresses in it she might want.'

'Yes, I bet there are,' she says sourly. 'No. I've no idea where she went. She didn't owe me rent, so I've no interest where she went.' She clearly wants to close the topic.

THURSDAY 21ST FEB

Brenda is making up for being a door-mat! She's got two more boyfriends now – but maybe only one after today! I knew about one but I didn't know about another called Malek. He turned up one night and I had to lie for her. It put me in a really difficult position! Why didn't she tell me? I look like an idiot now! It happened like this.

Brenda and boyfriend number one are on their way out coming down the top floor stairs as I exit the bathroom. I look up and up and we exchange greetings. The doorbell rings.

'That was the doorbell,' I say unnecessarily. It rings again. Brenda looks worried. She and boyfriend number one grind to a halt. Why? What's the matter with her? The Dragon is first to the door and grumpily admits the caller.

'Yes, come in, but I think she's got company up there,' she says.

Brenda suddenly hustles boyfriend number one back up the stairs and into her room.

'Tell him I'm out,' she whispers hoarsely bending over the bannister.

'Who?' I ask bewildered.

'Malek' she says.

'Who's Alec?'

'Not Alec. I said Malek! Never mind!' she spits in panic. 'Just say I'm out! Don't let him up!'

I stand there mouth open as boyfriend number two reaches the first flight. I block his passage.

INDEPENDENCE

'Are you Malek?' I try to smile naturally but it's false. He's attractive. I think he's Indian but later find out he's Pakistani.

'Yes… How do you know?' There is a trace of an accent.

'Er, Brenda asked me to tell you …she's er, she's… gone out. She had to …go for some milk'

'That's funny. Are you sure? The landlady just said she was in. She said she had some company.'

'Well she had … but then she went out …with a friend.'

'She told you to tell me that…? But, she didn't know I was coming – so why would she say that? I'll just try her door.' Then, ever so politely, 'Can you let me pass please.'

Without physically restraining him I couldn't stop him. Soon arguing was heard followed by stoney-faced boyfriend number one stomping down the stairs and out of the front door. Malek stayed.

SATURDAY 23RD FEB

Daytime: Brenda knocked at my door at 8.30 before I was up! I've hardly seen her lately. I made us tea and toast. I asked her about Wednesday and she explained she is now going out with Malek. The other one, Brian, is off, gone, chucked. I told her about bits from the diary but she was hardly interested.

We talk about Malek. He seems exotic to me. It's 1963 but 'mixed' relationships are still frowned upon. Many older people around were born in Victorian or Edwardian times and have retained colonialist attitudes and most have deep prejudices to some extent.

'He's good looking,' I say. 'But he's coloured!'

ROOM TO GROW

'I know. I know. And my mother would have a fit if she knew… but I like him. He's easy to talk to and he's intelligent and polite.'

'But…but… they're different….don't they think that women are unimportant in their country? They don't allow them out do they, and keep them at home like prisoners after they're married.'

'Malek's not like that….Anyway who's going to marry him! I only met him last week!'

'Ok, ok, It's not for me to tell you who to go out with, but people might stare at you. And you know, they do have different ideas in those countries, so be careful.'

'Those countries! What are you talking about Lizzie! He was born and bred in Manchester. He's a Mancunian like you.'

It's 1963. Civil Rights are becoming an important issue in America but mean little to me. Nelson Mandela is leading an anti apartheid movement in South Africa but I've never heard of him. There is overt racism everywhere, rejecting other ethnicities as inferior and much prejudice about 'mixed' relationships. I'd never met a 'foreigner' before, not one with a brown skin. But Malek was as British as me. I try to accommodate this conflict of perceptions.

Evening: Looks like Saturday night on my own again! Maybe Doris will let me watch TV with her. The only thing is she doesn't like people smoking in her room. Everyone in the bedsits except her and Bobby smoke. The walls in the hall and stairways are now nicotine yellow.

INDEPENDENCE

SUNDAY 24TH FEB

I did watch TV last night. *Morecombe and Wise*, then the News. It was all about the H bomb. She's worried about it, but I'm not because we'd win if there was a war. Doris can knit and follow the news without even looking at her fingers. Her budgie can swear but I don't know who taught him as Doris doesn't swear. She even told me off for saying 'Jesus Christ' when he flew out of his cage and landed on my head.

Doris's budgie was more interesting to me than the possibility of a nuclear war. Doris wasn't a lucky person. She'd had her house destroyed in the Manchester Blitz, her husband killed in action, had no family and lived on what was called 'National Assistance' and a small widows' pension. Her only child died at seven and she had a condition which made her skin break out in itchy weals as well as allergies to anything you could think of.

She was still convinced God was looking after her though, and went to church each Sunday in a neat matching coat and hat to thank him.

MONDAY 25TH FEB

Brenda and I huddled over my electric fire tonight to share shillings for the meter. My fingers are almost numb with cold. I like to write last thing before bed but there's not much to say and my hands are so cold I'm wearing gloves in bed. Youth has a built in thermal underwear effect, but even that was challenged. The cold weather was ceaseless.

TUESDAY 26TH FEB

This bedsitter gets colder and colder and that black metal meter swallows my money like a greedy monster. I think they can set it to whatever rate they like and I can hardly afford to keep warm! Today I found a solution, although I daren't write it down here. It's got to stay a big secret between me and Brenda forever or we could be in trouble. All I can think is – it serves them right!

Winter 1963 was the coldest recorded since 1948. A prolonged period of deep snow and freezing temperatures for weeks and weeks on end caused snowdrifts, road blockages, sheep almost starving on hills, skidding vehicles and elderly people making unwanted contact with the ground.

Temperatures plummeted, frost patterns appeared on windows in the morning and overland powerlines frequently weighed down. It doesn't excuse what I did this day. Morality is a fine thing when you're warm and well fed.

The big secret? Brenda and I were keeping each other company one evening when I went to feed the electric meter with shillings. I watched the little metal revolving disc that records the amount of electricity being used. It's responsible for cutting off the power after a shilling's worth; there'd be a sudden blackout and you'd grope towards where you think the meter should be and trip over things in the dark to reach it.

Hmm. I pondered. What would happen if I could slow or stop that revolving thing? I looked at it carefully. A little twisted wire fastened on top was the only thing that secured it. The rest was just screws, and even I could undo screws. I just needed a screwdriver. One had been conveniently left in the cutlery drawer, probably to puncture tins in case of tin opener failure.

I check it's still there. Yes, good. I squat before the meter and break off the little twisted wire tag that seals the top and unscrew the front. I could twist the wire back on. It wouldn't be sealed as before but nobody would notice.

Brenda watches in alarm as she realises what I am doing.

'Lizzie… stop it! What are you doing?'

'I'm just taking this off.'

'What if you electrocute yourself!'

'I won't, I'm not stupid. I'm just taking it off to have a look. If I touch anything I'll do it with paper… so I won't get a shock. Paper's not a conductor of electricity.' I say brandishing the screwdriver and trying to sound convincing. 'Isn't that right?' Actually I'm not sure. Brenda thinks.

'Yes I think so. I was good at science at school,' she says. 'You have to be careful you don't become part of the circuit! Or is it the other way round? The wrong way and your eyeballs light up!' We giggle at the thought. Calm down, we must be serious.

We revise what is and isn't a conductor of electricity, recalled from half remembered school physics lessons while the solid metal front lies harmlessly on the floor. Its little glass panel through which I'd watched the busy little thing looks smeary so I wipe it with a dishcloth.

We note how the disc speed changes when I put the electric fire on; much faster, so we experiment plugging appliances into sockets and noting: radio; hardly moves, iron; quite fast, electric cooker, spins wildly again.

I peer inside the meter, fully exposed now, its shiny, silver disc spinning merrily for all it's worth, preparing to demand yet more payment. We're thinking the same thing. What would happen if this little thing was slowed or stopped? If we handicapped its exploitive little game.

'What could we use to stop it?'

'Well we could use paper.' Brenda says forgetting her former anxiety. 'Sort of disable it with a wodge of paper?'

'Yeah… or cloth or plastic maybe. Something we could easily remove. Umm… yes probably paper.' I find some newspaper, fold it and stuff it under the disc, slowing it down a bit, then a lot.

'We'd need to keep the paper wedged in …we can't stand here holding it all day.'

'But what if *she* sees it?' She's anxious again.

'We'd probably be evicted …or even arrested. It's criminal I think. It's stealing electricity. We could end up in Styal prison.'

'Oh God no, some of the women are so hard in there. One of them decapitated her husband! They'd eat us!'

'At least we'd be warm and get regular meals!'

'Um. Yeah, but maybe not that great for job applications. Can you imagine. "Why is there a two year gap in employment here Miss Dale? Where did you work between 1963 and 1965?"'

'Yes well, we'd have to be careful and make sure that doesn't happen. You'd have to pull the paper out if you heard her coming and screw the front back on very quickly.'

'Just me? Aren't you going to do it in your room too?'

'Of course I am. Now we know how to do it.'

'We haven't tried it properly yet. Pass me that newspaper. I'll fold it and make it thicker.' I fold some sheets over and over to wedge nicely under the disc which slows to a dead stop. We mentally enjoy the success for a moment. 'That's done it. Let's wait and see what happens.' I fix the front of the meter on and twist the short piece of wire back. Its not sealed now, but it's not noticable.

'What if she comes upstairs? She's got keys to all the bedsits!'

'Yes but she always knocks and waits doesn't she. She doesn't come in when she comes for the rent. I could always ask her to wait a moment. I could say, 'Wait a minute please, I'm not dressed.'

'So you'd have to take off your clothes!'

'No silly. I'd just *pretend* I was getting dressed – while I took the front off, removed the paper and screwed it back.'

'Of course. You'd be under pressure though – anxious about getting found out.'

'Well yes. That's the downside – but better than freezing to death in these rooms!'

'I've thought of something else too,' says Brenda. 'We'll have to at least put some coins in for when she empties it. It's going to look funny if it's completely empty.' We both laugh thinking of a puzzled Mrs Bryson holding an empty coin box. We're pleased with our inventiveness. It's lifted the afternoon.

There are no more extortionist demands that afternoon and we celebrate our criminality with tea and chocolate biscuits. She will do the same with hers later. We'll do alternative days to reduce risks. I don't tell Janet. It's impossible for her to keep a secret, but I would like to tell Bobby but Brenda says not to, the fewer who know the better.

WEDNESDAY 27TH FEB

I've had Jenny's diary for nine days but don't think I'll be able to trace her. I've had another look and the name of the hairdresser is in there after all. I didn't see it the first time. It's in tiny writing in a part I didn't think interesting. It said 'cheque to Heidi's Hair Salon.' I don't know where it is and she may not go there anymore. Also, they may not be willing to give a client's address. What do I do now?

THUR 28 FEB.

Pity it's not a leap year then I could propose to Bobby! Really. Mustn't be pushy! The most noteworthy thing today, was Mrs Bryson's strange husband collecting the rent. He looks at your legs and mumbles and you can't hear what he's saying.

I'm leaving my room to go to the phone, but wait a minute, he's there padding up the stairs without a sound and I don't hear him until we're face to face on the landing. He's quiet, creepy and gives me a shock. He's collecting the rent unusually early. Mrs B usually does it as I don't think she trusts him with money, but I'll have to go into my room to find it and the rent book. It wasn't due until tomorrow but she's away. I should have told him to come back tomorrow but I panicked because of the meter!

Oh my God! He might want to come in and notice it while I'm locating the rent book. Is it in its proper state? Or does it have half the Evening News stuffed up its innards! I knew this would happen one day!

'Glad I've caught you,' he says. 'Have you got your rent ready?'

'No,' I say, thinking on my feet. 'I was just going to the bathroom. Ok if I bring it down in a few minutes?' He grins and looks me up and down.

'Anything's Ok for you, love,' he says. Yes I bet it is, I think.

FRIDAY 1ST MAR

Snowing as usual! Worked until eight o'clock. Time and a half. Next Friday I'll be rich! I've been in this bedsitter almost two months and it's is looking better with my posters and Mum's curtains. Still a bit 'brown' though. Going shopping tomorrow morning and evening to the Twisted Wheel with Brenda. I love Saturday nights out. Such special nights, after a weeks' work with a good lie in on Sundays to recover.

SATURDAY 2ND MAR

Good pay packet yesterday. Went to C&A on Oldham Street and bought a paisley dress for twenty-nine shillings and eleven and some boots. Had tea, cake and a cigarette in the upstairs Woolworths café.

It's a typical early sixties shopping morning. Lewis's department store, a well-known landmark is my first call. In classiness it is above C&A, and below Kendal Milne, it has call girls in its arcade, but attactive goods over four floors. I ride up and down on the escalators but don't buy anything. Then, a short cut cut through Littlewoods to Affleck and Brown on Oldham Street.

Piccadilly Gardens are just that, with flower beds and seats all around but I'm off to Lillie and Skinner now for boots. It's on Market Street not yet pedestrianised and crawling with traffic. The boots, red, trendy and knee length, are so comfortable I ask to keep them on. I'm in the city so I need to look good.

The buildings look cleaner these days. They've been 'stone cleaned' of industrial grime and given a beige facelift to the surprise of many who thought they'd been built black. Next, the Woolworth's café where smokers and eaters sit together with impunity, ash trays helpfully provided.

Evening: Went to the 'Twisted Wheel' with Brenda. It's another trendy club that hosts rising stars. Saw Wayne Fontana and 'The Jets'. Janet had gone out with Andy of course. With overtime money to splash, I treated myself and Brenda to 'Cherry Bs' (like sickly sweet red wine) which we think is the 'in' drink to have.

We indulge in even more bought for us by two young men we've got together with and exchange phone numbers with but leave the club without them. A potential predator's dream we stagger incapably drunk and fall into a taxi. As we arrive back at 1.30am, curtains twitch but we are too drunk to care. I go in and collapse onto the bed. I'm feeling sick and the room's going round.

INDEPENDENCE

SUNDAY. 3ᴿᴰ MAR

Had a nice lie in – but what a headache! Went for a walk but got a fright when a car skidded on the ice and came onto the pavement right near me! It's very slippy. Saw that bloke on the way back standing against a hedge again in the shadows, facing away from me. He crossed over and went down St John's Road when he saw me. Do I know him or not? I'm definitely going to speak to him next time – if I'm brave enough.

Evening: Saw Bobby and chatted for a while. I really do like him. I wish he would just put his arms around me. It's a pity girls can't make the first move. You must never appear 'forward' or lead them on, the well meaning advice goes. But maybe some need just that!

TUESDAY 5ᵀᴴ MAR

Fed up. Bobby asked me to go on the Aldermaston March with him at Easter. I can't because I'd have to have time off work and it's DOUBLE TIME on Bank holidays! I need the money. He is a good friend but he doesn't fancy me at all! How can I make him!! Perhaps I should ask Brenda. She seems to know what to do.

Bobby was attractive, had eyelashes a girl would die for and lovely blue-grey eyes – but not for me so it didn't do much for my self confidence. Brenda liked him too. His friendly interest in our hair and clothes created an easy bond so we treated him like a girlfriend. He'd make us laugh and cups of tea like a nice brother. He had a sweet tooth and I'd bring him cakes from the factory. He still hadn't told his parents about dropping out, and the longer it got, the worse. Unlike me he was interested in world issues and well informed – like in the following.

'Heard the news?' Bobby asks.

'Well I know nail varnish has gone up in Woolworths,' I joke. 'It was only one and tuppence last week.'

'Nail varnish? What? …No, no. Well, you know the Government is worried about the big march to Aldermaston at Easter …you know …the one to demonstrate for nuclear disarmament …to try and ban the bomb… The H bomb.' He emphasises it to make it clearer.

'The bomb could be a real threat to world peace and well, this is our chance to make our voices heard. Some people from my university are going. I'm still in touch with one of them and I'm definitely going.'

'I have heard of the H bomb,' I admit. 'But is it a good thing to ban it? Nobody's going to start a war with us if we have one are they? And anyway, we really showed how strong we were in the war didn't we? Winston Churchill really showed them didn't he? No-one would dare start messing about with us now would they?'

'No no. Lizzie, listen. It's much different now. A nuclear war wouldn't be like that last one – the one our dads were in. It wouldn't matter who was strong. It'll just take another nasty meglomaniac like Stalin or Hitler to set it off and we'll all be done for. All of us. Most of the world! And because we've got it – it's even more dangerous! Someone could set it off by mistake. And it's not going to save us if we lob one back just because someone's sent us one! I'm definitely going. It's so important. Why don't you come with me? We could march together. It would be great fun and a good cause. Come on. Say yes. It's only a couple of days.'

'I don't know. Where is Aldermaston? How long will it take? How do you get there? Where would we sleep?' But I can't go. I need to earn that double time at the bank holiday weekend.

WEDNESDAY 6TH MAR

My job gets boring sometimes. I wish I'd stayed on at school so I could get a better one. Pay gets better when I'm eighteen. Some of my friends work in offices but they don't seem to earn much more. Went out to get a five pack of cigarettes. I'm sure that bloke was there leaning against a tree this time. He was in its shadow but I saw his arm move. I'll speak to him next time. It's not that I'm being 'forward' I'm just curious.

I try and convince myself that I won't lose dignity by opening up a conversation. I'm not going to flirt or ask for a date or anything. What's wrong with that?

FRIDAY 8TH MAR

Met Bobby on the doorstep after work. I hadn't seen him for a while but didn't like to ask why in case he thinks I'm nosey. But I wonder where he goes some evenings. I suppose I'm jealous he may be seeing a girl. I told him about the diary and the money found in Brenda's room and he was interested. I knew he would be. We went through the notebook. The hairdresser's address problem is solved thanks to him.

'Hey Lizzie' he says. 'Glad I've seen you. Look, I got this big loaf today – still fresh. They let me take it or it would get chucked. Let's eat some in my room. I'm starving.' He hands it to me as if to pursuade me, but I'm hungry and don't need it.

'I'll bring some strawberry jam – and some tea.'

I carry the tea and jam to his room and watch while he makes jam sandwiches. I expect big, two handed 'doorstep' jobs, but he's doing dainty little triangles and laying them neatly in circles around the plate like afternoon tea at the Midland.

'Yum. They look lovely.'

'Come on then. Get stuck in,' he invites licking the jam from a spoon and handing me the plate. So delicious on an empty stomach! We devour the sugary treats like wolves and sit back relaxed.

'Anyway here's that diary I was telling you about.' I announce as he pours more tea. I open the little book and read out some interesting bits.

'See here – it's the name of the hairdresser's she goes to. I could go there and ask about her if I knew where it was but – that's the problem, I don't.'

'That shouldn't be a problem. It'll be in the telephone book,' he says in an instant. Of course! The telephone book. I hadn't see one since leaving home and had forgotten there was such a thing.

'Someone didn't replace the one here, but there'll be one in the library,' he says. 'I'll look it up for you on Monday.' Why didn't I think of that!

SATURDAY 9TH MAR

My friends are all out tonight with their boyfriends and I'm alone again *on a Saturday night!* My room is warmer and I've lots of food in so I should be thankful but I'm lonely. Bobby's gone out somewhere again. Wrote a letter to a friend in Gorton who's not on the phone. Her husband has a good job at Peacock and Beyer and they are going to buy a terraced house near a 'clearance' area where they're demolishing loads with no inside bathrooms or toilets, but theirs is Ok. Another friend in Moss-Side lives in one which doesn't even have running hot water, only a geyser. Most of the street is now shells of houses and rubble. Hers will be soon.

SUNDAY 10TH MAR

Went for a walk in Longford Park. I hadn't been there for years. Its coffee bar had gone. I wandered along to the children's play area and watched kids playing on the equipment. 'Will you push us on the roundabout Miss,' one asked me. I pushed it faster and faster, then jumped on with them. It was like being ten again. I wish I was. Life was good. I had lots of friends. Where are they now?

MONDAY 11TH MAR

I've now got the hairdresser's address thanks to Bobby. It's on Washway Road in Sale. I know that road because Janet and I used to go to the Sale Locarno, a dance hall which was once a cinema. I'll lose money but I'll clock off early on Friday and go.

Cinemas are becoming other things. One in Cheadle Hulme, a dance hall, another a funeral parlour; another a supermarket.

Everyone has television and cinemas will be a thing of the past but I hope the Gaumont isn't. There's a Gaumont and an Odeon in Manchester but they're a bus ride away and tickets more expensive.

WEDNESDAY 13TH MAR

Evening – met Janet at the pub. We wore our knee-length boots. Hers white, mine red. We ended up with freezing cold wet feet because they're only fashion boots. She told me about a cabaret club that's opening nearby. You have to be twenty-one but the bouncer is her cousin so he'll let us in. Denis showed me how to throw darts (the one who picked up my salt packet last time).

He asks me for a date but not for over a week! Talk about keeping a girl waiting. Did I really agree to him making me wait? Am I so desperate. I hope it's for a Saturday night.

FRIDAY 15TH MAR

Finished at three o'clock today. Told Ivy I had a dentist appointment and took a bus down Washway Road. The hairdresser's was easy to find. 'Heidi's Hairdresser's' it said over the window and the number of the road was marked on the door. It looked quite classy. I'd rehearsed what I was going to say and it worked well. I think I've found her.

The hairdresser is younger than I expected and welcomes me in a pink pinafore with huge pockets, large brush and comb protruding and various clips attached. Her auburn hair in a bob looks just done.

INDEPENDENCE

Free hairdressing is probably a perk; it's even more poorly paid than factory work so well deserved. She thinks I want an appointment and stands smiling, poised with pen and appointment book. 'I wonder if you can help me?' I begin hesitantly. I'm looking for a Jennifer Freeman. I know she comes here, so I was wondering…. if you could tell me where I could find her.'

'Jennifer? Well, yes, she's a client here… but what do you mean, where could you find her?'

I patiently explain that she once lived at the address where I live, and that I've found something of hers I want to return. If she could give me her present address I'd be really grateful. She looks unsure. She's not going to give it me I can tell. 'I don't think I should give out client's addresses …but I could tell her you called,' she suggests cautiously. 'Who are you?'

'I'm Lizzie Dale. She won't know me, but if you could ask her to ring me on this number…' I fumble in my bag for a pen.

'Well wait a minute…let me think. She'll be here for a shampoo and trim on Tuesday evening. We're open late, so you could ask her yourself, if you came then.'

'Yes, yes that would great. What time?'

'She's booked at five-thirty. She'll be here an hour at least, so – any time from then. Maybe we could make an appointment for you too.'

She's smiling, looking at my tousled hair, joking but serious. But it's a service I rarely use. I have shampoo, sharp scissors and a steady hand and eye. I'll have to go straight from work and I'll be tired – but it's worth it.

SATURDAY 16TH MAR

Daytime: Worked a Saturday shift then visited 'home'. I told them about finding Jenny and the money and diary but not about her profession! It's a bit too much for them! Mum had a surprise for me. A big, black ugly bike. And it was a MAN's! So old fashioned too.

Mum is beaming as I walk into the house. I can tell she can't wait to tell me something.

'I have something for you,' she says. 'You know you said you wanted a bike to save you bus fares?'

'Yes.'

'Well one of our neighbours has given me one. They were going to give it to the Rag and Bone man. It's in good condition though. They just don't use it anymore. Do you want to see it?'

'Oh yes please – show me!'

I picture myself upon a trendy, brightly coloured Raleigh bike, straight handlebars, three gears, hair blowing in the wind and admired by friends and pedestrians. What's propped against the fence in the garden is black, like the one the butcher boy rides, albeit without the great heavy front iron 'basket'. It is not trendy. It is not elegant. It has a pump, a bell, seat height for a giant – and a CROSSBAR!

'Mum. I can't ride that! It's a man's bike…a boy's!' Her face falls. 'Does it matter? It's a bike isn't it. You'd get used to it.'

'Do you want me to show my knickers to the world when I get on it?' I protest.

'Wear trousers,' she says.

'I haven't got any. Non of my friends wear trousers. I'd look silly – like I was trying to look like a lad.'

'There's a pair of your jeans here somewhere. The ones you used to wear for horse-riding.'

I've squashed her good intentions and spoilt the surprise by rejecting the kindly meant gift. I'm suddenly aware of how hurtful I'm being. Maybe, I suppose – if the rest of me looked feminine it might look just look alright. Anyway, only travellers to work would see me on the hidious thing, so I change my ungrateful response.

'Sorry Mum. It was really nice of you to think of me. I will have it. It will save me money and I'll get used to the crossbar like you said.' She smiles.

'You could wear bloomers like your grandma. Those great big pink ones she wears!'

'Yes, I could wear the matching pink corsets too and the hat.'

Dad appears. 'Oh hello Lizzie. So you've seen the bike. I've mended the puncture. I'll just adjust the seat height for you.'

'Thanks Dad.' I smile and resign myself to this monstrous contraption.

Later, I set off on it back to the house. It's not like any I've ridden before and has a mind of its own, it's a devil bike. At a road junction I try to stop. The brakes work fine but the pedals don't stop! I take my feet off and one clonks me on the back of my leg. Ow! I set off again.

Minutes later I'm sprawled across the road, the contents of my bag strewn all over. The helpful driver who'd almost driven over me picks me up. My arm is bleeding but I'm not seriously hurt. He makes reassuring noises, picks up the bike for me and continues on his way. The Dragon glares when I bring it into the house. She's been window watching.

'Where do you think you're going to keep that?' she demands.

'In the hall here?' I know this is not going to work. 'Outside in the back. I'll get a lock for it,'

Suddenly her tone changes.

'Have you hurt yourself?' she asks seeing my bloodied arm. She senses I'm almost in tears and hands me a hankerchief. 'I'll get you something to put on it,' she says kindly. I explain what happened.

'Oh it must be a fixed wheel bike,' she says.

What's one of those? I find out it is a particular type of bike you have to keep pedaling; even when stopped! You have to somehow try and back pedal. Its mechanics are much simpler than conventional bikes so they're much cheaper to produce. I park it round the back next to the dustbins and hope someone will steal it.

The bike disaster's tired me but I'm bored by the evening. Everyone is out including Brenda and Bobby. I'm fidgety. Am I interested in this radio programme about gardening? No, I'll reread this magazine or maybe try the crossword. No, I won't, I'll wash some smalls in the sink. No, I may as well do my journal, then I'll visit Doris and ask if I can watch *Morecombe and Wise*. At least they'll make me laugh.

SUN 17 MAR

Slept in until 11.00. Walked round to Janet's. Guess what. Andy was there of course. Felt a gooseberry so went for a ride on the

INDEPENDENCE

devil bike. I'm getting used to bruised shins! I rode round a corner right past the mystery man standing where I'd seen him before. I braked to a sudden stop in front of him avoiding the moving pedals, and wasn't sure whether to speak to him, but when I did, he asked me for a date! That's two in just over a week! It's a feast or a famine.

'Do I know you?' I ask. He looks up and pauses.

'You may have seen me around. I'm fairly local.'

'Oh, so am I… So where do you live?' I inquire for something to say. He hesitates then names an avenue I've never heard of.

'Oh, where's that?' He doesn't seem to want to answer, and I've run out of small talk so I begin to get on my bike. I'd only spoken to him to satisfy my curiosity.

'Wait a minute,' he says. 'Do you live in that house there?' he points.

'Yes. Why?'

'I was going to apply for a bedsitter there…and I wanted to see what it was like from the outside.'

I'm puzzled. He doesn't seem to realise I've seen him before. How many times does he need to see the outside of the house? I think about it for a moment.

'Actually… there isn't one to let at the moment.'

'There was,' he says. 'Maybe it's been let now. I've not seen you around though. Did you think you knew me?'

'Well, for a minute I did…but I have seen you here before.'

'Have you? Well if I'd seen you I'd have remembered it. You're such an attractive girl. Hope you don't mind me saying that. Bet you've been told that before?'

67

Not that often I think. Not as much as I'd like. But I smile and accept the compliment. I begin to get on my bike again but he stops me.

'Oh don't go yet. I'd like to talk to you some more …Yes I know – it's cold now and you want to go in. Would you like to come for a drink with me one evening, somewhere warmer,' he asks pleasantly. 'There's a nice pub round the corner with a fire.'

'I don't know. I don't really know you.'

I'm thinking about it. He is quite good looking. Tallish, dark haired, nice and evenly built, nice face, well dressed, with trendy spectacles that didn't spoil his face but make him look thoughtful and interested. A bit older than lads I've dated before but definitely attractive.

'You're not sure really are you?' he says catching my uncertainty. 'Tell you what. Let me have your phone number – there is a phone for the house?' he asks. 'Then you can think about it. Would that be OK?'

I can't think of a good reason not to, so I give it to him on a scrap of paper he's produced.

'Thanks" I say as if he's done me a favour.

'Well I'd better have your name…so I know who to ask for.'

'It's Elizabeth. Just ask for Lizzie.'

'I'll look forward to talking to you again one day I hope Lizzie.' he says and watches me walk the bike the last few yards from the shadow of the hedge.

TUESDAY 19TH MAR

Hairdresser visit. I made sure my hair looked Ok when I went to 'Heidi's Hairdresser's'. I'd shampooed it and put rollers in the night before but I must have pulled them out in the night as most were on the floor in the morning. I met Jenny and she was so grateful I'd contacted her. I didn't take the money as I didn't want to take that much to work and carry it around but we arranged a meeting so I could give it to her then.

I wait outside the salon in the rain. She arrives in a black cab. She's slim with long blonde hair; just a bit taller than me and and gets out of the car like a model, legs gracefully together, then balancing perfectly in her high heels. I call to get her attention.

'Jennifer… Jenny. Can I have a quick word? It won't take long.' She stops and looks puzzled. Within seconds I've related the circumstances and her face lights into a lovely smile. She'd written it off, but she remembers hiding the money and the diary when I tell her where I'd found it. I promise to bring it to her on Thursday when we agree to meet.

'Oh that's fantastic. I knew I'd left it but I didn't want to go back and face her …or him. Know who I mean?' Her face registers distaste. 'It was almost worth fifty quid not to go back for it.' I nod. I know who she means – but fifty pounds! I'd crawl on my hands and knees through hell, high water and humiliation to retrieve that much money!

'Come into the salon so we can chat. It's wet out here. What did you say your name was?'

'Elizabeth, but call me Lizzie. I'm glad I've been able to contact you. I'd almost given up.'

'Thanks so much, Lizzie,' she says smiling, showing perfect teeth. 'Did you come all this way on the bus too? That was so good of you.'

I'm offered a swivelling chair next to her. Heidi is busy with someone so we're free to talk. She's easy to talk to and I'm immediately at ease. She must be seventeen now like me, maybe eighteen but looks even younger with her blonde hair and shiny rounded cheeks that look as if they've been polished. Is she wearing make-up? No, she's naturally pretty – so lucky. I've forgotten about her 'work' as we chat about the Brysons and some past tenants until it's time for her shampoo. We arrange to meet on Thursday evening at the Seymour Hotel to hand over the money.

'Here, let me get you a taxi home.' She takes a pound note from a purse and offers it to me. 'You don't want to be messing around on buses at this time, and it's raining. Go on. Take it.' She pushes it into the bag I'm holding before I can argue.

'I'll phone one for you,' she says, 'It'll be here within ten minutes and you'll stay nice and dry.'

I'm grateful. I wouldn't keep dry in that Manchester drizzle; it's the type that soaks you before you realise it's raining, but a pound? That seems too much.

'I don't think it will cost that much. Are you sure? Can I give you some back,' I offer.

'It's Ok. Keep it. It's worth it for what you've done. I wasn't going to bother going back there but you've given me a way to get my money back – such a nice surprise... and I remember there's an address I need in the diary too, so it's been very useful. Thanks again and ...see you on Thursday then.'

'Yes, Ok, see you Thursday. Bye for now.' A black taxi appears and pulls up. 'Miss Freeman?'

'Well actually it's for me,' I explain, but he's opened the door and helped me in and I'm home in fifteen minutes.

INDEPENDENCE

WEDNESDAY 20TH MAR

I've thought about it. Yes, maybe I will. He hasn't rung yet but it's only three days ago. He looked in his mid- or late -twenties so probably too old for me anyway – and he's probably changed his mind. I'm not that bothered. I have another date on Friday with Denis.

THURSDAY 21 MAR

Went to the Post Office straight from work to draw out the fifty pounds for Jenny. I took Brenda along to prove I wasn't trying to keep it, although I know she trusts me, then we met Jenny in The Seymour. She wanted to give us ten pounds each as a reward but we said NO; There's no point losing twenty pounds after our efforts to reunite her with it. Brenda had to go early (boyfriend) so it left the two of us. We got on so well I knew I could make a friend of her despite what she does. It wasn't her fault she was abducted from a chlldrens' home and misused so badly. She must have had an unhappy childhood to be in one in the first place.

We have a long talk. She's wearing a black Astrakhan coat – very fashionable. I've wanted one for ages. She's made up, but not too much and looks good. I tell her I've had to read bits of her diary to locate her but she doesn't seem to mind the intrusion.

'Well you know what I do now – so I don't need to pretend. Yeah, the addresses are some of my clients; you were right about that. Hope it didn't shock you too much.'

'No, it was the most interesting thing I'd read for ages.'

I'm tempted to ask what it's like with different men each night but I don't. Too intrusive.

I do ask about names though, about Harold and yes, I was right, he was the 'sugar daddy' child abuser who'd introduced her to the trade. Just as I'd thought.

'And Earnest? Who's he?' I ask.

'Earnest? Oh…you'll know who that is…don't you? … Mr Bryson.'

'Mr Bryson! No!' I'm agog. 'But why were you giving him money? I mean, apart from the rent?'

'That was for letting little me rent the flat. I was almost underage.' She gives an ironically sweet smile. 'He was a friend of Harold's, so he paid him – as a friend, for his discretion. So … they were sharing some of my earnings and weren't they on to a good thing! Bloody parasites.'

'Good God… was Mrs Bryson in on this too?'

'Oh heavens, no. She'd have lynched them and evicted me! She knew something was amiss though when I ran away from Harold… The police got involved 'cos my friend reported me missing. I'd only been gone five days! Anyway, the police came to the Bryson house and were all over it, the cellar and everywhere, and it got in the local papers – so she knew what I'd been doing! That's why she doesn't like me. Brought the house into ill repute she said. As if it was a nunnery before!'

'So where did you run to?'

'My friend, Joyce's, in Whalley Range. That's where I live now. I didn't tell anyone because I didn't want Harold to know where I was – and I owed him money too, what you've just given me. I'd hidden it but I left in such a hurry I forgot to take it.'

INDEPENDENCE

'So glad I could return it – and get to meet you.'

'I'd gone missing once before you know – from a Children's home. Harold took me away from there. Not that they cared once I'd turned sixteen. They saw I'd got somewhere to live and were happy I was off their hands. You're on your own after sixteen you know. They'll usually find you a room but its often something grotty, or with people you don't like. Harold promised me something better. 'Soon,' he'd keep saying when I complained …but it didn't work out like that …so I needed a new start. I've found there's only one person I can rely on – and that's myself – and I've never looked back.'

'But you had an awful time didn't you?'

'Yes… but…I've got over all that….I've learned to look after number one.' Anyhow, I'll have to go soon. Sorry but I need to see someone at nine. Tell you what; it was lovely meeting you again. Phone when you get some free time. We could go out somewhere and enjoy ourselves. Here's my number.' She scribbles it on a beer mat. Yes I'll do that I think.

FRI 22 MAR

Went out with the lad I'd met at The King's, Denis, who's good at darts. I don't like him as much now I've been out with him. He's not good company – in fact he's boring! He probably finds me boring too, not enjoying darts or drinking so the feeling's mutual. I was so tired I just wanted to get rid of him in the end!

Denis, who'd supervised my uncoordinated attempts at throwing darts mainly missing the dartboard, thought I was worth a date.

He'd have liked to be the late James Dean; quiffed hair, 501 blue jeans, rebellious looks, but just an outdated teddy boy really, a relic of the fifties – or like the 'Rockers' who arrange local wars with scooter riding, short haired 'mods.' But he wasn't aggressive. In fact I couldn't imagine him wasting his energy on anything and his horizons didn't extend beyond a few beers and a dartboard. He liked a pretty girl though. We met by a shopping veranda.

'Hi. What do you wanna do then? Pictures, pub… or just a walkaround?' he says.

Pictures would suit, but am I expected to pay? Males are paid more for the same work but I'm not sure of the protocol. I settle for a walkabout.

'We can get a couple of beers if you like,' he suggests. 'We can sit in the park and drink them.' Is this a treat? A Dandylion and Burdock somewhere warm would be nicer, but sounds babyish. He disappears into the off-licence and reappears clutching two brown bottles. I've only tried beer once before and hated it but I must try and develop a more adult taste.

We stroll to the park; me tottering in impossibly high stilettos my mother says will ruin my back. I have to hang on to his arm to keep my balance: this enhances his macho image as he struts proudly along.

We sit on a damp bench where he produces an opener with a tiny triangular end to flip off the metal caps of the bottles. He must have shaken them, so frothy liquid erupts and dribbles down my sleeve. I try to maintain a neutral expression as I take a mouthful of the bitter stuff.

'Good beer this innit?' he asks. Is he joking! It's the vilest thing I've ever tasted. How could anyone like it! A bottleful gives him new boldness. Beery kissing and attempted groping follow but the beery breath fumes do nothing for me. He lights two cigarettes and hands me one. He holds his between his thumb and forefinger like a pincer. You never see girls hold them like that. It doesn't look elegant like when Brenda smokes and he makes an unnecessary sucking noise which gets on my nerves. The cold park bench is hard and I am overwhelmingly weary. I tolerate the discomfort for nearly an hour but it begins to show.

'What's the matter?'

'Nothing. I'm just very tired. You see I'm living away from home now – in a flat, there's more to do and…'

'A flat did you say?' I know this was a mistake.

'Well, just a bedsitter really.'

An adolescent vision of paradise is appearing. A girl! In her own flat; with a bed in it!

But it's hard luck for Denis. I feign a headache and he begrudgingly walks me to the front door. This one's a one track minder. I'm desparate to lose my virginity – and be like everyone else – but he's not even a contender.

SATURDAY 23RD MAR

Brenda said she'd go out with me tonight but she's seeing Malek now instead. Janet is out with hers. I said I didn't mind but I do really! I'm always in on a Saturday night. That's when I feel it most – Saturday nights. She had a strange silent phone call before she went. She's lucky. I don't even get silent ones!

I enjoy Saturday daytimes. I can have a lie in, go shopping, idly watch life go by on the streets or treat myself to hot chocolate or ice-cream in the jukebox café. Friends are around, fully available in the day but by early evening they disappear to preen themselves for the night ahead. Boyfriends come first now. They usurp us like cuckoos, take up our places so we fall to the ground. It's the default understanding between girls, but wouldn't you'd think once in a while, girls could consider their girlfriends; the ones they'd had for years and shared laughs, tears, secrets and joy with.

MONDAY 25TH MAR

Cold again. Will this winter ever end? I'm fed up with it although I still have that secret with Brenda! We thought it would only be for a few weeks but the cold spell has gone on and on. I spend time with Bobby if we are both around – and I often am these days. I hope he doesn't go. I know I'm falling in love with him but it's so one sided!

We sit on his single divan and he tells me Finefare want to train him as a supermarket manager. They've recognised his capability, above their usual expectations and I'm not surprised.

'And what did you say? Do you want to?' I ask hoping he'd said yes.

'I don't know. You know I'd really like to try another university – but I'm not sure how I'll explain why I left the one I was at.' He looks uncomfortable, as if he regrets saying it and fiddles with loose threads on a cushion.

'Why?' I ask. 'Just tell them the truth. They'll have heard it all before I'm sure, so just tell them. Why did you leave anyway? You've never told me.'

'Um… It's not that simple. I haven't told you… because it wasn't fair to burden you, that's why. I've not told anyone. I was in trouble you see… I'll tell you one day. Not now though.'

'But …I thought we were friends. You know you can trust me. Come on. Tell me.'

I don't understand the hesitancy, the wariness. My girlfriends tell me everything, he's a friend, so why doesn't he? Doesn't he trust me? Does he think I'll gossip about him?

'Well ….maybe one day.' He changes the subject. 'Let's cuddle up and keep warm. I'll put some music on.'

He switches on the Dansette record player. It holds about five singles which helpfully drop into place when one finishes and I sit with him, warm and comfortable, listening to the music and wondering why he doesn't kiss me. This would be the perfect opportunity. Am I so undesirable?

TUESDAY 26TH MAR

Work: Therasa is getting married on Saturday so I put half a crown into a collection for a present.

Evening: Walked out of the house with Bobby, then went separate ways. He's probably meeting a girlfriend. So envious. Janet and I played darts at the Kings. I don't get any better at it – like finding a boyfriend, it doesn't happen. 'Bulls eye' if it did. I kept my distance from Denis occupied with another girl, thank heavens!

THURS 28 MARCH

Jenny rang. Mrs B answered but didn't recognise her voice. She'd changed it and said she was Sheila! I do know a Sheila but couldn't think why she'd ring and was so confused until I caught on who it was. She was at a loose end, no clients and Joyce was away so we arranged to meet in the Seymour. She is so different from other friends.

We sit in one of the quieter rooms. Neither of us look eighteen, especially her, and the landlord's challenge provokes a cheeky response from her.

'We're only drinking bitter lemon but I've seen three underage boys drinking beer in the back room so what's the problem? Anyway we are eighteen. We just look young. We've had an easy life.'

I stifle a laugh. He looks at us, shakes his head and leaves us.

'Love your shoes,' I say to Jenny when he's gone. They're white stilettos, high and pointed.

'Yeah there's a story behind these. This client had bought them for his wife and forgot them so when he short changed me I kept them when I saw they were my size.' She laughs. She's very open about her work; the situations and personalities, the funny tales, the eager and hasty, the needy, the perverted. It's entertaining. I've never heard anything like it.

'There's one guy who just wants to be loved. He wants affection and sweet words, then praise for his performance. He's like a child and likes to sit on my knee afterwards. I can hardly wait to get rid of him sometimes but we have to go through this routine before he'll leave. Sad really.'

'Yes, but what if you get someone with nasty tastes?' She laughs. 'Lizzie, I'm wiser now. I don't have to see anyone nasty. If they are, I have the little bell.'

'The little bell?'

'Yeah, by my bed on the wall; a little electric switch. It's the old servants bell. I press it and Joyce is there in seconds, or Bill, her boyfriend if they're more difficult.'

I'm absolutely intrigued. She explains things humorously, in simple language without false modesty and I listen and learn, amused by the anecdotes of this alternative profession.

'What about you then? Your love life?' She's throwing it over to me and I can't really be coy after her frankness – or compete with her experiences!

'Me? … well… I haven't got one. In fact I've never had one. Not a proper one anyway. I've never …you know.'

'You're kidding. You've never had a sexual lover! Are you telling me you're a virgin – at your age! God. I was thirteen when I first did it.'

'Yeah … well I've just never met anyone …nice enough yet.'

She smiles. 'I could soon sort that out for you. I know nice men who'd pay a fortune to deflower you. I could find you one tonight – easy.'

'No. You see it's got to be someone special for me, the right one. I'm not brave like you and I'd feel bad about myself after – if I just did it with anybody – just for the sake of it.'

'You wouldn't be doing it for the sake of it! Lizzie. You need to change your thinking about this. It's a bodily function – a sort of procedure like having your ears pierced or going to the dentist, it's forgotten soon after just like that is. You don't feel bad after having your teeth or ears done do you? Of course

ROOM TO GROW

not. Same with your virginity, something happens to your body, then you forget about it, almost straight away. Did you wait for a very, very nice special dentist or doctor the first time you had a tooth out? She's used a mocking, baby voice – then back to normal as she answers. 'No. It's just womens' sexual guilt – been going on since Adam and Eve; it's for the benefit of men so they can keep the best for themselves. You need to free yourself from it.'

I'm lost for words.

'I've never thought about it like that… and I don't blame you. I know you've had to look out for yourself…and I admire you for it. All the same, I still want the right guy…It's sort of been ingrained. I can't help it.'

She gives a sympathetic smile. She thinks I'm a sad case but it's time to go. I've enjoyed this evening though. She's made me think.

SAT 30TH MAR

Went to the pub. Others were there too besides Janet and Andy so I wasn't alone for a change. When I got back there was a fight between Stan and Mr Bryson! I know bad things about Mr Bryson but I don't like to see him punched like that. I've never seen Stan so drunk before!

He sways up the path singing at the top of his voice at eleven o'clock, the same time as I arrive. He's been seen from the viewing platform by Mr Bryson who comes to the door. 'DON'T THINK YOU'RE COMING IN HERE LIKE THAT!'

Feeling challenged, Stan punches him in the face and I stand frozen as blood dribbles down Mr Bryson's face. He staggers looking dazed.

'Fuck off you shtupid bashtard,' slurs Stan. Olive has heard him and runs downstairs.

'For heavens' sake help me get him away,' she yells. 'He'll hurt someone. Help me get him upstairs.'

We half drag the incapable Stan up the stairs clumsily pushing past the bleeding landlord, Olive remonstrating with the drunken aggressor. The Dragon appears and seeing her bloody-faced husband thunders up the stairs.

'I'll have you out on the streets,' she shouts. Stan shouts back incoherantly. Olive and I manage to get him inside their door and slam it with us inside, backs to the door as reinforcement should the door break. We stand there panting with Stan slumped over us. Mr Bryson follows bleeding, noisily intent on having a fight. I plead uselessly for them to go away. On hearing the rumpus Bobby opens his door. The Beatles' 'All you need is Love' resounds through the house and continues its ironic mantra throughout the shouting. I foolishly open the door to plead with the Brysons to go away and Stan makes a miraculous but stumbling recovery and forces himself past us. He tries to grab the lapels of Mr Bryson who nuts him in the face. Olive futilely tries to separate them as Frank (ex GBH offender) bigger and tougher than everyone else, hears the rumpus, thuds down the stairs and succeeds. There's hardly room on the landing for us all. Mr Bryson wearies and backs off along the landing leaving a blood trail but the Dragon makes a lurch for Stan. Frank grabs her from behind, his arms reaching halfway around her large waist and wrestles her off him. Suddenly everyone's had enough. Stan is now slumped over our shoulders,

Mr Bryson has gone to bathe his face and Frank has pacified the Dragon. We retreat to our respective quarters. Admonishments and threats of eviction face Stan the next day who apologises to the Brysons, one arm firmly up his back by Olive. Poor Olive if she has to put up with this! We now have a new friend, Frank. Any problem with anyone, just let him know!

MONDAY 1ST APR

Work: My work mates are good fun. April Fools jokes all day, even past midday. Mary said I had to go to the flour store. When I went to see what I was supposed to do I 'accidently' got covered in flour. Ivy, the supervisor didn't think it funny. Miserable cow!

Evening: Someone asked for Brenda on the phone. Another admirer? Where does she get them! It could be an April Fool but you're not supposed to do them after twelve o'clock or you're the fool. It happened a few days ago too. I'd hoped it was the guy I met at the front but no. Olive took the call.

'Chorlton 5443,' she says. It's her telephone voice. She pauses. 'Hello, Chorlton 5443,' Several seconds pass. 'You want to speak to Brenda did you say?' She can't sustain the voice and lapses into city talk. 'You'll have to speak up. I can hardly hear you. Who shall I say it is?'

She looks at me puzzled holding the phone at arm's length.

'It's for Brenda. He's got a really weird accent. I can hardly make out what he says. Then there was a funny noise.'

'I'll go and get her' – but she's already on her way down. She's off out somewhere in her stiletto heels, hair piled high and full make up. She always looks good.

'Me?' she asks. 'Who is it?' She takes the receiver.

'Hello. Brenda here.' Silence. 'Who is that please?' Silence. 'Look, I'm in a hurry. If you don't answer me I'm going to put the phone down. She slams down the phone in irritation.

TUESDAY 2ND APR

Janet's 18th birthday party. She wants to get engaged but Andy doesn't! So they had a row – on her 18th birthday! Met Dave – her ex boyfriend. They're still friends. He kept looking at me while I was dancing then came over and bought me a coke. He asked if I'd like to go for a drink somewhere on Saturday. Why do they always want to drink? I'd like to go to a theatre or a restaurant and I'd go myself if I could afford it.

Well, better than staying in on a Saturday night maybe. But I'm watching him drink. He's already downed five pints and his speech is off key. How do five pints fit into one stomach? I don't understand alcohol. I come from a family where a bottle of sherry sits in a cupboard waiting for Christmas, then is consumed by the thimbleful, and I'm getting bored by drinkers.

'Sorry. Thanks for asking, but I've arranged to see friends on Saturday.' Some hope!

WEDNESDAY 3RD APR

Work: Marian is going to work at Parkinson and Cowan where they make cooker parts and things. I'll miss her in my lunch breaks when we gossip and share jokes. Today I had two cream doughnuts for 3d each. Then lunchtime, cottage pie and peas, then rice pudding – all for 9d. Not that much more when I'm eighteen. You wouldn't get that at Parkinson and Cowan.

Evening: The silent caller called again for Brenda and this time she answered it herself. Great isn't it. I'm waiting and waiting for a call from a guy while Brenda gets calls she doesn't want! It's not fair.

THURSDAY 4TH APR

Its so good to have just one friend who is not taken up by some guy! I called Jenny because I wasn't going out all week and needed a break. Bobby had been going out more lately so I haven't seen him. She organises life to suit herself and came by taxi to the Seymour and booked it again for ten-thirty – to take me home too. Pubs can get boring but we had another interesting talk about work. Mine this time.

'So how much do you earn at the bakery?' she asks.

'Eight pounds, ten shillings a week.'

'I could never manage on that. I'd spend that on taxis, hairdressers and manicures.'

'Yeah, well the rent's cheap as you know.'

'Yes but they charged me enough didn't they – Ernie and Harold. Bloodsucking sharks. I wouldn't put up with it now!' She scowls at the memory. 'Harold wouldn't dare come to my place now. I've got good back up. Woe betide him if he even sets foot down our road…. But anyway…. eight pounds ten shillings did you say? What, forty hours a week doing boring work on your feet all day… that's exploitation! That's just an existence

INDEPENDENCE

Lizzie. Don't you want a better life? For God's sake find a rich fella…or more than one. Even better, get one's who'll pay you!'

'I can't do that! You know that. I'd be terrified …and it wouldn't be right for me.'

'Stop being Miss Goody Two-Shoes. It won't get you anywhere you know. And if you're getting bored with pubs we'll go to a night club in Manchester and I'll introduce you to different people, people who have money.'

What does she mean? Who does she know in night clubs? Should I look forward to something interesting or risky?

FRIDAY 5TH APR

Got to do different things at work so enjoyed it more. I was late to clock on – but someone had clocked my card (by mistake?). Ernie, who works a mixing machine told me he'd dropped a biro in the Country Fruit cake mix! His workmates think it's funny. Anything goes with these folk to liven up the routine and Mary was so crude – but she makes us laugh.

Factory routine begins with 'clocking on at 8.00' at the latest. A minute later and you're 'quartered'. No, not some medieval execution technique, just a quarter of an hour's pay docked from your wages. You feed a card into a machine which stamps it decisively leaving indelible proof. They're mechanically accurate, but the cards, kept openly in alphabetical order in racks, are vulnerable to misuse like 'clocking in' for late friends. A quarter of an hour's pay buys a pint of milk and a tin of beans so I am usually punctual.

A shapeless white overall and a turban has to be worn covering all hair. Hair and dandruff are not hygienic, but dandruff looks like dessicated coconut so I don't see the problem with the coconut cake. High temperatures would kill any self respecting organisms anyway. So, in this garb, I dash up a flight of stairs, grab my card, and queue at the 'clock', exchanging greetings with fellow workers. Ker–lunk, ding! Clocking in begins as 'Dirty Mary' arrives, so called because of her ultra coarse jokes which could make a sailor blush. 'Hello Bridget,' she calls to a young Irish woman behind me. 'How's that boyfriend of yours? Did he give you one last night?'

Bridget grins widely. She's learned how to handle Mary. Most people take the ribald teasing and factory horseplay in good humour. It livens long hours of repetitive work. New or young workers have to adapt to it – or be eternally embarrassed.

'Yeah, sure he did Mary. Wouldn't I just tell him to piss off home if he didn't.'

Mary roars with laughter and looks around for her next victim. I studiously examine the numbers on my card, fervantly hoping she won't notice me.

'Ha Ha! Smile if you had it last night?' she shouts, turning round to her captive audience. 'Aha,' she continues, pointing to Ernie, a nervous looking little man who's been unable to resist smiling.

'I bet she gave you a good bouncing Ernie. I bet you're black and blue this morning aren't you Ern?'

Ernie's smile turns into an embarrassed grin encouraging the cackling Mary even more. She can outdo any of the factory men in course banter and poor Ernie is an easy target.

INDEPENDENCE

SATURDAY 6TH APR

Went for a meal at an Indian Restaurant with Brenda and Malek. Malek knows I don't like Saturday nights alone and asked me to go with them which was so nice of him. I'd never had a curry before – or any sort of foreign food so poppadoms and chicken bhuna were really new and exciting to me.

'On your own tonight?' he'd asked. 'You don't need to be you know. Come out with Brenda and I. We're going for a curry.'

'Yes, come on, Lizzie,' Brenda encourages. A dual invitation sounds more acceptable with less chance of not being wanted so I perk up.

'You'll love the restaurant. It's so…so…different. People call it an Indian restaurant but Malek's uncle owns it and his family are from Pakistan …but people don't know the difference so they call them all Indian. You'd think they'd know about Pakistan in nineteen sixty-three wouldn't you? Partition from India was fifteen years ago for God's sake! The food is really good though whatever you want to call it.'

'But I don't want to play gooseberry to you two… I'll be Ok here,' I protest weakly.

'Oh there's nothing wrong with gooseberries,' Malek says with a smile. 'Sometimes a bit sour, but you're not. Come on – we want you to, really. You're welcome.'

Curry? I've only ever had a packet of dried ingredients, of what I'm not sure, which said it was curry on the packet. It tasted of something vaguely spicey with raisons and a little portion of rice in a separate packet. Almost as disappointing as dried packet soup with little chewy bits posing as vegetables.

'I'm not sure,' I reply. Is it like those Vesta ones? 'Will it be very hot?'

'Oh those. They aren't proper ones like we make. They're just flavoured rubbish. Come and try some authentic food – and there's lots to choose from. You'll like it, I'm sure you will.'

So three of us board a bus past Platt Fields to Fallowfield along the main A34 to Manchester beginning to be known as 'The Curry Mile'. The restaurant's name is emblazoned in dark red and gold letters. You can't miss it. The senses get hit straight away. Eastern type music plays subtley in the background and you breathe in a spicy aroma as you enter. Cubes of brightly coloured sweet delicacies make eyecatching displays in the window and colourful depictions of eastern creatures, myths and scenery adorn the walls creating a magical feel. But I'm slightly nervous. Actually, I've never eaten in any restaurant before never mind an Indian one. The Café Royal on Peter Street was the nearest at the wedding reception of a relative when I was about ten so how am I supposed to behave? Will I use the cutlery correctly? Will I understand the menu? Will it be in English?

Dark skinned waiters greet us warmly. They know Malek and his family so we are treated like important guests and I am helped and advised about dishes so I can relax and soak in the atmosphere as I enjoy my first taste of foreign food.

INDEPENDENCE

MONDAY 8TH APRIL

Work: Marian has changed her mind about leaving the bakery so I'm happy. She's counted her blessings, it's not that bad working here and the money wasn't much better there anyway. They make you join a union as well. I don't know what one is.

Evening: The Dragon must have seen one of Malek's visits from her viewing platform. She stopped me on the way out and asked me about him. Nosey cow! She pulls me discreetly to one side as if we are conspirators.

'Here a minute love.'

I'm 'love' when she wants to know something, or she wants a favour like clearing the snow from the path, or to pay her newspaper bill if she thinks I'm 'popping to the shop'.

'Is your friend upstairs going out with that coloured boy?'

She's caught me unprepared again. Should I lie, or say 'yes — and what's it got to to with you,' or keep her guessing. I decide on the latter.

'I don't really know …Why don't you ask her?' I say innocently. She senses evasion and it's not going to get anywhere so walks off muttering about 'foreigners' and 'keeping to your own sort'.

The pay phone rings. I rush to answer it in case its 'that guy' for me.

'Chorlton 5443,' I trill. Silence. 'Hello. 5443. Hello, hello… Who is this?'

There's a noise like shuffling papers but no-one answers. Did I hear breathing? Who on earth is it? Who'd play games like this? So annoying.

'Hello,' I repeat. They hang up.

TUESDAY 9TH APR

The weather is beginning to get a bit warmer at last. Well, warmer than that long winter with roads constantly blocked and cars getting stranded every night. The daffodils are out, nights are lighter, trees are blossoming. Brenda's romance is blossoming too. She smiles more and has that look of contentment which I can't help feeling envious of.

I try to analyse where I might be going wrong. Am I too serious? Too chatty? Too shy? Too ugly? Bad breath? No, I don't think any of these so, what's going wrong? Someone once told me you give out vibes when you're looking for love, and it puts males off. I wouldn't know how to prevent vibes even if I had them – so that's not helpful. Perhaps it's just lack of opportunity as I don't actually go anywhere much.

What would the Agony Aunts say? Follow an interest, join a club, join the local church – they do clubs. OK then: Youth club? Too old now; Young Wives/ Mothers' Union? Unqualified. Church Choir? Can't sing. Bible classes? Not interested. Horse riding. Love to, too expensive. Would night clubs with Jenny count as clubs? Perhaps I'm just destined to be celibate like a nun. I couldn't be one though. My thoughts aren't pure enough and I'm irreligeous.

WEDNESDAY 10TH APR

Something upset me a lot today. That man I gave the house phone number to – Brenda thinks it's Colin! She's so annoyed with me

INDEPENDENCE

and it's not my fault. I didn't know who it was. Anyway it might not be – then she'd be sorry for accusing me. It spoilt our meal together.

We're sharing this meal because Malek has told her how to make a five ingredient, plus rice, spicey dish, so I'm the Royal Taster. At least I don't have to make anything for myself tonight. While she dishes out rice I tell her about the latest silent telephone call.

'Maybe the phantom caller's latching on to you now,' she says, pausing, spoon in hand. 'It's funny that fellow never rang you isn't it?' She's looking strange now as if she's suddenly thought of something. She spoons rice onto the plates then reaches for a tea towel to lift the pan of something smelling delicious.

I taste the rice. A little different. Is it slightly perfumed I wonder. It's subtle and quite pleasant. I wait for the curry and she serves it without a word. It's spicier than the one the other night – different but still not too spicey.

'Ummm. This is really nice you know,' but she's not listening.

'You don't think it could be him – your guy, making the calls do you?' she asks.

'He's hardly my guy. I've only spoken to him once – and why would he do that?' ...I take another mouthful... 'and anyway the phantom's always asked for you not me. I just happened to answer the phone this time.'

'What did you say he looked like?' she's frowning a bit. I know her now. Something's going on in her head.

'Did you you say medium height, quite smartly dressed… black rimmed glasses?'

'Yes. That's what I remember. Like Buddy Holly glasses.'

'How old did he look?'

'Oh, in his twenties, late twenties probably. A bit older than us I suppose. But hard to tell with people sometimes.'

I want to concentrate on enjoying the new flavours and wish she'd stop asking me things.

'Did he have sort of darkish wavy hair. Sort of shiny?'

'Yes. Well I think so. Can't remember that well, but I think he had. Quite nice it looked.'

'And he was smoking?'

'Yes. Each time I saw him.'

'Did he light his cigarettes with a silver Ronson lighter?'

'I don't know. I didn't notice. I wasn't that close. He might have done. Hey, what's all this about? Do you think you know him or something?'

'Yes. I think I do! And you've given him the house phone number haven't you!'

'Yes. Well?... Ok. So what?'

'You fool Lizzie! You absolute idiot! It's Colin, I'm sure! I think it's him snooping about. I bet it is! And you went and gave him the number! Did he say his name was Colin?'

'He didn't give me his name. I never thought to ask.'

'So you gave our...the house telephone number to a complete stranger ...when you know someone is trying to get at me!

It isn't a question. I'm stunned by the anger. It puts me off my food.'

'That's why he's snooping about. He's found out where I live and now he knows the phone number as well thanks to you!' she snarls. She hardly speaks to me while we eat.

Later, I think about it. The man I spoke to seemed really nice once I'd got him talking – encouraging without trying too hard

INDEPENDENCE

– and so pleasant. He couldn't possibly be the nasty, jealous Colin, so she's wrong about that.

FRIDAY 12TH APR

Brenda is still annoyed with me even though I've apologised and still don't even know who the man was I gave the phone number to! I don't think it was him anyway. Well I'm not going to bother with her until she gets over it. I did some overtime at double time but was on my own in the evening. Bobby is on the Aldermaston March today. I wish I'd gone with him now.

But I didn't, so that's the bank holiday weekend spoiled. I try counting my blessings. I am not a refugee, blind, stupid or suffering from some horrible disease. I have friends even if they all have boyfriends. I have food and a good book, and now the awful weather has gone I feel warmer despite increasing heating costs since giving up the 'winter secret'. I'd started to feel ashamed about it, even though blatant extortionism necessitated it, and there's always the worry of getting caught. But it's Spring – less need to do it, and things could be much worse. Read your book and think yourself lucky. Despite the rationalisation I'm still lonely.

SATURDAY 13TH APRIL

Worked a Saturday morning shift at double time so wages should be good next Friday. I don't think Bobby will be back until late, or even tomorrow. Everyone else has somewhere to go and someone to go with. It's bad enough being alone on a Saturday night – but a bank holiday as well! These should be with someone you love.

Yes, Saturday nights and bank holidays are special. They're for putting on stylish clothes, spending ages doing your hair and make-up and being with people you like – or are in love with. I'm in love with Bobby and can do the dressing up bit but can't make him interested in me. Not as a love item. How come Brenda always has someone? Men make a beeline for her, eating out of her hand within minutes yet she's so casual it's almost rude. Same with Jenny. Maybe I should be more direct, more frank, say what I think and want and to hell with them. It's not me though. It would be a façade.

SUNDAY 14TH APR

I thought I was going to spend the whole Bank holiday alone but Bobby came back from the Aldermaston march this afternoon. I was looking forward to seeing him so much even though he treats me like a sister. I've been waiting and waiting and waiting for it to change! I really wanted him to be my first real 'lover.' I knew he'd be understanding and gentle, so I tried to tempt him but it didn't work out and left me flat and disappointed.

I was low. All my friends were in relationships now: Janet, Brenda and schoolfriends too. I envied them and felt a freak for being on my own and a virgin. No-one else in my circle was.

INDEPENDENCE

It was 1963 and attitudes were changing. Well, maybe not for the older generation, but certainly amongst mine and I was head over heels in love with Bobby. Something had to change. I had to do something. The answer lay less than six feet away, through a wall!

So I decided I must act – tonight. I know he won't be going out so I put a shilling into the geyser knowing it won't have time to heat the water. Ugh, it's luke warm and the bath cubes don't dissolve properly but I'm getting in. I shampoo my hair so it will look good when I dry it and spray it. I step out of the bath, put on my 'Baby Doll' pyjamas – a short two piece job, slightly see through which I thought he'd like, and apply 'Outdoor Girl' peachy pink lipstick and some perfume. Nothing too obvious. This has got to work. My hair is still damp but I can't wait any longer.

I knock at his bedsitter door. His light is on and he lets me in straightway like we do for each other. The room is cold so he's been reading in bed fully dressed.

'You may as well get in,' he invites pulling back the covers. 'It's more comfortable than that bashed up settee.' I don't hesitate. A brilliant opportunity!

'I was going to get an early night, ' he says. 'Where've you been? Whatever's that…perfume?'

'It's "Remember", by Goya. 'It's my best one,' I add. 'I was with Janet earlier, but then her boyfriend came and they didn't want me as usual so I went. It's always the same. Everyone's got someone – except me. Always the spare part, the hanger on. Anyway, you know Bobby…' I begin. 'I've been thinking'.

'Oh careful now. It strains the brain,' he jokes.

'Not sure if I've actually got one,' I joke back.

But I don't want to joke and I snuggle next to him with my arms around him. It's the closest I've ever been to him: then closer, and to his surprise begin stroking his shoulders over his Tee shirt. Gentle caresses. Lovely little light strokes – but no reaction! He stays perfectly still. I stroke his upper arms, his chest, then tentatively a little further down his body.

'Lizzie! What the heck are you doing?'

'I thought it was obvious…Don't tell me you don't like it… Bobby…don't you think I'm attractive?' I'm slightly worried now. He gently removes my hand.

'Of course you are …but we're friends aren't we?'

'Yes, but friends can get closer can't they?'

'Yes, but… Look this isn't going to work Lizzie …I don't want to hurt you but – I'm not the one for you. You need to find someone …someone nice…but it won't be me.'

I'm mortified.

'I think I'm in love with you if that makes it better. Oh, I'm fed up with not having anybody. I feel so different to my friends. I'm sick of being the only virgin in town. I wanted you to be my first time. Someone I know who'd be kind. Who I could trust. You don't have to be in love with me or anything…and I wouldn't demand anything… or expect a great romance or anything… so what's wrong with me?'

My self image has plummeted. I'm disappointed, rejected, a failure.

'Hey, hey, hey. There's nothing wrong with you…and you can trust me, but you don't understand. There are …things… things I've not told you… It wasn't fair to burden you with them… so I didn't.'

'What things? Tell me, why should anything make a difference?'

'Lizzie... I don't love girls!...I like them as friends – but nothing more. Do you get me?'

'What do you mean?' It begins to dawn on me what he is saying. 'Are you...do you mean you're a ...'I can't even say it and he senses my monentary confusion.

'Yes. 'Fraid so Lizzie. Sorry... So sorry about that. Are you terribly shocked?'

'No...I'm just ...surprised. I've never known anybody like that before. But ...I'd never have guessed. As long as it wasn't me that put you off. I'd hate myself if it was.'

'You wouldn't put any bloke off. You're lovely. I'd help you if I could – as a friend, but I know it wouldn't work. It would be a complete flop!' We both laugh at the double meaning.

'That's why I had to leave university.' He looks serious now. 'I had an affair with a tutor – a man. You know it's against the law don't you? The physical thing I mean? When they found out they threw me out – well, asked me to leave. You must promise not to tell anyone. You do know how important it is don't you?' he asks earnestly.

'Oh Bobby... I'm sorry. I didn't know. I never thought ...All this time too...It makes sense now. Why didn't you say before? You should have told me when you had chance. I would have been kind about it.'

'Well, there it is. I hope we'll still be friends. I can love you as a friend you know.'

'Thanks ...and I'm sorry ...I promise I won't ever try and seduce you again. We'll just cuddle up now and keep warm. Don't worry. I'll never tell anyone what you've told me.'

'I know you won't,' he says. I nestle down nursing my disappointment to internalise what I've learned and have to accept.

MONDAY 15TH APR

Last night I found out why Bobby had to leave university. We will only ever be friends and he'll never love me the way I want. I know that. My phone call never came from the man I met outside either, whoever he is. Not even the silent calls are for me! Brenda is still cool with me and I fell off my bike again. I'm not feeling happy at all.

Easter weekend was not a good one. Lonely, a rejected seduction attempt, my friend not speaking to me, no phone call from the guy I'd met outside and a bruised leg and elbow. I'm low. What more could go wrong.

PART TWO
Colin

WED 17TH APRIL

Such a surprise! Mystery man was waiting for me outside the house when I came back from work. It is Colin after all! I found out his name but he's not like Brenda said at all and I'm sure she exaggerates! He seems really nice. I'm going to go out with him – just once to prove what he's really like. I'm sure he's alright and just once won't do any harm will it?

'Oh it's you,' I'm a bit surprised as he suddenly appears from nowhere as I arrive back from work.

'Don't look so surprised. I said I wanted to see you again didn't I? Remember?'

'Yes, but that was weeks ago and you said you'd ring.'

'Well I lost your phone number. So, I thought you'd be getting home about this time so I waited, and I was lucky wasn't I.'

'You never told me your name.'

'You didn't ask.'

'Are you Colin by any chance?'

'Now, who've you been talking to? Let me guess. Brenda?'

'Well – are you? Colin?'

'Yes – but this is nothing to do with Brenda. Her and I were finished some time ago. It's you I came to see. That's why I'm here.'

'But you told me you were thinking of renting a bedsitter here. Why would you if you and her were over?' It doesn't make sense.'

'Lizzie. I'm so sorry… Listen, I had to lie to you. Yes, at first when you saw me I was hoping to see Brenda. I really loved her you know, and …although we'd parted, I sometimes, sort of… had a need to see her, to see if she'd change her mind. I didn't want to admit to you that I was hanging around for a girl – like a love sick puppy. So I made the bedsitter excuse so you wouldn't think I was pathetic.'

'You needn't have done that. I'd have understood.'

'But then, after I spoke to you, something changed. You looked so young, so pretty sitting on that big black bike. And so natural to talk to. I thought…there's something about that girl I like and I knew straight away I had to get to know you. A voice was telling me you'd been sent to make me forget about Brenda – if only you'd give me a chance.'

'You took your time to come and find me if you thought I was so nice!' I'm not sure whether to believe him.

'I know. I didn't want to rush things in case it put you off. I was giving you some time. Did you think about it by the way? Whether you'd come out with me? You said you might.'

'Sort of, but I've been waiting for you to ring …but first tell me truthfully, have you been making silent telephone calls, to Brenda… and me the other day when I answered it – because it's not a joke if you have.'

'What calls? Silent calls? Me? No of course not. I couldn't

have. I've told you I've lost your number. That's why I've had to come here in person …Have they been bothering you?'

'Not me. Brenda. She thought it could be you.'

'She said that! She should know me better! I'm not afraid to speak to people.'

'Well I'm not giving you the number again – even if it wasn't you. I'm not risking making her angry again.' He listens and thinks about it.

'Well how will I contact you then? Come out with me – just once. See if you think I'm capable of funny phone calls.' He smiles at me. It's a nice smile I think, warm and friendly with just a touch of teasing. I think it's sincere.

'I suppose we could meet here tomorrow if you like. Maybe go for a quick drink.' I suggest.

'Ok, Lets say seven. We could go to The King's Arms.'

'No, not there. I know people there. I wouldn't want to meet you there. They'd wonder who you were.'

'OK, a bit more discreet. Wherever you want then. Oh yes. Something good to tell you. I got some expenses from work. For the whole past year! So I'm buying a car at the weekend. It's a Jaguar. I've paid a deposit on it, done the paperwork and I'm picking it up on Saturday. Tell you what, let's leave it until then and we can drive out somewhere in Cheshire.'

I can't resist. It's the best offer I've had for a long time. A Saturday night and I won't be alone for once.

FRIDAY 19TH APRIL

Evening: Brought Angel cake home today for Bobby and talked

for ages. I'd always wondered about my earlier encounters at fifteen with a boy from school and it was useful to have my suspicions confirmed – just as I thought! I do know what happened but I'm not good at using the right words. Bobby is though. I can talk about anything with him. He's a soul mate.

My doubtful status as a fully fledged woman of the world came up quite naturally in conversation.

'So I'm still a virgin – like I told you that night.' I said. 'Well at least I think I am, but maybe I'm not. I don't know. I'm not really sure.'

'Lizzie, slow down. What do you mean – you're not sure if you are? That lad you told me about; the one with the cosy cellar in his parents' house. What was his name? Didn't you go out with him for a while? Well didn't you do anything with him?'

'Yes… But I'm not sure that was it.' He tried but … I don't think it worked. It didn't feel how people said it would. He…it…didn't really go anywhere…do you know what I mean? We had to stop.'

'You mean he couldn't get it up?' Now there was a phrase I could use.

'Yes. He couldn't get it up…. get it to go up… inside me.'

'Do you mean – he couldn't maintain an erection?' he says with superior phraseolgy.

'Yes…well I'm not sure. I think he could. You see he tried… but I must be the wrong shape or size or something, so it didn't actually go anywhere …know what I mean? So he gave up. I'm not sure if that counts.'

'Doesn't sound very successful to me. Sounds as you're intact. It doesn't sound as if either of you had much idea of what you were doing either!' he laughed. I'm quite glad really. He wasn't the brightest spark. I tell myself I want to lose that thing – to someone nice but also competant please!

SATURDAY 20TH APR

Morning: Went to the local shops and bumped into Janet. I didn't tell her about tonight in case she sees Brenda because I know she cannot keep a secret! She was surprised when I turned down the offer to meet her and Andy at the pub.

'Why? Have you got a better offer?

My excuse. 'No. I'm a bit broke.'

Late afternoon: Spent ages getting ready and actually, when I looked in the mirror, I'm not that bad now. I'm getting a nicer shape, my legs are slimmer and my hair's longer which suits me better. I've felt so dowdy lately. It's a real treat to get dressed up. I'll even wear my stiletto heels. He'd better be nice!

Late Evening: He was! And I've had the most wonderful evening! He was a real gentleman and his new car is gorgeous! A real Jaguar with leather seats and a shiny wooden (walnut?) dashboard. We went to a very nice pub in Goostrey in Cheshire. A lovely area with very smartly dressed people. I don't know if I should see him again, but I think I'd like to because I'm so excited! I haven't written so much for ages. Seven-thirty and he's waiting for me outside in his new car

'Oh Colin it's lovely,' I exclaim through its window. 'A Jaguar, how classy – and it's got a silver Jaguar at the front,' I say admiring the silver leaping feline on the bonnet of this gleaming machine.

'Yes. I'm going to polish it every week. The car's not brand new, but the last owner didn't do a high mileage so it's in mint condition and it moves like a bomb. You should see me on a nice empty road! Beats that company car they dumped on me.

I'd never been in a classy car before. In fact not many cars actually, but this was quality, I could tell. He's puffed up with pride, dying to show off his new possession and I'm sharing in his delight.

'Yeah, It's a Mark Two. It has a two-point-four litre engine. That's powerful – and you'll love the real leather seats. But, come on. Get in. We'll go to Goostrey.'

Goostry? It might as well be on the moon. I don't know where it is nor care. Away from here must be a better place. I step in and breathe in the leathery seats smell. It even has a little record player that plays singles. I relax into the comfortable seat and we set off passing Wilmslow and Alderley Edge, speeding through pretty countryside; windows open, 'The Searchers' blaring out their hit, 'Sugar and Spice'. It's windy and exhilarating and I'm tingling and excited.

'There's the Lovell Telescope,' he says pointing out the huge dish we're about to pass. I've heard about this famous telescope but never seen it before. It's involved in ground breaking research and I'd like to stop and look at it but zoom – we've past it.

We enter a quiet bar with a real coal fire; not a bit like the Horse and Jockey or the King's Arms. Conversations are quiet, tasteful music plays in the background, there are no rowdy youths and only conservatively dressed people. Expensively dressed people in fact. Just look at that dress. You wouldn't get that in C&A, and that suit is more than Burton tailoring.

'What would you like to drink?' he asks.

Gin and orange sounds sophisicated, so I ask for it even though I'd really like a coke. He returns with a tall glass clinking with ice-cubes and embellished with slices of orange. So icy, pretty and delicious. I actually liked it and had another enjoying the heady feel as we swapped selected personal information, edited for embarrassing bits but as open as necessary.

I return home slightly inebriated, uninhibited and unsnogged. I get a kiss on the cheek and that's it. He knows why I don't ask him in and doesn't question it; such a gentleman. We've both enjoyed the evening. The best Saturday night I've had in ages. I'm as high as a kite, fluffed up as candy floss.

WEDNESDAY 24 APR

Brenda has sent a peace offering – naan bread and a chicken dish from Malek's uncle's restaurant left outside my door, hot, so I couldn't refuse it. I could smell it as soon as I reached the stairs to my room starving as usual. Probably Malek's idea but it was nice of them. I haven't dared tell her about last Saturday night – about enjoying myself so much – I know what she'd say!

I'm glad she's coming round though. I suppose it was silly of me to give our phone number to a complete stranger, especially under the circumstances, but she's obviously forgiven me so I enjoy the food; delicious, just the right spiciness level for a beginner taster like me. She's given me a recipe for it but I don't have the ingredients.

Neither do most local shops.

'Gar...um...mas...al...a?' asked an assistant trying to pronounce it. 'What's is it? I don't think we sell it. Is it one word?'

Same with tumeric. I tried to explain, then settled for garlic which she'd heard of, could pronounce and had some in store.

'I can't stay long.' Brenda says as I thank her for the treat. 'I'm meeting Malek.'

Good, I think. I don't have to lie or explain anything, even though it's been going round and round in my head like a tape recording; those small details: the icy gin, the smell of the car, the neat little pattern on his tie, the matching silver cigarette case and lighter, as if it was an hour ago. He did ask me out again, 'soon' he said but didn't say when. Best kept quiet for now.

THURSDAY 25TH APR

Morning: Late for work because of an accident on Seymour Grove. I'll be docked half an hour's pay that could pay for a meal! Good job I can eat at work.

Evening: My dilemma. Should I go out with him again? I felt so good to be out somewhere nice on a Saturday night with a good looking man – in a nice car too, so I think I will. Who can it harm? But I will have to tell Brenda this time as I don't want to lie or pretend with friends. You get found out and it makes things worse.

She's horrified when I tell her. Her eyes widen in disbelief.

'Lizzie – you must be careful. He's …very …plausable. He'll be wonderful at first, believe me. He'll treat you like a princess, and before you know it you'll be under his spell and going along with everything he says. Don't let having a good time pursuade you. Take my advice. I don't want you to get hurt or bullied like I did!'

'Look it's just another date. I wouldn't let him hurt me anyway. He just wants someone to try out his new car with… and I'm far too young for him …and probably not sophisticated enough either. He's not going to want me for long. Why would he want to keep seeing a seventeen-year-old girl?'

'Because that's what he likes! As young as legally possible so he can be boss! They don't argue as much. He can direct things and get all his own way and and they'll just go along with it. He'd go for pre–pubescents if he could get away with it!'

She's exaggerating I can tell. Is she jealous? Is this 'dog in the manger' syndrome? Besides, there are two sides to everything. I know she's a terrible flirt …and a two-timer, so it's no wonder he got cross with her sometimes. I'm not sure if he actually did hit her but I wouldn't let him hit me! I'd be off like a shot if he did. And did he really stop her going out? How can you stop someone going out? My parents never managed it with me!

She's probably trying to blame him because it didn't work out and turned sour, but I'm going to make my own mind up. Anyway, ten years older than me isn't that much. Same as my mum and dad and they were OK.

'Lizzie I'm warning you,' she says, her face serious. 'You'll regret it. I know you will.'

I nod to show I'm listening. She means well, but I'm nearly eighteen and don't need this advice.

FRIDAY 26TH APR

Ate out at a 'Bernie Inn' with Colin. Steak and chips and new forest gateaux! Expensive compared to canteen food. Today, a good two-course lunch for under eighteen-year-olds costs less than a shilling.

He has to work away for a while soon. He's an insurance assessor whatever that is, but I think it's a good job. He's worked his way up so he must be steady and reliable. The evening was a lovely surprise. He just turned up!

His car is there, as I arrive back from work, and he's sitting reading a newspaper. He's smoking and every spot of ash goes into the ashtray, the tidiest smoker I've ever known. The car is immaculate as if he's polished every shiny inch of it, and the British Racing Green colour – so classy and tasteful. I loved going out in it last Saturday. I wanted people to look and say 'Who is that lucky girl with such a handsome man in that lovely car?'

He winds down the window.

'Hi. Do you fancy something to eat?'

'I don't know. I'm not really dressed for it.'

I compare my flat heeled shoes and plain clothes I wear under my overalls to this well groomed driver but he doesn't seem to see the contrast.

'You look fine to me. Can't you just go up and change if you're that bothered.'

'What did you mean, something to eat? Shall we go to the chip shop? I wouldn't need to change for that.'

'No. We'll do something better than that.'

'But that'll be expensive won't it?' I haven't worked out cost sharing protocol on dates and don't like to admit my money is carefully budgeted for the week and I won't get a wage increase until I'm eighteen in two months.

'Oh, that won't matter. My treat because I've invited you – I'd love someone to eat with. I never enjoy eating on my own – so I pay.'

'But Colin... you paid for our drinks last time... so I think I must contribute something. It's only fair, and then there's the petrol. I must pay towards that too.'

'Well that's only about five bob a gallon at the moment, but besides, no girlfriend of mine ever pays for anything when we go out. It's against my principles. No, you won't pay a penny. I won't hear of it. I'd be offended it you did,' he asserts carefully stubbing out his cigarette into a newly cleaned ashtray.

I don't argue too much. We wouldn't go far on my money. Did he just call me his girlfriend?

It's cold and I'm getting hungry so I'm a pushover.

'Just give me a few minutes to get changed.'

SATURDAY 27TH APR

Alone on a Saturday night again. I'd rather our date had been tonight rather than last night – but at least the whole weekend's not been a complete flop. I keep wondering where he is and what he's doing tonight. He's such a gentleman, and not at all like Brenda said. He seems to be on his own too, like me, so it's nice for both of us and I can't wait to see him again. Today is such a dreary contrast to last night.

The rest of the empty day looms. A book might pass the time so I walk to the local library in a Manchester drizzle. I've just read *Doctor No* by Ian Fleming. Doris had lent it me and I want *Goldfinger*, but it's not on the shelf. It went straight out, the librarian said and would I like to reserve it. Not really. I want something now. She guides me to similar fiction but I'm not interested and leave as dampened as the day wondering what to do with the rest of it.

I return *Doctor No* to Doris in the hope of a TV invite later, even though it might mean watching *Bonanza*. She's alone as usual with her cheerful budgie bashing it's reflection in its tiny mirror then dancing along its perch chattering non stop. Her room is always warmer than mine which makes me wonder if her meter is set at a different rate and if so, why? There's a cruxifx on the wall with the usual dejected looking Jesus – not cheerful viewing but it's her choice of ornament as are the flying ducks, so I'd never comment. My posters of Liverpool groups don't exactly exude good taste.

'Come up later if you're not going out,' she suggests. I'm relieved. I didn't like to ask. So I join her and she knits and natters throughout the programmes, but anything's better than sitting alone. I leave Doris about ten-thirty not wanting to outstay my welcome and find a note cellotaped to my door.

'Lizzie, someone left something for you. I've left it in the hall,' it says in scrawly writing. I run downstairs and find the

COLIN

package by the payphone. Inside there's a box of Newbury Fruits and a card. 'Sweets for my sweet,' it says inside. 'The Seachers' hit we'd been playing in his car last night sweetly combined title and message. 'See you Monday,' it added at the bottom. He must have been here? Well that was lovely of him wasn't it.

SUNDAY 28TH APR

Another nice surprise! The weekend has got better. Jenny rang and asked if I could go riding with her in an hour's time. In an hour! Not much notice and I didn't know she liked riding or where we would be doing it. I found she was looking after a client's horses for the weekend and it was such a lovely day she fancied a ride. I'd not been riding for six years. I love horses but can't afford anything to do with them so what an opportunity! I found my old jeans and wellies and cycled down to 'Jackson's Boat' (a pub by the River Mersey) and found her sitting on a bench outside with a shandy, an elegant chestnut mare and a sturdy looking piebald grazing beside her.

'Hi Lizzie. The piebald's yours,' she says and hands me the reins still seated on the bench.

'He's lovely,' I enthuse patting it's smooth coat. It looks up briefly then continues it's grassy lunch. It looks well cared for; solid looking with a shiny coat and well trimmed mane and tail; not short, just tidily groomed. It grazes calmly, oblivious to being stroked, or the antics of some passing noisy children.

'He's called Jester,' Jenny informs me. 'He's bomb proof, you won't have any trouble with him.'

113

ROOM TO GROW

In contrast, the classy looking chestnut steps nervously sideways as a stray carrier bag takes off in the wind. I wonder how such a large, powerful animal can be seriously spooked by a paper bag. It watches anxiously as it blows away. I pat it's soft, velvety nose and get a snort of appreciation – or perhaps disdain.

'What's this one called?'

'Do you want her stable name? It's "Golden Dawn" but just call her Goldie.'

'Goldie,' I whisper to her quietly.

She doesn't mind the abbrieviation. She's spotted another hazard: a man approaching with a lively dog. She steps away as it attempts to sniff her.

'How did you know I liked riding?' I ask.

'You told me. Don't you remember? You were wearing those jeans you said you used to ride in. You said you'd gladly swap your evil bike for a horse. It made me smile so I remembered it, and I don't know anyone else who rides. It's more fun to ride with someone, so …I thought of you.'

'So who owns them? Will they mind if I ride one?'

'They're Charlie's; he's an occasional client, a local councilor. You've probably seen his picture at local election time. We do each other a favour occasionally. It's an advantage to know a councilor sometimes and no, he won't mind if tell him you're a friend of mine, and a competent rider.'

'Well maybe six years ago. I may not be now, but this one seems nice and quiet.'

'Yes, he was Charlie's daughter's until she left home. I could ask him if you can look after Jester when he goes away again, if you like.' Jenny offers. 'Then you could ride him other times.'

I don't respond. I don't want Charlie's favours. He might want one back! We ride single file along the riverside paths, Goldie skittish and suspicious of anything that moved, Jester steady as a rock.

'Let's have a good canter,' shouts Jenny without any consulation.

'Oh God no! It's been so long – I might fall off.'

She doesn't hear me in the wind, but my body recognises the rhythm as if I was twelve-years-old again and we're off, exhilarated, wind in hair, sun in face, memories revived.

Home, and I'm greeted by Olive on her way out. It's Sunday, with shops closed except off licences but she has a shopping bag so probably going for Stan's booze. I wouldn't buy him booze. I've seen what it does to him.

'A man was looking for you,' she tells me. 'Glasses, in a dark green car – he stopped outside about an hour ago.'

I know who that was. But why did he call? I hadn't expected him. I thank her and stagger up to my room beautifully exhausted from the horsey exercise.

MONDAY 29TH APR

Went out with Colin tonight. A beautiful evening so we went for a walk in Longford Park and sat in the rose garden, all very quiet and deserted as if it was a Sunday. He questioned my weekend whereabouts which puzzled me a bit.

'So you were in on Saturday night then?' he asks.

'Yes, I've already said.'

'Well your light wasn't on when I drove past that's all.'

What's that in his voice? Something odd that shouldn't be there.

'Oh … well that's because I watched TV in Doris's room so it wouldn't be.' I explain. Where would he think I was? I wouldn't have asked him that. I wouldn't have thought it was very interesting.

'It was nice of you to leave the sweets by the way, I didn't know you'd be in the area though. I thought you were catching up with work all weekend.'

'Yes, I was…but I needed a break so I went for a drive.'

'Down my road? Why there?'

'I wanted to see if you were in, as you said you'd be.'

'Well I was.'

'And I wanted to get away from my boss who's always around. He thinks I don't see him. Huh!'

'What do you mean?'

'Oh, he's watching out for me to make a mistake so he can fire me. He wants to get rid of me. But look, I don't want to talk about that at the moment. Tell me about Sunday.'

'What about Sunday?' I want to ask more about about his boss but he doesn't give me chance.

'I called round and a woman – a tenant, I don't know her name, said you were out.'

'Olive. Yes she told me – and I was. I go out sometimes.'

'You didn't say you were going out on Sunday.'

'I didn't know I had to. Anyway a friend called and we went horse riding,' I deliberately don't name her or encourage curiousity.

'Horse riding! I didn't know you liked riding – well that's an expensive hobby. How much did that cost?'

COLIN

'Nothing, or I wouldn't have gone. She was looking after someone's horses and wanted somone to ride with – so I got a free ride.'

'I see.' I don't understand the question mark in his voice. I've only really started seeing him recently. Brenda said he was the jealous type. Does he think I'm seeing someone else? Chance would be a fine thing wouldn't it!

TUESDAY 30TH APR

Work; The usual stuff. Evening – really great. Went to see *The Birds* at the Gaumont with Colin. The first time I've been to the cinema this year. It was a brilliant film about birds becoming evil and flocking and attacking people. I clung onto Colin's arm at the scarey bits even though I knew it was only a film. The people behind us must have filled all the ashtrays fixed to the back of the seats they smoked so much, plumes of smoke billowing over our heads the whole performance. Why so many? We're smokers but we only had two each from his neat silver cigarette case.

He was really nice as if to make up for questioning me last night. We had a long snog in his car afterwards. He's getting quite amorous!

There are long lingering kisses and murmourings. I'm so young and pretty, I have lovely soft hair; I was meant for him, I'm beautiful! Wait a minute. Who me! I don't think so. He says God is on his side – whatever that means, and He will guide him to make the right decisions? What is he supposed to be deciding. Is it about me? Deciding whether or not to continue this or something? It's not the first time he's brought God into a conversation but I'll swallow my cynicism as belief is a personal choice for people.

Then there's the birds. 'The action of those birds,' he says. 'Do you think Hitchcock wanted to show God was trying to punish those people – for sins they may have committed? What did you think?' I wouldn't have thought that. What would they be being punished for? But I'm not a film or book critique. I just enjoyed the exciting film and said so.

WEDNESDAY 1ST MAY

It's May Day. I went for a walk this evening and it was good to see the bluebells out in the wooded area off Hardy Lane. The May-tree blossom is out and it's such a beautiful month with all the new leaf and spring flowers and it's good to be alive.

The urban area comes to an abrupt end at the start of the Mersey flood plain. Nice for locals to experience some greeness without going far and I've always loved May. Our local church used to have a May Queen. She'd be paraded around, strewn with petals, in a specially made dress, white and virginal like a bride with goody goody little girl attendants and everyone would go to watch her ride past in a decorated pick up truck. My friend was one once, fresh and pretty with long blonde plaits as if she was in the Hitler Youth.

Mayday seems to mean different things to different people. Bobby told me the Communists celebrate it, and in olden days, virgins were said to have frolicked naked in the woods at dawn and would find out the names of their future husbands. I've never been tempted, too cold and wet at dawn. A future husband might have been interesting though.

'Don't 'cast your clouts till May is out,' but does that mean the month of May, or the tree? Hedge your bets I think. My Grandma said they used to decorate horses' harnesses and bridles with coloured ribbons in the old days, as well as all the frolicking. They liked free entertainment too like skipping round a maypole or following a procession or a band. The Manchester Whit walks still draw hundreds although we have a sedentary substitute now – television.

THURSDAY 2ND MAY

Out to a really nice pub in Wilmslow with Colin. He is a gentleman, opening doors for me, guiding me past people and pulling out the chair for me. The boys I've known would never do that for you; they'd let the door slam in your face and you'd sort your own chair out. I had gin and tonic with ice and lemon. I'm beginning to like this sharp tangy drink that quickly goes to your head.

Suddenly, I'm seeing a lot of him. A casual date has become an established relationship which amazes as much as pleases me. It's only been about three weeks or so but it's wonderful, and just what I've been waiting for. I still wonder what he sees in someone young and unsophisticated like me; it must appeal to his masculinity and make him feel protective which is so nice. No one else has ever looked after me like this before and I can't believe my good luck to find someone so caring. He's working away soon for a few days, so not sure when I'll see him but can hardly wait.

FRIDAY 3RD MAY

Work: Something went wrong with some of the machines so we had an extended break in the afternoon while electricians fixed them. The new Pepsi Cola machine in the canteen swallows coins but doesn't always deliver. Three of us complained but Chris said it wasn't anything to do with him, but we don't know who it is to do with.

Evening: went to the King's to meet Janet (and Andy of course!). Colin appeared about ten o'clock. How did he know I'd be there? He bought a round of drinks and met some of my friends.

'Hi, didn't know you were coming,' I say casually as he appears unexpectedly. I'm actually dizzy with pleasure and want to gaze into his dark brown eyes – but I mustn't seem too keen. They say it puts them off so I daren't risk it. I need to keep this lovely man.

'Well, I wasn't doing much – so I thought I'd come and see where you go sometimes.'

'OK… it's nice to see you but, how did you know where I was?'

'I asked someone from your address, I was just passing and saw this lad and asked if he knew you. He said you might be here.'

'Was it Bobby? Fair-haired lad?'

'I didn't ask but he certainly knew you. Who are all these people?' he asks looking round. It's noisy. Little groups of people sit or stand, chatting, joking, drinking. Does he think I can name them all?

'They're not all with me. Just Janet and Andy – oh and Mike there, and Sarah over there.' I introduce him to those I know and he nods greetings.

'They seem to be on the house beer,' he observes. He studies them carefully then orders a round of drinks for the ones I know.

'Right, who is he then?' queries Janet while he's at the bar. You've kept this quiet. Thought I hadn't seen you for weeks! Nice looking eh? A bit quiet though. Is he your type? How old is he? He looks older than you but ...you still look good together.' She's weighed it up quicker than a tote machine and wants answers.

'Well not much older,' I say defensively. 'And quiet is better than a noisy show off.' 'Like Andy,' I feel like adding but don't.

Colin returns and distributes beer among my friends busy now in their own bubbles, any thanks hardly heard above pub chatter. He sits next to me.

'I wanted to see you – before I go away like I said. I'm off tomorrow.'

'Where to?'

'London. It's a work thing, like I told you the other night, nothing interesting. I wanted to make sure you'd be around when I got back. It's been good hasn't it?' He pauses and looks at me. His eyes say it all.

'Yes, it has. That would be really nice. I'll look forward to it.'

That's an understatement. Does he know how much! He drives me home and we stop for soft, lingering kisses.

SATURDAY 4TH MAY

Did some shopping in the afternoon then called at Janet's to see if she wanted to go out while Colin is away. Andy is at a family party without her which she is not happy about as she thinks it shows he is not serious about her. It's great to see her without him. We've not seen each other much because she's always with him. Her mum made us egg and chips and we ended up staying in and watching TV. I told her about Colin and the things Brenda had said about him. 'Oh ignore her she's just jealous,' she said. Janet always takes my side. I love Janet.

We sit close together on the settee like sisters watching TV sharing a pack of Maltesers. Rex, the fox terrier, watches and salivates in doggy anticipation. He stays perfectly still except for two eyes following hand to mouth and back again. He raises one paw to look cute.

'Chocolate's bad for you,' Janet tells him. He doesn't care. A long thin streak of saliva hangs from his mouth and he gives a little whimper. I give him just one which he bolts without chewing then cocks his head appealingly.

I tune my ear in to the TV where the Minister of Transport is discussing 'The Beeching Report' all about road transport being the way ahead. Oh not that stuff again. Who cares? Janet's mum does. She swears at the proposed train line axing and local station closures, Chorlton Station near here probably being one of them.

'What you worried about? Dad's just bought that nice Ford Cortina,' Janet says, lighting a cigarette a bit close to my hair.

'I do go out without him sometimes you know,' she says, 'and

COLIN

I can't drive. I'd have to learn – and you know what he thinks about women drivers. Shouldn't be allowed on the road!'

I don't know any women drivers so don't have an opinion. I'll probably never learn to drive.

SUNDAY MAY 5TH

Six days to seeing Colin. I used to count down to Christmas like this; anticipating the pleasures and sensory delights to come, unable to sleep with excitement. Now I think of the warmth radiating through his shirt, the thrill of prolonged eye contact, the slight brush of lips against my ear. Don't be long Saturday.

MONDAY MAY 6TH

Five days. Restless and counting but a wisp of memory flashes. There is was, then gone. It was a bit unsettling. I couldn't quite catch hold of it but it was something to do with his questions the other night. Forget it. I must ring Jenny. We could go out somewhere and she'll distract me.

TUESDAY 7TH MAY

Jenny and I went out straight from work. I'd not seen her for some weeks so we caught up with news – mine about my fast developing relationship and hers about a relative in Ireland who's become a priest. A priest! I wonder if he knows what she does.

Her confessions would knock his dog collar off. She was sitting neatly at the bar, legs crossed and stiletto heels showing off her shapely calves. She'd made up her eyes with black eye liner and mascaras and wore her smart Astrakhan coat; yes – just to go to this pub in! It made me feel underdressed in my plain denim jacket and just washed face.

'So, you're going to see this guy again when he comes back?' she asks after hearing a glowing account of my new found romance and how happy I was.

'I think so. But my friend Brenda, you know, the one I told you about, thinks he's weird and treats women badly and she doesn't approve… but I think he's OK. He's been great with me.'

'Well that's up to you then isn't it! You can't let other people decide what you do. If you want to see him, you've got to please yourself.' She pauses. 'But where did you say he was going?'

'He's gone to London. He has to go away with his job sometimes. I don't really mind. He gets well paid for it.'

'Umm, are you sure he's not married? I've heard that one before…about working away. I'd be careful if I were you.'

'I don't think he's married. I'll have to trust him for now, but if I found out different I'd drop him – of course I would.'

'OK, but why get yourself involved with someone doubtful in the first place? If Brenda doesn't trust him I'd wonder why if I were you. Keep yourself free, like me. Play the field. Better still play the field and make them pay! Tell you what, if ever you do, I know just the client for you. Lovely man. Lonely. I used to see him. He treated me like his girlfriend; you know, flowers and gifts and things …as well as pay of course. If ever you need some cash – I'm still in touch with him. I could fix you up easily.

COLIN

'I couldn't do that.' I'm horrified at the idea. It's not for me. Accepting what she does, and admiring her independence is one thing, but joining her 'profession' – a different matter entirely!

'Just think about it. Would it be so bad? You'd be doing a lonely man a service – just for lending your body for an hour or so. What's so wrong about that? You won't get struck down from above or anything you know!'

That's Jenny – she can turn a moral on its head and be convincing. It does makes me think about whether I could actually do that though. No; I couldn't, I decide. I'll have to wait for my special man, but yes, she has a point, it wouldn't hurt anyone – and if I got desperate – who knows what choices I'd have to make.

WEDNESDAY 8TH MAY

Three days to go. Mary on form today. She was singing some really rude songs including a truly disgusting version of The Eton Boat Song but everyone happily sang along loudly and got told off! Ivy said she couldn't hear herself being paged and could we please shut up. Miserable cow. She hates it when we're happy! No wonder her husband is having an affair with a bar maid at the Lloyds.

We've heard the gossip about him; second, third, fourth, fifth hand etc, changing in detail each time rising incrementally: a friendly hug, a passionate embrace, a lingering kiss, thrashing around on the floor after closing time. We love something to gossip about. It could be me if I'm not careful. Look at her with her fancy man and his flash car!

THURSDAY 9TH MAY

Talked with Bob tonight in my room. We had a sort of meal cobbled together from what we'd brought home back from our jobs. He told me more about leaving university. It's not fair the way they treated him. He could have done so well and it's all wasted if he can't get another place.

He knocks at my door and I'm glad for the company. I've another two days to wait to see my boyfriend. Boyfriend, I like to say it. I savour the word in my mouth. It sounds nice. I've got one – at last. I open the door to Bob holding a greaseproof bag.

'Look, we can make sausage butties,' he says handing me the pack and looking pleased. I have a 'reject' cake to contribute, wrapped, but battered as though someone's trodden on it. Jam and fake cream have squidged into the sponge but we devour it like wolves after the sausages. I make some tea as he prepares our meal and the topic turns to his ejection from university. 'But why didn't they throw out the tutor?' I ask. 'He was as much to blame. In fact more – because he was in a senior position. You were only a student, so why only you? He thinks…

'They didn't want a scandal …and he was powerful. He was the head of department and doing important research. They didn't want to lose him so they let me keep the rest of my year's grant and bought my train ticket to Manchester to get rid of me. I could have protested, but then everyone would have known about it – and they would have won anyway, so it was better kept quiet.'

COLIN

'Yes but wasn't that awful for you. You must have been devastated....your whole future threatened. But ...how did it happen anyway? Why did you fall for him? How did he know you were... like that.' I can't bring myself to say puff or queer, and homosexual sounds stark and clinical. No usable words come to mind. 'How could he tell?' I continue. 'I mean it's not obvious. You're not like Kenneth Williams or anything. Did you let it slip talking about something else?'

'No...People like us sort of...give out vibes. Even if you don't say anything – it somehow communicates itself. I wasn't a very confident student so I enjoyed the attention; him being nice to me and that. He was very good at raising my self esteem. Always gave me good marks. Said I was the brightest student he'd ever taught. I always felt good after seeing him...as if I was worth something.'

'Flattery got him everywhere then. He must have been deliberately working on you. Then lets you take the rap when it gets difficult! What a bastard.'

'I guess so. So, now you know my secret and you musn't tell anyone. I know you won't and I do trust you. People can get into serious trouble...even now in 1963, like I did. People would shun me. I know they would...and those two downstairs would throw me out. My parents wouldn't understand either. I've already got to tell them I'm no longer studying but I don't think they could cope with that as well. I'm going to have to lie. I can't tell them. They would be devastated.'

I love Bob but it's changing. We're confidentees, soulmates, friends. I have like butterflies in the stomach for someone else now.

FRIDAY 10TH MAY

He's back tomorrow. I've been thinking about him every day and can't wait to see him and share more outings to nice places, more whispered nothings, more excitement. He has changed my life in ways I'd never dreamed of.

It's the beginning of something exciting. I can feel it in my bones, my stomach, my nether regions; a fluttering sensation. My mood soars – and stays on that high until I'm too happy to sleep properly. I'm restlessly counting down the hours now and cannot be bothered to eat or get involved in anything else.

SATURDAY 11TH MAY

He's back. He brought me a silk scarf from London. It's long with tiny flowers in yellow and blue and feels soft next to my skin. I've never had anything in real silk before. He seems to think his boss wants to sack him and that must worry him but it's nice he can tell me such personal things.

I thanked him profusely for the scarf. So nice of him and I'd never expected a present so I'm truly touched. He explained how he made the choice.

'I hear people sometimes you know. Sort of in my head. They give me ideas…talk to me, help me make decisions. They told me you'd like that one.'

I'm holding it to my face and enjoying its silky fabric sensation and the beautiful colours.

COLIN

'Well,' I say, 'doesn't everyone hear something like that, when they're trying to decide things. You have to sort of discuss it with yourself…It's like your own thoughts. They call it the inner voice,' I say knowledgably offering an excuse for something I think I understand. 'Everyone has one I think. Especially if you're a creative person.'

'I have several. So I must be very creative. I hope it doesn't put you off.'

'No. Everyone is different, and I'm not going to be put off by something so…ordinary and unimportant. What does it matter if you hear things others can't?'

He pauses.

'It can be a bit unsettling when they say bad things though… like my boss spying on me, or that people are reporting what I do.'

'Why would they do that? Do you really think he's spying on you?'

'I do. I told you. He's got it in for me … trying to catch me out. The voices tell me to watch out for him and be careful. There's one voice – she's called Lucy, who can be very nasty. She tells me some of the awful things he says.'

Hmm. I think. That's a bit different to what I thought…but maybe it's just his way of explaining it.

'Well don't listen to them then,' I suggest. 'Ignore them. If you're doing nothing wrong there's nothing to worry about and it will probably stop when you stop worrying about it.'

'You think in such a delightfully simple way Lizzie. You're good for me. I know you are.'

MONDAY 13TH MAY

Went out with Jenny. She'd rung because she won't be able to make our arrangement for Friday so she invited me to her place tonight instead to meet her friend Joyce. She is more than a friend I discovered. She is a MADAM! She's a strong, outspoken sort of woman but easy to talk to and it's certainly interesting knowing these people and their lifestyles. They live in a lovely big house in Whalley Range.

Mrs B shouts up about a taxi arriving for me and gives me a quizzical look, nosy cow, but I try to look nonchalant, as if taxi hiring is normal for me. It's a surprise as I meant to catch the bus to Jenny's who is going to do my hair as if I've been to a salon, and show me a range of expensive make up which I'll never be able to afford. She's paid for the taxi but when I try and reimburse her she won't take it! I don't insist too strongly as I can't really afford it but I don't like to exploit her generosity which she'll practise at any opportunity.

The house is beautifully Victorian, built for rich Manchester heyday cotton merchants, unlike the one that I live in deteriorating by the week. It has a manicured garden with proud stone lions sitting on gate posts and a driveway neatly outlined with tasteful miniature shrubs. I'd like a guided tour like a stately home but I'm ushered to the sitting room by Joyce who's introduced herself, and offered me a drink as Jenny appears in a haze of perfume and plonks herself down next to me. 'I see you've introduced yourselves,' she observes cheerfully helping herself to gin and topping up with tonic water. 'Want a top up?

COLIN

You said that guy introduced you to gin – so go on spoil yourself,' she says pouring more into my glass. She turns to Joyce.

'Lizzie lives where I used to. You know – when I worked for Harold.' Joyce pulls a sour face.

'That place,' she says. 'You don't want to live there, it's a death trap. And that creepy Ernie Bryson! Don't be fooled by him. He's no innocent little henpecked man. He's a nasty piece of work so beware. You know he rented Jenny a room so he could be in on the business with her and Harold don't you?'

'Yes, Jenny told me. I did think he was creepy, but not that bad. It was *her* that scared me – Mrs Bryson. We call her the Dragon – me and my friend, when she gets angry. And so nosey! She watches everybody coming and going from her window. But him! He looks such an ineffective little weed and he's terrified of her.'

'Yeah, well you'd be well out of there for various reasons. There's a room going here soon,' she says. 'Lovely room, back view over the garden, nice trees and things. One of the girls is leaving to live with one of her clients! I introduced them. How about that? I'm a bloody matchmaker now! Anyhow, think about it. You'd be really welcome.'

A room? Is she making a kindly offer? Or would there be strings? And can I keep it as a sort of reserve strategy in case nothing else turns up, or times get hard?

TUESDAY 14TH MAY

The Dragon has been benign lately but I heard her cursing Stan for leaving the lid off the dustbin. Next door's dog had tipped it over, strewn the contents over the path and made off with a

ROOM TO GROW

chicken carcass. It's smart that dog and never misses a trick. I like dogs but not this one. It growls and has a scowling face.

I've been staying in tonight catching up with the journal. I sometimes wonder why I do it but I always feel sort of satisfied and calm afterwards – like after having a warm bath. The routine makes me feel in control and it's something to look back on and remember. Sometimes I don't get time and have to remember a weeks' worth!

WEDNESDAY 15TH MAY

I realise that I've never spoken about Jenny to Colin. In fact I don't think I've mentioned her name ever. He only likes innocent girls, and Jenny isn't one. So I've avoided it in case he asks questions I'd have to lie about – like where does she work? What does she do? It's not that I'm ashamed to know her. She's good company and I learn from her even if I don't take her advice, but I'll keep quiet. I've told Janet. I hope she keeps her mouth shut, and of course Brenda knows because we found the diary together. Yes, she's best kept a secret. I only see her occasionally so it shouldn't be that difficult.

I feel better now I've written it down and aired it. It is like having a discussion with yourself but isn't that like hearing another voice? Like Colin does? Except I know it's me and I'm in control of it.

THURSDAY 16TH MAY

Life is great at the moment: restaurants, cinemas and drives out to places. He's going to take me to London and I can hardly wait!

I've always wanted to see famous places like Trafalgar Square and Buckingham Palace, and the fashions on Carnaby Street. Blackpool is the furthest place I've ever been.

He takes my face in his hands – that loving gesture he does. Then he lights two cigarettes and hands me one.

'I thought about you in London you know, when I had some free time. I wished you'd been there, exploring that great city with me.'

'I've never been to London,' I admit. 'Is it sort of very busy ... and trendy? Did you see the Palace and the guards?'

'You've never been to London? Oh my sweet little parochial. I must take you there, very soon, but let's go and eat now. I thought we'd try this other little restaurant I've found.'

I'm going to put on weight at this rate. I've never eaten so well in my life!

FRIDAY 17TH MAY

Tonight we passed a little church somewhere near Macclesfield and stopped. He knew this church and wanted to walk round and look at some of the graves. On the way back we stopped and snogged for about half an hour! It's getting quite steamy! Not sure how long I'm going to resist him. He's not been too demanding but I know 'it's' going to happen soon. I just hope it doesn't hurt!

This tired-looking old church down a side road is familiar to him. He stops the car and helps me out. We go through a gate and up the path. There's a solid oak door with out-of-date notices locked with a huge padlock. Many of the graves lie untended with faded inscriptions and overgrown with weeds and I've noticed two tiny sad gravestones of young children. How long have they been the forgotten dead? How many generations before nobody's even heard of you?

He's walking purposefully reading aloud from inscriptions; about God taking souls, dead people reunited with love ones, children resting in the arms of Jesus or taken to heaven. I think 'dust to dust, ashes to ashes,' but don't say it because I don't want to admit I'm a non–believer and emphasise our differencies. Best stay quiet.

'My grandmother is buried here,' he announces. At least someone's remembered her. 'I'll show you where she is,' he adds leading me between gravestones leaning at odd angles and stopping at a stone angel guarding a headstone.

'It's here. She's here.' He reads the sad epitaph aloud and turns to me.

'This is the church where God first spoke to me you know.'

It's an unexpected change of context and I don't know how to respond.

'He spoke to you? Here? Why would he speak to you?'

I don't like to question why, out of millions, in fact billions, of deserving equals he should be spoken to by God, as if he's universally special. It seems conceited of him to think he is so unique. Does he even go to church to enhance his heavenly chances? I've not known him to.

'Well he did speak to me,' he replies. 'It was his voice – a kind voice. It told me I would see her in heaven – so it must have been him.'

'Well you probably thought it was – and if it comforted you it was a nice thing to believe. People need that comfort sometimes don't they?' There, I've smoothed it.

He does say some odd things. We travel back quietly then enjoy some frantic kissing

SATURDAY 18TH MAY

Colin took me to a nightclub in Manchester last night called 'The Piccadilly'. You can have food and drink there and there was an entertainer. I wonder if this is the club Jenny mentioned? The people here must be quite wealthy to afford the expensive drinks and food and look so elegant in their evening wear. I wore my one, simple, but nice little black dress of the sort you can wear anywhere. We had a slow, slow dance at the end to 'Misty' that Johnny Mathis sings so beautifully, but then, so did the pianist/singer. We were dancing very close indeed!

It's hardly dancing. Hardly moving in fact. I can feel it having its effect on him. I nestle into his neck and enjoy the comfort of his warm body as we sway slowly to the music. It is emotionally magic but I don't ask him in when we get home. I don't want to bump into another dose of disapproval from Brenda – but kissing goodnight takes a lot longer these days and it would be better somewhere more comfortable than in a car! We know where this is going and I'm glad.

TUESDAY 21ST MAY

He was waiting outside after work again. I'm going to give him the phone number. Those silent calls have stopped but it can't have been him anyway if he'd lost the number. It's silly if we can only arrange to meet outside and can't speak to each other in between.

'Thought we could go to The Bull's Head tonight,' he announces.

'I'm not dressed for going out.' I protest. This is why I must give him the phone number, so I can get ready properly after work and feel fresh and good.

'It's only a pub; no need to dress up. But you're gorgeous, I love you as you are – but go and put something nice on if you like. I'll wait here for you.'

'Did he say I love you! Really? I'm too taken aback to reply. I rush inside, briefly wash, find something to wear, drag it over my head and dash down the stairs passing Bob carrying something in a Fine Fare bag.

'Hi. Where are you rushing off to?' Then, to my retreating back, 'I like that dress!'

'Can't stop. I'm meeting Colin. He's outside.'

'Oh pity… I've brought us something. There's plenty for both of us. I'll save you some.'

I've passed leaving the last words in the air. 'Sorry, not this time. Must go.'

He watches me go, disappointed.

COLIN

THURSDAY 23RD MAY

I've told him not to wait for me outside after work. I have given him the phone number now so there's no need to just turn up. I need time to relax and get ready properly without a rush but there he was again. I asked him in while I got ready. I'm past caring now whether we see Brenda or not. She knows anyway. He wasn't impressed by my room at all.

'I've found somewhere else to eat,' he says. He knows my weakness. I'm always starving.

'Come on in,' I say through the open car window. 'I have to hurry if you're waiting there and it makes me anxious. It's time you saw my room. Don't expect a palace though – and it's very small.'

He follows me up the stairs into the room.

'Sit here while I go to the bathroom,' I order as I collect a towel and clean clothes. He's looking around critically.

'A bit cramped isn't it? Very small. Why don't you look for something bigger?'

'I will do one day, but it's Ok for now. I can manage'

There's a knock and a familiar voice at the door.

'Lizzie? Are you in? I've got something for you.'

I let him in.

'Come in Bob. This is Colin. Colin – Bobby.' They nod a greeting to each other.

'Oh, sorry Lizzie. I didn't know you had company.' He looks uncomfortably at Colin, pauses, then at me. 'OK… Well, see you later maybe?'

He retreats leaving a pack of my favourite Cheshire cheese.

I go to the bathroom but someone's in it! I think it's Olive. She'll be ages!

'Olive,' I call through the door. 'Will you be long?'

'Won't be a minute. I'm shaving my legs.'

Oh God, there'll be leg hairs all over the bath.

'Can I come in a mo – just for a quick wash? I'm in a hurry.' She lets me in and we stand there occupied in our respective ablutions. I return clean but I'd like to be glamorous for a change! No time for that, damn him.

Colin tells me 'voices' have told him to find me a better flat. I ignore it. He hears these voices but it's just his own mind again telling him things. It's like when you wish for things – or want to get your head around something, so you sort of discuss it internally with yourself like I do when I write. As we leave, Mrs B's head appears round her door. She's noted the man in tow and that I look nice. I deliberately hold his hand as we walk to the door and we're off out somewhere. There's passion and murmurings in the car again.

FRIDAY 24TH MAY

I'm excited but nervous. Something tells me 'it's' going to happen soon, if not tomorrow. I can tell from the way he looks at me and what he says. There is sexy subtlety – but we both know. It's time I got this over and I know Colin will make it OK for me, but I'm not really sure exactly what I'm supposed to do! Do I close my eyes? Or say anything? Am I supposed to take my own clothes off? Or leave some on? Is it grown up to cry out if it's painful? I wish I wasn't such a novice! He seems so wordly.

My hormones are in robust health and dominating most thoughts and actions but I'm wondering, is this love or infactuation? It's pretty strong whatever it is affecting my appetite and sleep making me dazed and distracted. I imagine conversations we might have and plan what I'll wear tomorrow to look good. I'm getting my hair trimmed in the morning at Janet's hairdresser and I'll put perfumed bath salts in the bathwater and scented lotion all over my body. It'll be so special.

SATURDAY 25TH MAY

No wonder he didn't think much of my bedsit! The contrast! He took me back to his much classier flat. It's on the attic floor of a large house in Didsbury and has a living room with a tiny kitchen and a double bedroom – and no nosey landlady on the premises! We made very good use of the bedroom! (Yes, at last.) He'd been waiting so patiently and the thing I was so keen to lose happened easily and naturally. I don't know what I expected but was no great event.

If I'm entirely honest about it, it wasn't that good. A hot chocolate or a manicure would have been more enjoyable. It was all a bit messy and disappointing, and the protective device that looked like a wet deflated balloon was almost comical. A bit like the Christopher Robin story when Piglet presents Winnie the Pooh with one as a birthday present (a balloon not a condom). At least Pooh got a useful honey jar as well! What is all the fuss about? Why do males seek this out so ardently? How curious copulation would seem to an onlooker from space!

SUNDAY 26TH MAY

Bob is thrilled because Manchester United won the Cup Final yesterday. They beat Leicester three to one and it's all over the papers and news but I had been 'otherwise occupied' at kick off time. I thought I'd got to know Bob well in the last few months but didn't know he was such an avid Manchester United fan.

Saying the best team in the world were playing at Wembley should have been a clue, but I hadn't picked it up and said, 'Oh Wembley, really, glad it's not a home match because the buses would be chocked full and everywhere crowded with noisy fans.' Today, with time to spare together he relives the event, to his captive audience, me. I'm not a football fan and there's no escape but I listen and indulge him. 'Bobby Charlton is such an asset to that team. In fact they were all fantastic; and that final goal! Wow, you should have seen it! Matt Busby is a brilliant manager you know,' he asserts enthusiastically. 'The best they have ever had! The way he's built that team up since the Munich crash. You should have come and watched it with me and Doris. You would have enjoyed it. We watched it again on *Grandstand* later as well. You wouldn't think she was a football fan would you? She was so excited, cheering them on and making comments about tactics and things. I've never known her so animated before. It was such a special day for them. I'll never forget it.'

'Yes it was,' I weakly agree, thinking back to yesterday. It was a special day for me too. I'll always remember that cup final too – but for different reasons than Bob's.

COLIN

TUESDAY 28TH MAY

Too nice to work today. All the blossoms are out on the trees and the Spring flowers. The weather is warmer, it's almost my birthday and Colin says he loves me. He told me God had told him to love me. Lovely, but a bit strange. He's definitely religious. I blur my atheism so as not to antagonise. I told him I loved him too. I'm so much happier now.

I'm on a love boat. A slow, soothing vessel gently rocking me to oblivion. It heightens my mood like a drug and I wallow in its haze. 'Lizzie's in love,' say my workmates. 'Are you with us Lizzie?' Even Mrs Bryson's features have softened. She smiles at me sometimes now. She's only 'The Dragon' when she's not being nice. My libido is improving a bit too! I hoped it would.

FRIDAY 31ST MAY

Took today off as I had a day's paid holiday left from last year. I met Brenda in town who had left-over luncheon vouchers so we used them in her lunch hour. There are Chinese restaurants in the George Street area now and I had chicken chow mein for the first time. The Chinese hold rice bowls up near their faces and shovel it in but I tried to use chop sticks. It was like trying to catch tadpoles with slithery sticks.

Brenda has had parent trouble. They don't like Malek because he is too foreign! She's also overheard workmates talking about them. And Malek's family have changed their mind about her because she's a different religion!

I think about it. Why should it matter? People think differently about all sorts of things so why not religion? Last week they seemed to like her. And her gossiping workmates. Have they nothing better to talk about! A strange turnaround for us two. My love life is good now – hers is rubbish!

SATURDAY 1ST JUN

Staying with Colin tonight. This afternoon we went to see *West Side Story* the musical about teenage gangs. Brilliant storyline, dancing and songs. It's so good being with Colin and going to all these places. Then he cooked for me at his flat. I'm so lucky. I could hear him conversing with the 'friends' I'm not able to see as he fried and chopped things. I've never known anyone like this before. He's certainly a bit eccentric.

I think about this word…eccentric. A sort of stretched circular shape, almost like an oval, less circular than a circle, but eccentric people are unusual, peculiar, sort of straying from the norm in behaviour or tastes. He is definitely that, but so were many successful people. Leonardo Da Vivci was eccentric, so were Einstein, William Blake, Howard Hughs, Van Gogh and many others so it can't be such a bad thing.

Talking to yourself isn't that abnormal either. My Grandma used to do it as she got older. I've heard her many a time chatting to herself.

'Who were you talking to?' I once asked.

'Myself of course. Who else? I'm the only one I can make any sense of now,' she said, turning to look at me so she could lip read better.

I have a sneaky chance to catch up with notes for the journal. I use a little notebook while he cooks. I extend it into a journal later. It's a small one so I can slip it into a pocket or bag if he comes into the room. I'd hate him to see what I write!

SUNDAY 2ND JUN

I've been seeing him most nights for ages now. I love him a lot but I'm beginning to miss my friends, especially Janet. I've not seen Jenny for ages either. I am more puzzled by the 'voices' now even though I'm not going to make an issue of it. It's not quite as simple as I thought. It's usually a man who 'speaks' to him – and he says odd things – like his boss (Ellis) is spying on him. Does he really believe this? Why would he? He also sees 'signs' which I can never see the significance of.

I had heard of schizophrenia, but I thought it was a raving, foaming at the mouth thing – an absolute. You were or you weren't. Unless someone is conspicuously 'loony' they seem alright to me.

MONDAY 3RD JUN

Had my tea again with Bob today. We ate nearly three packs of

ROOM TO GROW

boiled ham due to be cleared from the shelves. Yesterday I found a neat half of a trifle outside my door covered with a tea towel. It's a a varied menu but I never know what it will be. We talked about the news I'd watched on Doris's TV about the Profumo affair, then Brenda came in a real panic. I can't put in writing what was wrong but we fixed it!

'Who is John Profumo?' I ask. I know he's something to do with the Government but I don't know who's in the Cabinet.

'Oh he's the Secretary of State for Defence. A really important position.'

'So what's all this about him having to resign? Why did he have to?'

'He's in big trouble. He lied in court about something and got found out, but there's lots of other stuff coming out – and other people. It's going to be a big, big story! And there's another man called Stephen Ward…'

Knock knock. It's Brenda. I open the door to her anxious face.

'I need a screw driver.'

'Anything I can help with?' offers Bob.

'No. No. I've just lost the screwdiver.' She's gabbling her words. 'Can you lend me one – quickly.'

I guess the problem immediately, take the tool Bob offers and follow her upstairs. The front of the electric meter lies detached on the floor complete with screws. Mrs Bryson is due any minute to collect last week's rent as she couldn't do it on Friday.

'I thought we weren't doing this now the weather is warmer. We said it was too risky.'

COLIN

'I wasn't – but I ran out of shillings. But then I forgot about it and I couldn't find where I'd put the screwdriver to put it back on properly. I didn't realise she'd come on a Monday. She's coming now! Any minute!'

She's fumbling, panicking and talking too quickly to be effective.

'Come here. Let me do it.' I get it on – seconds before the knock on the door.

WEDNESDAY 5TH JUN

A frank talk with Colin today: 'Why don't you ignore these voices if they say something you don't like.' I said. He told me not to worry, the voices he hears now are mostly pleasant, and that's all because of me! I'm glad about that but I don't really understand. How can you hear people that aren't there? He's a bit old for invisible friends! Mine had gone by the time I was about five. When Brenda first mentioned his strangeness I didn't think it was like this. I thought it was something artistic.

'They like you, you know.' I don't know who he means so I look round. We're the only ones in a city bar so it can't be anyone here.

'Who do?'

'The friends who speak to me sometimes.'

'Which friends do you mean?' I don't know any of his friends. I've never met any, in fact has he got any? But I know what he's talking about and choose not to acknowledge them.

'Most people don't believe me so I don't tell anyone these days – but I trust you. I know you will listen and won't judge me.

There are three of them, a man and a women. Occasionally there's been a child too. They comment on what I do or – sometimes what they think I should do. They advise me and warn me.'

'What kind of things do they say?'

He pauses.

'Well you know when I first met you, and I was still kind of hooked on Brenda? Well they said she'd met someone else. The voices came night and day. I had to listen to them. That's why I was waiting outside sometimes. I wanted to see her to see if it was true.'

What? I'm confused. I didn't think she was seeing anyone then. Was it just his suspiciousness? Something he just thought had happened? I'm going to ask him.

FRIDAY 7TH JUN

Tonight I tried to get to the bottom of what Colin had said about voices telling him Brenda had met someone – before she actually had. It left me even more baffled. 'I didn't understand,' I challenged. 'The voices said she'd met someone? But she hadn't then had she? So they weren't accurate were they? Even more reason to ignore them if they are unreliable and tell you falsehoods.'

'No, but sometimes they talk about the future. They knew it was going to happen. They knew she would be meeting someone. I was waiting for it to happen. And then she met that coloured bloke didn't she, so they were right. He wouldn't have been good for her either.'

COLIN

'You mean Malek. Colin! Are you saying you think Malek wasn't good for her? He's a really nice guy.'

'Yes. Ok, Ok, Ok. I'm not bothered about it now. That stopped when I met you. It's you I care for now. I must look after you now… you're not like her. You are good for me and that's why they say I must look after you, protect you, find you a better place. It's best to listen and take their advice.'

Protect me! I know he's ten years older than me but do I need protecting? Imaginary people saying I need protection? It could be funny but he's serious.

SUNDAY 9TH JUN

I've thought about Colin's voices and decided it's a bit like Father Christmas or the Tooth Fairy: it's not going to do us any harm, so I'm not going to react. It's sort of part of his individuality, like the way he matches his tie to his shirt, or is fastidiously tidy. It is just a bit weird. I don't want anything to spoil things between us when I'm having such a fantastic time. Life is so much better now – even though lately, he does hear them more often.

'I don't know why I'm hearing them more often,' he tells me. 'Nobody else can hear them and I only tell you because you're so special. They are good people you know, Lizzie, especially the man, Godfey. Not so much the woman though – she's mean. But Godfrey knows what's going to happen and is often right.'

'Oh really? Ask him if I'll ever get a better job.' I say frivolously.

TUESDAY 11TH JUN

The Beatles are becoming very famous and popular now. 'She Loves You' is already at the top of the charts and girls are mobbing them and screaming wherever they go! I watched them the other night on Doris's TV. They are brilliant and I especially like Paul.

Went shopping with Brenda. She warned me again about Colin but says it's up to me now. She doesn't want us to fall out but I'm still careful what I tell her. She's not afraid to ask though.

'Have you "been" with him yet?' she asks me directly in the trendy coffee bar we end up in.

'Yes. In fact I have.' What is she going to say now? I couldn't really fudge it or think of a suitable lie in time so she's cornered me.

'Oh Lord, you're truly netted now,' she says and shakes her head in mock incredulity. She's still disapproving but it's modified now. I can cope with that. I go to the jukebox and put in sixpence as a distraction ploy and we begin hand jiving to records. Within moments she's smiling, any disapproval forgotten. The friendship's intact.

THURSDAY 13TH JUN

He was waiting for me after work. I'd already given him the phone number so we can make arrangements. How many times do I have to tell him! I DON'T WANT TO GO OUT STRAIGHT FROM WORK. I've told him again. He also seems jealous of Bob. Why I don't know.

COLIN

'I didn't expect you so early again,' I begin. 'Why didn't you phone?'

'I thought you'd be hungry, and you know I don't like eating alone. I didn't want you to eat, then not want to later.'

'Thanks, but if I knew we were going out for food I wouldn't! I don't like rushing out without time to rest or get ready properly. Sometimes I want a bath and to put my make up on without hurrying.'

'You don't need make up. Don't you know how pretty you are? In fact don't wear it. It just makes you look tarty. I think I'll have that make up bag off you when I get chance! You're beautiful just as you are.'

Is he joking? I'm flattered but unsettled by the threat of taking my make-up. Please don't. It helps my confidence.

'Let's go out early this time,' I say patiently, 'but …can we do it later next time? Just ring first or arrange with me in advance so I can be ready.'

'As you like. By the way, that lad?… Bobby?'

'Bobby…Oh, you've met him, remember? He's in the next room to me. He works in the new supermarket. That's why he left me that cheese. He sometimes gets free food.'

'You seem very friendly with him.'

'That's probably because I am. He's a good friend.'

'I see… Do you see a lot of him him then?'

'Depends. We keep each other company if we're not doing anything else. But not always, only when it suits. We're good friends. But that's all. It's you I love – you know that don't you. But I've not had that much time to see anyone lately have I? I keep seeing you all the time.'

'Suppose so. I bet he's been trying to see you though. Bet

he's hanging round all the time; biding his time.' I ignore these remarks. They're baseless and ridiculous. And there's Brenda too. 'I've not seen much of Brenda either while I've been seeing you so much.'

'Hmm. Brenda. It's just as well. I don't think she's a very good influence on you y'know.'

'Why ever not. She's a great friend,' I reply indignantly. He doesn't explain, just frowns.

'Never mind. Let's just go and find a nice restaurant.'

Well everyone is grumpy sometimes I suppose. I just wish he wouldn't have such a downer on my friends when he is.

SATURDAY 15TH JUN

So happy still. Someone loves me at last. I have a smashing boyfriend – good looking and with a car and not short of money. What more could I want, and I've never had such a good time in my life! He is stlll very suspicious about Bob, though I can't think why and I can't reassure him without revealing what I promised never to tell anyone! That's a promise I'll always keep.

SUNDAY 16TH JUN

Stayed at Colin's last night. I've been staying there lately at weekends. There's more room and the bed is bigger and doesn't squeak like mine. It's eerily quiet though and I don't think I'd like to live there, even with no resident landlady or landlord. Tenants in the house are not friends like where I live. They turn away and don't acknowledge him when they see him.

We walked along the riverbank this morning, then had Sunday roast cooked by him. He's a much better cook than me! I found some pills in the kitchen by accident but he didn't say what they were for.

I'm wiping the surfaces in the kitchen as my cloth swipes foils of pills covered under a serviette. I look at them curiously.

'What are these for?' As I gather them together he's moving closer and his hand goes firmly over them.

'Oh nothing. They're just something for me,' he says, then; 'Hey look what I got you.' He quickly pockets the pills whilst indicating an unopened box of 'Black Magic' lying by the kettle.

'I knew you'd like dark chocolate. We could have one with our coffee... If you're willing to share,' he says playfully. I thank him, but I recognise a distraction ploy when I see it. What were they for?

TUESDAY 18TH JUN

Something about John Profumo was on the *Home Service* tonight. Lots of serious talking and so boring. Tuned in to Radio Luxembourg instead. I'd just boiled a kettle of water to wash my hair when Jenny phoned. We were both free and hadn't seen each other for a while so met up in The Seymour. I told her about my love life and she had funny anecdotes as usual about hers!

'It's so great to see you Jenny,' I enthuse. 'I've really missed you – and all my friends lately … since I've been…well together properly with Colin. We're much closer since last time I saw you. I know him much better now. I know I wasn't sure then but… I've found my special fella and I'm so happy.'

'Good for you,' she hugs me close. She's grinning when she releases me. 'So, are you saying you've got to know him…in the biblical sense?' That makes me smile.

'Yes, yes and I won't regret it. He's such a gentleman – and I'm having such a lovely time. Best time in my life I'd say.'

'Yeah, well let's drink to that then. Things can change but – enjoy it while you can.'

She shrugs. She can be cynical but I think I have her blessing. 'Thanks. I'm sure I will.'

'Are you interested in the room at my place by the way?' she asks. 'Only Joyce was asking again. That girl has moved out, so she wants to let it – and thought of you – if you want it that is.'

'I don't know. The thing is…what did Joyce have in mind? I mean… the girl who left? Is that what would she'd expect of me? Was she offering me a job as well?

'What did you say about me? I would like to find a better place – but not with the arrangement she had.' I need to make it clear. It's like the anticipation of opening an unexpected parcel. What's inside? It could be good or unwanted. 'Listen, Joyce has an eye for what could be good for business, but she tests people first. She always waits to see if they're capable of adapting to any role she has in mind but she's not mentioned anything like that has she?'

'So, what would happen to anyone who didn't want any kind of arrangement other than wanting to rent a room? Would they just stay and pay rent?'

'Actually it's not happened before – but she'd find them other accomodation I'm sure. She knows a lot of landlords. I think she was offering it you because you were a friend of mine and you were having to put up with the Brysons. It would only be a temporary offer anyway as she's thinking of moving to London.'

'London? Why London?'

'Business opportunities. She's just inherited a legacy – so she's buying something there. I might even go with her. I don't know yet. Take the room if you want it. She'd be fine with you.'

I'm almost tempted again but it's confused me again. Would this be a way out of my tatty bedsitter? But if it's only temporary – what would I do if they moved to London? Anyway I don't want Jenny to move to London and hope she doesn't go. She is my only unattached friend and I'd miss her.

WEDNESDAY 19TH JUN

My eighteenth birthday is nearly here but I'm devastated because I've quarrelled with Colin. I started it too. I wish I hadn't got angry. He has to work away in London on my birthday as well which makes it worse!

'So sorry Lizzie,' he says sad faced and gentle toned. I have another meeting. I tried to get out of it but can't. And on your special day too. I'd take you with me – but I'd be working and you'd hardly see me. I hope you won't be alone.'

ROOM TO GROW

'No, it's ok. I can go to The Horse and Jockey, with my friends. They'll celebrate with me – and we can do something together when you get back.'

'I'll buy you something really nice to make up for it.' He kisses me on the forehead and gives me a little hug. 'I've got something in mind,' he says tantalizingly. I resist asking. I like a surprise.

'It'll be fun in a way – with Janet and Andy and others – and maybe Brenda will come.' At the mention of Brenda his face clouds over.

'She'll be too busy with that Pakki,' he says nastily.

Something's uncomfortable. I know nicknames are often used in fun. There's Taffy at work, a hilarious Welshman, and Paddy on the ovens, but it seems worse when applied to dark-skinned people. I haven't got my head round racism yet, it's nebulous and I've only recently heard the word for it. I just don't like him being rude about someone as nice as Malek.

'Don't call Malek a Pakki!' I snap.

'Well he is isn't he? From Pakistan?'

He's trying to make me think I'm being touchy about shortening a place name. He thinks it shouldn't be offensive – like calling a Scotsman a Scottie. But there's a hint of nastiness in his voice I don't like.

'Well answer me – he is from Pakistan isn't he?'

'Well actually it's his parents who came from Pakistan, but you don't need to be rude about him – even if he had. And, Brenda can go out with whoever she chooses. She doesn't need your approval. And come to think of it, she's not that keen on me going with you if you must know.' I add vehemently.

'Oh isn't she?' He's getting indignant now. 'I told you she was a bad influence on you. She hates me so she's trying to split

154

us up. I wish you didn't see her! She'll say all sorts about me; I know what she's like.'

'Well maybe she's got good reason. You were jealous of everyone weren't you? Like you are with me over friends. She told me about it. You think Bob's chasing me and …that I encourage it!

The argument continues. He's looking angry. Claims and counter claims are made about what Brenda has said or done, whether she's a liar or a trouble maker and if he'd ever hit her. He grips my arm, squeezes it hard until it hurts.

'Get off my arm! Yes, I think you may have hit her! Are you going to hit me too?' He grips harder furious at my outburst then suddenly lets go.

'Of course I'm not,' he says angrily, then pauses to gain composure. He's thought of another approach – the indignant innocent.

'Well, if that's what you think there's not much point in continuing.' He reaches across to open the passenger door. 'You may as well go now if that's what you think of me.' He doesn't bargain that I'll call his bluff and go.

'Yes, well it is what I think…and that's fine by me, and I'll go, right now!' I get out and slam the door loudly. He's not going to criticise my friends and hurt my arm like that. I go to my room, curl up on my bed and weep.

SAT 22ND JUN

I've done it now haven't I? Back to lonesome Saturday nights because I couldn't keep my mouth shut. It's rained most of the day so I couldn't go out. Bob's gone out somewhere so I can't talk to him. I've read both my library books and run out of cigarettes so I can't talk, read or have a smoke.

SUN 23RD JUN

Went 'home'. They'd bought me a camera for my birthday on Tuesday. It's a 'Brownie 127' model two. I don't remember ever wanting a camera but I'm pleased with it. My dad gave me a lesson on how to operate it.

It's more modern looking than a 'Box Brownie'; black plastic with a round lens at the front. My dad, Handy Andy the gadget man, knows how it works and how to put the film in. He'd love to take it to pieces but no-one lets him.

'Don't you dare!' says my mum. 'You might damage it.' We go into the garden to experiment.

'Smile,' I say pointing it at her.

A blurred face against underwear on a washing line appears when the film is developed.

MON 24THJUN

Not heard a word from him. Heartbroken. The only good thing in sight is my eighteenth tomorrow. I'll get 'full' pay but the men get much more for the same work which doesn't seem fair! But I'll manage a bit better now. It's been so hard even though the devil bike has saved me some bus fares.

COLIN

TUESDAY 25 JUN

My birthday. Too drunk to write!

WEDNESDAY 26TH JUN

An uneventful day – but my 18th birthday yesterday wasn't!

Daytime: (Tuesday) At work they pinched a cake and put sweets and candles on it for fun! They lit them in the canteen and I nearly set my hair on fire blowing them out. Marian bought me some Coty L'aimant cream perfume. I tried not to think of my quarrel with the love of my life but it kept slipping through chinks in the defences.

Later: An unplanned 'party' in the evening, after the pub! I only meant four quiet friends to come back but Janet may as well have announced a 'party' by loudspeaker. More turned up with bottles! Lucky the Brysons were away at a funeral until the next day!

The 'party' begins quietly. Janet, Andy, two other boys and me enter the front door. We've all had plenty to drink especially me – the birthday girl. I usher them up the stairs and into my room which Janet has strewn with balloons and a 'Happy Birthday' poster. But the doorbell rings and six others from The Horse stagger in and make their way upstairs incoherent with alcohol, singing a tuneless 'Happy birthday.' I know them all and haven't the heart or common sense to turn them away. There's hardly any room for them and the whole house can hear the noise!

I don't know where Bob's gone. I've borrowed his Dansette and someone's turned it up so Chubby Checker is twisting at full volumne. Olive and Stan appear, Stan wielding bottles of Newcastle Brown and a bottle opener, thrilled at an excuse for excess drinking. He pours beer into my new set of Woolworth's tumblers then rolls himself an untidy cigarette and throws the dead match into the waste bin. At least I think it's dead but the raised noise level is alarming me so I forget it. My ineffectual shushing sounds are drowned out by merriment and soon Frank comes down attracted by the noise.

'Im shshso shorry Frank.'

'Oh that's OK. I haven't been to a party for ages. Happy birthday. Hey, I've got a bottle of whisky upstairs. I'll go and get it.' He returns with whisky and shots glasses. He's big but he's grown huge in the crowded space. By now the 'party' is well alight and spilling out onto the landing. Someone is in the bathroom being sick and a couple are in my bed doing God knows what. Doris comes in and out several times like a Swiss clock. She goes to bed early so it's late for her. I've never seen her frown before so she's disapproving. I call out a drowned out apology. She'll probably never let me watch her TV again, but it's a blurry thought and I'm immediately distracted by Andy.

'Lets go into the garden,' he shouts.

'Yeah! Come on – and open the window wide so we can hear the music.'

We troop noisily downstairs to continue the revelling. The next door neighbours are brilliant. They don't complain and bring folding chairs for the legless. Later they help to shoo everyone home and clear up the debris. Somebody goes home on the devil bike which will throw him off for sure.

COLIN

THUR 27TH JUN

Jenny's mock posh voice comes over the phone. It's to deceive the Brysons should they answer it and for a minute I'm confused. She apologises for forgetting my birthday although I don't remember telling her and she's going to buy me a present for this 'special birthday' with something horsey in mind! Horsey? I wouldn't put it past her to buy me one, but where would I keep it? I haven't had many presents but when she was eighteen she had expensive ballet tickets and a room chock full of red roses. How does she do it?

'Old enough to drink and vote now,' she says. 'You can do all sorts at sixteen without parental consent – but not get married until twenty-one. What kind of a daft law is that! But you weren't thinking of getting married were you. I wouldn't if I were you … unless to a millionaire. So…anyway what did you do? I hope you had a good celebration.'

I tell her about the party.

'Party!' she exclaims. 'Why didn't you invite me? I love a party. Any tasty men there?'

'I didn't invite anybody. Janet opened her big mouth and the whole world came and tried to squash into my room. I was too drunk to stop them!'

'Sounds good. What about lover boy? What did he do? Did he buy you anything?'

My face falls. I tell her about the row but she doesn't sympathise.

'Oh for God's sake. Tell him to get lost. Attention seeking children – the lot of them.'

I don't want him to get lost, I'm upset. Please tell me how to get him back – but someone is waiting to use the payphone so we end our chat. She usually cheers me up but not this time. My heart will ache forever, recovery is unlikely, and life will be downhill all the way.

FRI 28TH JUN

Bad news: I've not heard from him. Good news: I'm on full money at last. One pound, seventeen and sixpence more in my pay packet today. If I spend it all on rent on a new place I'm not going to feel richer so must be careful. I've forgotten how expensive eating out and entertainment can be as he always paid for me. In a fairer world I'd pay for my own entertainment and be totally independent. But that's wishful thinking. Back to one Babysham a night now, and six o'chips after the King's as a dining out treat.
I try to forget it. I count my wages and feel the extra coin weightiness in the small brown envelope. My budget is still relatively paltry but a bit more will make a difference. I can buy small things I want rather than need but that's about all. I need a better paid job but there aren't any.

SATURDAY 29TH JUN

We've made up. I'm so happy I could hug the world. He bought me a lovely necklace and matching bracelet from London and said he missed me very much. Not as much as I'd missed him but don't say it. We had a romantic make up and began a lovely evening. But then I told him about the 'party' and his mood changed. I could feel it darkening like before a rainstorm before he verbally launches into my friends at the King's who he thinks are very immature. I have a bad choice of friends. 'Well that was such childish behaviour,' he says. 'Getting so drunk you don't know what you're doing! Obviously out of control from the start.' He folds his arms and glares. 'And all those gate-crashers behaving like that! What if someone had called the police? What if the landlady had been at home? You could have been evicted!'

'I doubt if they'd have got through the front door!'

But what he says is true. It was out of my control, some were disgustingly drunk and it probably was immature, but he's like a finger-wagging parent, making me feel ashamed, so I'm not going to tell him it was actually good fun.

'It was a one-off. My friends don't usually drink like that. They're ok.'

'They don't sound it to me. Going to that pub every night? And making all that noise just because they're drunk! They should have grown out of that by now. I don't want you to go there anymore. Get some decent friends. I don't want you associating with people like that. And keep away from Bobby too when I'm not there to keep my eye on you. What with all this ...Do you know...I'm really glad I'm not going away for a while. Who knows what you'll get up to when I'm not there!'

A warning light comes on. Don't react. I'm not Brenda. I'll handle this better than her. He'll be ok if I don't antagonise him. He likes to think he's been listened to, that I'm going to do what he says and bend to his wishes. I can be clever too. I smile sweetly and look repentant. Sure enough his voice softens. He turns to me.

'I'm so glad you like my present.' he says, 'It looks so good on you. It suits your colouring; against your skin and hair. You look lovely.'

It is beautiful. I've never had anything as beautiful. The necklace has little golden hearts suspended on a delicate chain and the bracelet sits prettily on my wrist. It's proper gold, not fake stuff like I buy. It must have cost a fortune!

MONDAY 1ST JUL

Lovely weather today so after work Colin and I played with my new camera in the park. Someone offered to take our picture together and he took some of me. He has an inbuilt sense of picture composition whereas I just point and snap. Duff photos create expensive trips to Boots for me. People caught in peculiar poses, grimacing, or with ugly objects in unwanted backgrounds appear in a roll of twelve I've had developed! He patiently moves me around to get a better light on a rose bush.

'Lizzie, look ahead now. What can you see?'

'A beautiful rose tree.' I'm ready to click the shutter.

'Yes, but someone's had a picnic there. There's litter. And it's windy. The flowers will be blurred unless you wait.' His interpreting eye is impressive. He's a natural.

It was a lovely evening. The party wasn't mentioned and only one discordant moment.

'Can you see the park keeper over there?'

'Yes …picking up litter I think. Why can't people pick up their own.'

'He's been watching us. Well me actually. He'll be reporting to Ellis I've been in the park.'

WEDNESDAY 3RD JUL

Work: Getting busy again but the overtime is welcome. Colin and I went to the new Club that's opened near here. Freddie and the Dreamers were on stage. We were on the front row. Freddie sang: 'You were made for Me' and smiled at me when he was singing! Colin had some weird ideas about this.

'Is he smiling at you?' he asks. 'Do you know him from somewhere? You haven't been meeting him or something have you?' Freddie is a local lad so I suppose there was a remote chance of knowing him, but I don't.

'No. It's the first time I've seen him in person. I think he smiles at anyone who catches his eye.'

'No. I think it is a message.' Colin says. 'He's trying to give you a message I can tell. He's working with my boss and thinks you shouldn't be here with me – that I'm dangerous that you shouldn't be with me. I understand these messages Lizzie; I have this gift. I can pick up things others can't. Believe me. They're trying to ruin me.'

I must humour him. I know how to handle him now. Just nicely tell him we're together and his boss and a pop singer are not in league, or going to split us up or ruin him.

He's silent, but I can tell it's on his mind.

THURSDAY 4TH JUL

Went to see Jenny this evening; my secret friend. Most of my friends are now. But Jenny is the most secret secret. If he thinks Brenda is promiscuous, what would he think about her! He'd hate her with a vengeance.

I met two of the other girls too. We had some wine (ugh) but I drank it to be social. The room is still available if I want it but I've decided definitely not. It could cause misunderstandings and I want everything clear.

Colin would never understand the situation, or the friendship behind it he doesn't know exists! He'd wonder what I see in her. Even I do sometimes. Do I want to be like her or do I simply admire her guts? I look forward to her funny stories and outlook on life. We make an unlikely pair; me poor and trying to earn an honest living and Jenny who sells sex and would happily enrol me as a colleague! Me, who was desparate for a man; Jenny who doesn't need one, unless it finances her aims. We meet in secret like adultrous lovers, but as my lovelife gets more intense, meetings get rarer.

FRIDAY 5TH JUL

Rooms / flats: He keeps bringing me adverts for flats I can't afford. I wish he'd leave it to me! I want to filter them and organise them myself. I want to question landlords and negoiate rents without someone speaking on my behalf as if I am a child or inarticulate. He calls it looking after me.

'This is a good one.' He hands me a note he's scribbled down from a newsagent's window card. 'First floor flat. £5.10 shillings a week. Own kitchen, etc etc.'

It sounds quite nice but it's too much. I'll get the paper myself tonight and look myself.

SATURDAY 6TH JUL

Went 'home' today. Mum was not looking at all well and the doctor doesn't seem to know what's wrong with her. She's taking time off from her book-keeping job at the Gaumont which is a good idea as long as it doesn't leave them short of money. I'm a bit worried about her. Our family usually have robust health and don't look ill even when we are. She's probably a bit run down.

Something's different when I look at her: the paleness, the droopiness as if it's hard work to stay upright, and the short sentences, as if she'll run out of energy if she says more. She says she's tired and I've no experience of illness so I don't know what does or doesn't look serious. She'll go back to work soon perhaps.

MON 8TH JUL

With Bob today after work. 'Rhythm of the Falling Rain' played on my radio and it suddenly started pouring down so we laughed. We had a good talk and he made me look differently at things, like doing more with my life, although I'm not sure what. I'm stuck in a poorly paid job in a shabby bedsitter and couldn't see a way out. That's my situation. His? He's not told his parents about leaving university.

'Bob – you must tell them soon,' I urge. 'What if they find out from someone else!'

'Like who? No one else knows. Anyway I will. It's the end of the summer term – I'll go home as if I've only just left. If they disown me I'll go abroad and work.'

'Where would you go?… Why don't you do the management training at the store?'

'No, it's not for me. I'll probably go to Europe somewhere. I can speak French a bit, but somewhere where I could teach English. You could come for holidays,' he adds cheerfully.

'Teach English? I wish I could do that. I'd like to teach English – or anything else. I'd love to be a teacher.'

'Do you? Really? You never said before. Well, why don't you then …What's stopping you? Don't be afraid to go after something. Do it now, soon, or you'll just get married and have babies!'

'I know. I wouldn't make a great mother anyway.'

Not a young one anyway, I reflect. I've seen them before, some of my schoolfriends, pushing those prams with big spokey wheels, youth and freedom gone, confined to the house, old at thirty.

'But I couldn't get on a teacher training course,' I add defeatedly. 'I've no qualifications. I couldn't leave school fast enough, and I never took it seriously. They did warn me. Now I'm in a dead end job like they said. Looks like that's me now.'

He looks astonished. 'Don't just say "Oh I've got no qualifications" and do nothing – go and get them; anybody can.

COLIN

You can go to evening classes and take O'Levels. You don't need that many to do teacher training – and you're capable. You could enrol for September. What's to stop you?'

'Colin would,' I say with a sigh. 'He wouldn't take kindly to me… organising things on my own… doing things without him…planning things without consulting him and spending less time with him.'

'Lizzie. Don't let him dictate what you can do. It's your life: plot your own path through it. Have a goal and work towards it. Never mind what he thinks!'

WEDNESDAY 10TH JUL

A terrible day. My poor mum was taken into hospital urgently with meningitis. I was there and it was the worst day of my life. So frightening. Her face was grey and she was incoherent. There's no guarantee she won't die. My family are traumatised.

My sister has called in a panic. The drama peaks as I arrive. Ambulance men stretcher her off accompanied by my grim-faced father leaving Ruth and I with William. In a six-year-old's innocent self-interest he asks,

'Who's going to take me to Cubs?' We can't think of the mundane and don't answer.

We just watch dumbstruck as ambulance doors close like in a TV drama before racing away out of sight. I cannot believe what I've just witnessed. An ambulance! They carry anonymous people we don't really care about; other people,

167

not my mother! We watch it speed away, bells ringing, cars moving aside for it. *Touch your collar, when you see one,* say older people.

'We didn't do touch our collars,' says Ruth anxiously. 'Will it make it worse?' It's a superstition but we do it anyway. Better late than never. Then the empty wait.

FRIDAY 12TH JUL

Visited mum in hospital. Colin drove me or it would have been two bus rides. She is still in danger but stabilising. Thank heavens I have Colin because all that way on two buses after work would take ages and be exhausting. He's stopped looking for flats for me now as I am too preoccupied with this to think about that.

SATURDAY 13TH JUL

Ruth and Dad are coping. The neighbours have been very helpful. One has offered to take William to and from school. Ruth has always been very good with small chlldren so she'll help look after him really well.

Ruth's strong maternal instincts equip her well for surrogate motherhood. I've always preferred animals to small children but I'm called on today. Dad is going to the hospital and Ruth is out. I've arranged to meet friends at the jukebox café so I'll have to take William. His eyes light up as if I'm offering a trip to the moon.

'Can we stay there a long time?'

'Yes. There'll be big boys and girls there. You'll have to be good.'

'Oh, yes, yes, I will be!' he promises. 'Do they have ice-cream there?'

He walks and skips alternatively along asking impossible questions.

'Are those clouds in Manchester? How do they make buses?'

My friends ply him with coke, sweets and ice-cream. He is sick on the way home.

SUNDAY 14TH JUL

Hospital visit: Mum is out of immediate danger but is still very sick. She's dreading the lumbar puncture they are going to do as part of the diagnosis. She must feel at least a little bit better to want to argue about it.

She's witnessed them before as a nurse and knows they can be frightening and unpleasant. She's threatening to withhold permission until a kindly doctor reassures her it isn't as bad these days and that it will speed up her treatment plan.

MONDAY 15TH JUL

Saw our family doctor today. He told me Mum's illness was caused by TB bacteria that had gone to her brain. He showed me a microscope photograph of one in a book looking like a little maggot. He said all our family will have to have skin tests and chest XRays to see if we have, or have had, TB. He's a lovely doctor, Irish and very kind and helpful.

'But how has she caught this awful disease?' I ask.

'Well, I understand she was a nurse in the war at Bagley Sanitorium. She would have been exposed to TB there – and it's possible she could have harboured it for years. That can happen sometimes.'

'So it lay there for eighteen years – then decided to activate?'

'Yes it could have done.'

I'm amazed. She would have had no idea microscopic killers lurked in her body ready to attack her brain.

'Or, it could have been something she'd been exposed to more recently, and so, possibly you too,' he added.

'Do you mean I might have TB?' I ask anxiously. I think of a friend who lived for two years in Styal 'Open Air' School in the 1950s and people looking wan and pale and reluctant to admit to it. The stigma of this disease associated with poverty and overcrowding still exists to some extent.

'You look very healthy to me,' he says kindly. 'But we can test for it now and it can be treated, so there's nothing to worry about. Twenty years ago, yes, but we have a very effective antibiotic for it. It's called streptomycin.'

A skin test showed I had immunity so I needn't have worried.

WEDNESDAY 17TH JUL

Visited Mum in Bagley Hospital. She's going to recover although it may take a long time. I'm so relieved. Colin drove me. It's ironic she may have picked up the TB bacteria in this hospital!

We drive up the long road to the hospital which is undergoing work linking it to the larger, more general hospital. We find a space on the road to park where he waits like a taxi driver as visiting is restricted to close family members only. Inside I watch the nurses at work in an immaculately clean ward. So organised and efficient. A schools' careers worker trying to justify his job once said I'd make a good nurse. Everyone laughed. I don't like being instructed, would fall asleep on nights, be inaccurate over drug doses and – those neat envelope sheet corners, what a fag. I'd be disastrous.

FRIDAY 19TH JUL

Friends and workmates are so kind. They don't even know my mum but have had a collection to buy her some nice things to have in hospital; bath salts, handcream, body lotion, a frilly waterproof cap and matching face-cloths. I'm touched by their kindness.

Will I ever find such a good set of mates? They don't have much but there's always something for anyone in any kind of difficulty. Sadness, sickness, loss, death or bad luck they'll stump up hard-earned cash to soften the situation. One of them runs the work's 'Hospital Fund', a pre National Health scheme still operational for workers' hospital expenses. It's about sixpence a week.

SUNDAY 21ST JUL

Mum's looking a lot better this week. She looked wistfully out of the hospital window at my little brother today. He's too young to be allowed in this specialist hospital and doesn't really understand why she's there. He waved his little hand at her.

I've seen the best side of Colin since Mum's illness. He has given up a lot of time to help with transport and been a tower of support so I've decided I must stand by him through his own difficulties. With love and help from me I think he will abandon his silly fancies so we can be happy together.

TUESDAY 23RD JUL

A new group called The Rolling Stones is on the scene from London. Bob thinks they're great. He's bought their first record, 'Come on'. He keeps playing it and thinks they'll rival The Beatles. I watched them on *Top of the Pops* with Doris who thinks their lead singer has a sulky face and doesn't like them.

'Look at that one,' she points at Mick Jagger. 'What a great big mouth! Ugh. And writhing round like that. He'll never get famous. Who wants to watch that!'

'Well he is on television – so someone thought he was entertaining.'

'So sulky looking too. Why can't he smile. No, I'm turning over to the other channel.' We have just two channels here; BBC and ITV. America has lots. But her TV – my hard luck. We watch *The Virginan*. I think I'll rent a television.

WEDNESDAY 24TH JUL

Hospital visit after work. I've been going twice a week now to see Mum, driven by Colin. He tried to explain things he says – like the voices telling him she will be fine and home in a few weeks etc.

'I'm glad your friends think so,' I say. 'Your imaginary friends,' I add deliberately. Today I'm going to be a source of realism which I think is another way of helping him. At other times it's better ignoring them. Either way I'm irritated and wish they'd stop.

He looks sideways at me, annoyed.

'Don't doubt me like everyone does. I know they're real. I can hear them right now – and they're listening.'

'Do they have names?' I'm suddenly curious. 'Friends have names. What are they called?'

'The main one is Godfrey. I call him God.'

I stifle a laugh. Is he joking?

'So when you say God tells you to do something…it's him? Not the Almighty?'

'That's right. But God speaks through him. That's why I always listen to him in particular.'

'What?' …It takes a moment or two to process what he's said – but then he's thought of something else.

'And did you see the man putting up a "one way" sign in the car park?' he adds. 'Godfrey said it was a message that your mum is going to be alright. She's going one way; one way towards home. Didn't you see the way he smiled at us? He heard God speaking. You'll see I'm not the only one.'

I'm beginning to tire of this nonsense. I love him and accept his individuality but it's getting too complex. Imaginary friends, people signalling things, boss persecuting him. His imagination has run riot, gone wrong, warped and crossed into dreamlike realms.

'What about the others'. I ask. 'The woman? What is she called?'

'Lucy. What does that tell you?'

'Nothing. It's a female name.'

'What was God's fallen angel called?'

The penny drops, but I don't want to encourage him any further so stay quiet.

THURSDAY 25TH JUL

Colin has started finding another bedsit for me again. It's far too small he says, and it's in a poor area. But I think it's to get me away from Bob who he thinks is lusting after me. I should be so lucky!

'You could live in a better area than this,' he declares. 'The crime rate is high. I'd hate to have to insure my car in this area.'

'But I like the area and I don't have a car. It's convenient and I haven't actually been a victim of crime and…all my friends are round here.'

'Exactly. Your friends. You know what I think of them don't you?'

'Yes but you're wrong. They can be high spirited but none of them have ever been in any real trouble – and I can depend on them.'

'Can't you depend on me?'

I ponder. 'Yes but…' I don't get chance to finish.

'Well why do you need them then. You have me now. Aren't I enough?'

'Yes but … I need other people too but it doesn't mean I don't need you.'

'Godfrey thinks this is a bad place.' Oh no. Not him again.

'Haven't you noticed the seat has gone from the front garden?'

'What's that got to do with it?'

'It's gone – it's been moved.'

'Yes? It was rotten. You'd fall through it if you sat on it.'

'Don't you see? … Its being moved is a symbol. It means that you should move too. It was a sign from God to tell to me what to do. Whoever moved it had heard his instruction.'

I doubt God would have to use such abstract communication with all his alleged power, but I know I'm going to have to go along with it. He'll get upset if I question it. He looks so hurt if I say I don't believe him – or pour cold water on his fantasies.

'I do want to move eventually,' I say, 'but not now. I'll start looking at the end of the month. There's no rush is there?'

FRIDAY 26TH JUL

Brenda, her latest date and I, went to see a Rolling Stones concert. They played on a boarded floor over a local swimming pool in Urmston and looked very short with shaggy hair. We paid half a crown entrance and hoped the boards were strong enough. I don't know if they drained it first.

I sneak out this evening using a visit 'home' as an excuse to avoid disapproval of going out with Brenda.

'I'll pick you up later,' he offers.

'No, I'm not sure how long I'll stay – and I like to walk if the weather is fine,' I lie.

I'll have to practise lying because I'll need it. I just hope to hell it doesn't rain.

Brenda's boyfriend has been watching this up and coming group making waves in the pop scene. She's treated him to this concert because it's his birthday, it's cheap, and we want to see it too. I enjoy watching their extrovert performance with Mick Jagger strutting along the stage and much head shaking from the others. People get up to dance dropping their cigarette ends onto the floor first then grinding them in firmly with their feet. We follow and the floor withstands throbbing beats and dancing feet and everyone stays dry despite, possibly, six feet of water below!

SATURDAY 27TH JUL

I wanted to look for a flat but Colin was on the case before I had a chance. I'd enjoy scanning papers and newsagents' windows and it's summer, so it would get me out in the fresh air. I don't need to be taken everywhere by car. I could ride on the devil bike or walk but there he was, with an advert marked in red, wanting me to view it with him!

'Look. I've found this one for you,' he says passing me the evening paper. 'Four pounds a week plus electricity. And it's in a nicer area. There are buses all along the main road so you could get to work easily. And the shared bathroom is with only one other tenant.

'Yes but Colin… its nearly two pounds a week more. I'd have less to live on, and I'd rather have a bit more to spend each week.'

'The landlord would reduce it for you. I know he would.'

'Don't be silly. He's running a business. I wouldn't even ask him.'

'Ok, I'll give you two or three pounds each week if that would help. You know I'll always help you. I love you. I want to improve things for you.'

It would help. It's so tempting. I think of having a nice flat and some spare money for a hairdryer, and a new bag, but something's holding me back. What if it finished between us? I'd be struggling again. I'm pulled in both directions. Then no. I'm going to say no. It would be nice but I'll manage as I am.

'No thanks,' I say decisively. 'Not a good idea right now. I know you mean well, and I'm so lucky to have you to care about me… but it's better if I pay my own rent. I'm good at budgeting and besides… you help in so many other ways… I don't want to take advantage of you.'

'Let's just go and view it,' he suggests.

'Colin, there's no point. It's out of my range.'

He's not going to accept it. I can tell by the shape of his mouth. He's going to try and persuade me or insist. But no, wait a mo, he's thinking about something.

'I know the landlord will accept less if we ask. I'm certain of it.'

We? Who said we? I thought it was me!

'No, I've already said, I don't want to do that… And anyway, how do you know he'd take less?'

'God told me. He said the landlord had sent signs … that he wants you to have it above all others. That landlord is an immensely wealthy man…He'd never miss two pounds.'

'Look, you can't keep saying God tells you things just because you want it to happen. You mean Godfrey don't you? But you said Godfrey wasn't God! That makes it so confusing for me. Don't call Godfrey, God, I don't know what you mean and its getting silly!'

'I've told you before – God speaks through him – that's what I call him. God. It's just shortened Lizzie….and he does speak to me. I hear him. Believe me.'

What was initially a delightful idiosyncrasy is becoming a tangle of nonsense I can't unpick. I neither want to listen or view the flat so I feign hunger and we go for an unnecessary meal.

MONDAY 29TH JUL

Viewed a flat after work today. I'd rung about the advert yesterday but didn't tell him so I could do it myself. It was a lovely flat but out of my budget range. Two single bedrooms and a kitchen, which is ideal for two to share but who with? My only friend without a partner is Jenny and she's OK where she is, so that's out.

I consider advertising for a flat mate then change my mind. Too chancey. What if you don't get on, they hog the bathroom, don't pay their share of the heating, don't clean up, want their

COLIN

boyfriends there all the time etc! I think what it would be like to share with Brenda or Janet who are very dear friends – and I know I'm being picky, but not likely!

TUESDAY 30TH JUL

Daytime – two new girls started today. I was asked to look after them a bit and show them how to pack and seal. One had worked at Simpson's meat products factory but there's a sweeter smell here she says. The other came from Woolworths and didn't like working Saturdays.

Evening. A warm evening so drinks at The Horse, then a walk down Chorlton Meadows. He was strange again tonight, the signs and symbols thing again. I know that the full moon, or any kind of moon is not linked to madness – but Colin claims to be affected by it – technologically! It's yet another of his weird ideas.

'Look,' he says looking up on the way back. 'Look at the moon. What do you notice?'

'Nothing…Well, it's the moon – a full one. It's lovely.' The disc of light hangs in atmospheric dusk and I hope he's going to say something romantic. But no.

'It's following us. That's a warning – that I'm going to be followed.'

'Colin – that can't be possible. It just *looks* as if it is! It follows everyone. There's a scientific reason for it …which I don't know … but you're more educated than me – so you should!'

'I know, science is a wonderful thing. Don't forget the moon does have great powers though. It can turn tides – and they can use it to transmit television programmes now. You know like Telstar – signals bounce off it. It can transmit messages to people – like it does to me when the voices come through my television set.'

For a split second I'd thought he'd abandoned the delusion. It does have powers and we do have Telstar. It doesn't pass personal messages through TV sets though.

WEDNESDAY 31ST JUL

A sixteen-year-old girl called Pauline Reed, is missing in Gorton. She's been missing for days – just disappeared into thin air so they think somebody might have taken her. It must be awful for her parents. It's worrying for me because it's relatively local and I have a friend, Anna, in Gorton. I must tell her to be careful, but I bet she's read about it already.

The news disturbs the Manchester area. Awful warnings are issued. Girls are advised not to walk alone at night. It's on the news a lot and then dropped – until another one, a boy, disappears soon after.

'Take care,' says Bob. 'I'm always around if you need an escort, but don't let it stop you going out and being independent. And don't forget – you're more likely to be murdered by someone you know than a complete stranger.'

'I'd better watch out for you then!' He pulls a weird face and pretends to strangle me.

'You couldn't strangle a dishcloth.' I laugh as I fend him off. I leave quickly. The off licence closes in ten minutes and I need matches for the gas. I walk off confidently enough, but a passing car innocently slowing down unnerves me, so I cross the road casting suspicious looks at its driver.

FRIDAY 2 AUG

Busy at work with priority orders including a large run of swiss rolls with our supervisor begging people to work overtime until eight o'clock. I said no, because I'm going out with my boyfriend. 'Boy friend.' I like saying it for the pure pleasure of having it in my mouth. I never thought I'd have one.

Had a nice variety of jobs today. I stamped, wrapped, spread jam, grabbed, parcelled and packed. If I had a driving licence I'd have delivered them too, for better money – but that's always done by men. 'Grab and bundle' comes first. I grab six wrapped cakes from the belt and arrange them into neat rectangular shapes for someone down the line who scoops them up in one easy movement, plonks them onto sheets of brown paper for the next person who wraps them into neat paper parcels. Then there is taping and grabbing of parcels and dumping them in already opened boxes. Then someone parcel tapes the boxes shut. All done at high speed with occasional chaos of escapees and pile ups.

Jam spreading is best. It drops in sticky blobs onto flat sponges you ambush as they charge along. Someone then makes them into neat rolls. You'd think there'd be a machine for this! It's nineteen sixty-three.

We need silly distractions sometimes. The day before Therasa married the security guard we 'dressed up her coat' with coloured ribbons, cards with ribald slogans, and long twists of coloured crepe paper and made her walk home like that. It's a cheap fun, factory / mill tradition. We sing, we joke, we banter, we laugh to pass the day. Dirty Mary is at the other end of the belt. I can hear raucous laughter as Ernie disappears to the 'ovens' floor of the factory where everyone permanently drips with sweat.

SATURDAY 3RD AUG

Still no news of the Gorton girl. It's been so hot the last few days that Brenda's wearing her shorts. Her legs look great and she showed me a bottle of expensive tanning lotion which smelt awful. I'm going to do it the natural way, in the garden. She's lucky being fair-haired because her leg hairs hardly show. Mine are like gorillas' legs if I don't deal with them.

I'm envious of Brenda's long, sleek hairless legs. I'd like fabulous legs too so I change into an almost outgrown bikini and plonk myself on a towel in the garden. The mid-day sun turns my shoulders bright pink, but my legs stay milk bottle white. I persevere, undo the straps of my top so I don't get stripes and turn over. Almost second degree burns later it's becoming very uncomfortable. There's an interruption.

'Lizzie, a word.' The Dragon's head protrudes from behind the back door of her flat. 'The neighbours can see you y'know.'

COLIN

'Well aren't they lucky then,' I reply smarting from the sunburn but the legs are beginning to colour at last. Inside, Brenda lends me some Immac hair remover which I generously apply to my legs. It is absolute agony but I'd rather this than hairy legs, all for the sake of vanity – it's what we girls do.

SUNDAY 4TH AUG

The skin is peeling off my legs and they are so sore! They don't even look nice after all that pain! Stayed overnight at Colin's as usual on a Saturday night. I made us a roast lamb Sunday lunch but over-cooked it! He says I should move in while I look for somewhere. That's what Brenda did and it didn't work out and look what happened, but I think I can handle him better. The voices and strange ideas are even more frequent now and he needs my help facing reality. Who else is there for him? I'll help him over this phase because I love him.

Weekends are nice here and moving in tempts me sometimes, but a warning light always comes on. About what? It's probably because I'm not sure whether I could cure him of his fantasies or even help to, but what if they got worse? What if he gets strange ideas about me?

It's all about Ellis, his boss, at the moment who he says stays outside watching his movements and sending nasty messages through Godfrey via his TV set. He's convinced Ellis intends to bankrupt him. If he sees anything has moved, or changed in the garden, it is a sign that he's been there.

Ellis is a Free Mason. Colin thinks they believe in satanic rites and could take control of the government when they have sufficient members and funds. He's read up everything about them and thinks he's an expert. In the sixth form he'd had a thing about communists and accused a teacher of holding seditious meetings in the staffroom. Now it's his boss. Most of the time it's OK and I can often divert him with either food, TV, playing cards, going out somewhere, or conversation about something he might be interested in.

In fact, sometimes he'll be normal for days – as if he's recovering well and all will be fine. Then he's so attentive and caring it's a pleasure to be with him. I wish it was like that all the time though.

TUESDAY 6TH AUG

I've not written anything about work in my journal recently. That's because it's the same most days and I can't keep writing the same thing. Janet was amazed I do it at all.

'Why would you want to write things?' she asked.

'It's a hobby like collecting stamps or knitting. I like writing.'

I regretted telling her because she told friends who asked about it. She cannot resist telling people things and it's very private. She needs to develop some sensitivity. I take notes and keep them in a hidden compartment in my handbag so Colin can't see my anxieties about him.

THURSDAY 8TH AUG

Wow. There's been a train robbery with over a million pounds stolen! The poor train driver was coshed on the head and is lucky to be alive and the robbers got away. A million pounds! It's the most that's ever been stolen. The police have no idea how the robbers knew there was so much on that train. So far they haven't had any tip-offs from their usual informers. It's all over the papers and televison news which Doris let me watch tonight. It's exciting as I watch the footage. In fact I cannot sleep thinking about it. News is sometimes so dry I can't be bothered paying any attention. But I've been a vacuous little airhead long enough and I am going to try and take interest in the news and other important things. Bob will explain things I don't understand.

FRIDAY 9TH AUG

Something strange is happening here – but trivial compared to yesterday's train robbery. It's worrying because it's personal – it's happening to us tenants! Some are finding things disappearing from their rooms such as watches, money, records etc. Everyone is suspicious of each other. Brenda, Bobby and I trust each other, but the others?

I consider them. Frank? Well stuff like this wouldn't be worth him getting out of bed for, but Doris is odd. She's living on something called National Assistance which I hadn't heard of, but it's not much. She must be lonely with only a swearing budgie for company and rarely going out. She stays in bed all morning with her clothes on reading paperback novels emerging sometimes to check the post. I know this because Brenda and I peep in occasionally when her door is ajar and see her lying surrounded by piles of books. She wears large spikey rollers – silly if she never goes anywhere. It must be like sleeping on a porcupine but – she's an unlikely thief and we like her because she lets us watch her TV. No it's not her.

Olive and Stan in the large first floor front room are OK and I get on with Olive although Mrs Bryson is not impressed. She's pregnant which infuriates Mrs B because she must have known it when she read the advert saying: NO CHILDREN NO ANIMALS. Olive is annoying because she takes too long in the shared bathroom, leaves hairs in the plughole and tide marks in the bath. But she's not a thief.

Her husband, Stan? He drinks a lot and once had a fight with Mr Bryson. Mrs Bryson says he fills the bins outside so they overflow attracting mice which Mr Bryson then has to kill. 'Tidy it up yourself then,' Stan said to the Dragon. That doesn't make him a thief either. But someone is.

SATURDAY 10TH AUG

Colin still thinks I should move in with him. I've not looked for anything lately but someone's breaking into the bedsits and it's not nice. What with that and his hatred of Brenda and jealousy of Bob it could be a solution to keep him happy. But something is telling me not to. Perhaps I have an inner voice too!

I've arrived at Colin's immaculately clean flat on a Saturday afternoon.

COLIN

'Have you eaten?' he asks.

'Well Bob brought something to share at lunchtime from the supermarket.' Before the words are out of my mouth I'm regretting it. Too late. Why didn't I think!

'Bob did? Why does he bring you food?'

'I've told you. They let him have things if they've been in the store too long.'

'You don't need food handouts you know Lizzie. Don't I look after you well enough? And I've been thinking. It's about time you moved in here with me. There's plenty of food here and no burglaries.'

I think about his tidy pristine fridge and well stocked cupboard. Tempting.

'Yes but …it's a bit soon isn't it? I hesitate. I'm unsure. 'We've not been together long. Maybe in another six months or so. Shouldn't I look for my own place first?'

'What! While someone possibly dangerous might break into your room! Don't be ridiculous. You know I have to protect you. My friends told me I must.' Not them again.

MONDAY 12TH AUG

The thief has struck again and Mrs B has reported it to the police. A detective turned up and interviewed us but he doesn't think it's any of us. Doris's radio has gone missing but not the TV she rents from Radio Rentals thank God. Olive's purse has gone with seven and sixpence in it and Bobby's 'Please Please Me' Beatles album and his *Guiness Book of Records*. I've been lucky so far.

ROOM TO GROW

I enjoy contact with a real-life detective. It's exciting as if I'm starring in a soap opera or police drama. I answer his questions eagerly and hope he'll come back. I don't think it's going to be a priority police investigation as it's just petty thievery – but it feels threatening to me and I'd hate to lose my radio.

TUESDAY 13TH AUG

I saw the thief today! He broke into my room while I was in the bathroom. He thought no-one was in the house and didn't get chance to steal anything because he heard me and panicked. I was within about two feet of him: the man who'd left owing weeks of rent.

I'm standing in the shared bathroom putting on make-up when I hear something on the landing. It doesn't sound like any of the other tenants. It is distinctly furtive. I don't want to be stuck in this bathroom with someone nasty out there, so I edge along the lino, bare feet sticking to it and creep towards the door to peep out.

A scruffy looking man is trying my door unaware I am yards away. I've closed my room on the yale lock but this isn't deterring him. He slides something between the lock and hey presto, he's in and I'm wobbly and frozen to the spot wondering what to do. I pluck up courage and tip-toe shakily past, then rush downstairs to summon someone – but everyone's out! He hears me and in seconds he's rushed down the stairs passing me in a lightning getaway – but I've seen his face. He's pale and gaunt and looks more scared than me, as if he'd collapse if I said 'boo'. The moonlight flitter is a pathetic scrap of a man. He didn't get time to take anything so I've been lucky. I told Colin but wish I hadn't!

WEDNESDAY 14TH AUG

I reported this to the nice policeman who'd visited before.

'Yes, sounds like the Flitter,' he says with a sigh. 'It's typical. He leaves owing rent, taking the front door key with him, returning at a later date to steal things. He's done it before and is well known for it. But he's difficult to catch,' the policeman explained. 'He changes his address frequently so we don't know where to look.'

I'm disappointed. I wanted weighty detective work, fingerprinting, witness tracing, watching and reporting of suspects; something exciting I could talk about. Mrs Bryson is furious about advice to change the front door lock because the thief has a key.

'Do you know how much that will cost,' she berates the policeman who nods sympathetically.

'Sorry Mrs Bryson, but he may try again and we can't take the key off him because we don't know where he is.'

We're given obvious advice about locking our doors properly – as if we hadn't, and keeping our eyes open!

THURSDAY 15TH AUG

Mrs B has not been a dragon lately but she was back on nagging form – about tea-leaves this time! Such a fussing busybody. The

ROOM TO GROW

sooner I find somewhere else without a landlord/lady on the premises the better! Colin never has this trouble at his place. His landlord lives miles away.

'You've bin chucking tea-leaves down the bathroom sink haven't you?' she begins. 'Yes, I thought it were you.' I nearly jump out of my skin. She stands before me, a triumphant smirk on her face. I clutch a little brown tea-pot tighter to my chest its warmth spreading and heating my already reddening face. 'N... no,' I stammer. 'I've just brought it back from Bob's room.'
Brenda has come out and peers as the voices curl up the stairs. She's wearing Dusty Springfield-thick eye make-up and a Susi Wong dress. So fashionable. I look up and catch her eye. It creates an overwhelming urge to laugh, but I don't.

'My 'usband 'ad to take off the U-bend last time,' she continues. U-bend? I look at her puzzled. I've never heard of one despite the self descriptive name.

'And it's not the first time either. We shouldn't have to come cleaning up the bathroom after you.'

'Something the matter?' Olive now steps out at the loud voices sounds. She's in a quilted floral housecoat as if she's not been up long and holds a cigarette so close she'll melt a hole in its nylon material. She's also looking bulgy round the middle.

'I'll tell you what's the matter,' says the Dragon. 'Tipping tea-leaves down the bathroom sink. That's what's the matter. Left a right mess.' She turns back to me. 'Everyone's got to use that bathroom y' know. It's not just yours y'know. It's not an 'otel!'

'I know it's not. I've not tipped anything down the bathroom sink!' I protest. 'This teapot isn't empty. Look. It's full of tea leaves. I'm taking it back from Bob's room. We've just had a brew!'

190

COLIN

'That's right,' says Olive rising to my defence. 'If that's full of tea-leaves, how can she have put them down the sink? Anyway,' she continues. 'Why is it worse to empty them down a bathroom than a kitchen sink. Don't kitchen sinks have U-bends too? They all go to the same place don't they? And nobody blocks them deliberately!' She's surprising me. Stan gets her tongue but she's usually so quiet with everyone else.

'Don't get bloody cheeky with me!' comes the immediate retort, tea leaves forgotten, focus now on this tenant's audacity.

'That's not cheeky. I'll tell you what is though.' Olive counters. 'It's cheeky to come shouting at people when they've not done anything. Oh yes, and it's cheeky to listen in to phone calls in the hall like your husband does. He does you know.'

'Don't you speak about my 'usband like that.' She wags her finger in Olive's face.

'I'm only telling the truth and you don't like that do you?' she retorts. 'Well I'm not scared of you, and I didn't shout at you either…so talk civily and get your finger away from my face.'

The Dragon is agape. Accusations and counter accusations fly. Who doesn't put the lid on the dustbin? Well who wouldn't buy enough dustbins to fit all the rubbish? Who plays loud music after 11.00 when respectable people should be in bed? Yeah, well that's not late if you're in the twentieth century. And what about using all the hot water in the morning when someone else has put money in the geyser? Hot water! It's not only me that uses it. Tell that to the one who's always in the bathroom when you're bursting to go to the toilet!

An insistent doorbell interrupts everything. The Dragon, too nosey to miss anything, clomps down the stairs to confront a hapless tenant who'd forgotten his key again. It's Frank. We can hear him being told off as he comes in. It slides off like an oil slick. He doesn't get aggressive with women.

FRIDAY 16TH AUG

Colin is pestering me to move in with him again but I can't. I know he'll see it as a rejection if I find somewhere else. I've cut out an advert for another bedsitter and hidden it. Some of the things Brenda warned about are happening and it's the clothes he's now objecting to.

I'm getting ready to go to the birthday party of a friend's child. We've had a lovely week going out places and everything's fine with us. He looks me up and down. I smile. He must be admiring my appearance so I give a little twirl. I scrimped and saved for this new dress.

'Why are you dressed like that?'

'What do you mean?'

'That dress. It's far too short and revealing.'

'Short will be here in a big way soon,' I say as I daub on eyeshadow. 'Just wait and see. Shorter and shorter now. Hems are well up… maybe I'll be the first with this round here.'

'You don't need to set the fashion Lizzie. You're trendy enough without flaunting it!'

'Flaunting it! I don't call this flaunting it! It's just a shorter style.'

'I just don't want you to look tarty that's all. As if you're … well, anybody's. Put the grey one back on. It suits you much

COLIN

better. And do you need make up plastered on like that? Makes you look like a painted doll. You're pretty enough without it.'

I sigh and comply. Keep him happy. Don't argue. Hide the advert for the flat. Don't spoil a pleasant week.

SUNDAY 18TH AUG

My make up bag has disappeared! I'm in a bar, bare-faced without make up which I don't mention as I'm not sure what happened to it. He's probably taken it because he doesn't like me wearing make up! Just like it was with Brenda. I wish I'd listened to her. We finish a bar meal and I want to go back to my room as I usually do on a Sunday to prepare for work and do little jobs but:

'Stay another night,' he demands. 'Go back tomorrow. What's another night.'

I give in and we go to bed. I notice him locking the door and pocketing the key. Does he usually do this? Why turn the key and take it away?

'You're locking it?

'Yes.'

'Why's that? What if anyone calls or anything and I want to open it?'

'No one's going to call in the middle of the night! It's to keep anyone out who might be trying to get at me. I've told you before. It's for our safety I'm hiding the key.'

I hear him open a kitchen drawer. Must be the hiding place. I'll remember that.

But *for our safety?* I don't feel safe locked in! It's out of my control and makes me uneasy. I sleep fitfully waking to hear him prowling around like a restless animal. Why isn't he sleeping? What's he doing? Rustle rustle, crackle crackle. I identify the sound. Oh God! He's going through my bag. What if he discovers the secret compartment! My notes! What if he reads what I've written about him. What if he sees the newspaper cutting for another bedsit!

I hope he hasn't found the discreet inner pocket. It's large but flat and inconspicuous, the same colour as the lining but he could find it if in a good light if he was thorough. It's probably safe? No? Yes? I think it's OK. Yes. I hear him fasten my bag and return. What was he looking for? I feign sleep when he returns and he doesn't mention it in the morning. In fact he's charming and affectionate, brings me tea in bed and takes me to work so it must be alright. Phew! I won't carry such stuff in future.

MONDAY 19TH AUG

I'm thinking more about changing my job now. Mum will be coming home soon so I won't have to visit hospital and I'll have more time to look. Most of my friends do typing but I got thrown out of the typing class at school so I can't join a typing pool. I'd tried to write poems instead of single letter boring drills and got found out so I had to do needle work instead.

Work was fun today, singing along with 'Housewives' Choice.' This 'Light Programme' programme is good for worker morale

COLIN

so we listen to it over loudspeakers each morning. We sing in various levels of tunelessness to popular songs interspersed with cheery comments from the presenter. Intercom paging messages get noisily drowned out.

I have my lunch in the canteen with workmate Marian. We chat over the generously subsidised meals and share a cigarette on the other side of the canteen to the men's table they've extended to fit their number. We're territorial over our regular places, tutting, and looking annoyed should anyone innocently sit there which is not welcoming for new workers. The men laugh in loud masculine voices, roll their own cigarettes and play cards. Their pungent smoke drifts over and mingles with ours. I stub out what's left of our cigarette in the regulation ash tray on every table. I wouldn't want it behind my ears like the men do.

'I'm thinking of looking for another job,' I tell her.

'Oh, what do you want to do?'

'I don't really know. Something where they pay more, something different. I'm going to get the *Manchester Evening News* tonight.'

'The jam factory pays a bit more y'know,' she says. 'And there's the Vimto factory near here too. They were advertising for workers.'

'Yes, but it's still factory work. I might get bored with that too.'

'There's a cotton mill in Oldham that wants mule operatives.'

'Mule operatives? What are they? Donkey drivers!'

She laughs. 'Mules are big spinning machines. Actually I don't think you'd like it. It's very noisy. There's lots of mills in

Oldham but it takes ages to get to there so don't leave. I'd miss you!'

I still buy the Evening News that evening.

TUESDAY 20ᵀᴴ AUG

The jobs in the paper are not paying well, difficult to get to, or want qualifications that I haven't got. There are shop, factory and mill vacancies galore but nothing interesting. There's one at a mail-order company dealing with orders and filing things. Colin, he wasn't keen on this, and of course his voices had to come into it. They're butting into everything these days.

'Why do you want to work there?' he asks as I show him the advert and a map. 'You'd have to go all the way to Ardwick on the bus – and Ardwick! It's a really downtrodden area.'

'Its not exactly Chelsea round here.'

'Yes, but better the devil and all that. At least where you work I don't think you'd go off with any of the men there. They're all so…so…working class. All that heaving things out of ovens and sweating. That's enough to put a girl off surely…and they give you gifts don't they? I'm not happy about that. Why do you let them do that?'

'Gifts! You can hardly call little packs of cocoa and coffee gifts.'

'Oh, You're so young sometimes Lizzie. Don't you know what men are like?'

'Yes I do, but not these men. They're…family men. They're not interested in me. Not like that.'

'Oh but that will be in their minds – trust me. Even if they don't do anything they'll be thinking about it. My friends tell me about them and we know what's in their minds.'

The invisible kind he means. I've told him not to talk about them, so I don't respond, but he continues anyway.

'Lucy would have them baked alive in their ovens.' He's watching for my response. I can't contain it any longer.

'Colin! That's not nice, it's nasty and it's not real. Lucy doesn't exist. She's a voice in your head.'

He doesn't answer. He knows I don't like listening to this nonsense but he's muttering about her under his breath.

WEDNESDAY 21ST AUG

It was uncomfortably hot again today at work. Thank goodness for the new Pepsi machine which randomly swallows sixpences but sometimes you win and get a cold drink. I stripped off under my overalls.

Mary did too, her ample bosoms almost pouring out and shining with sweat. We slog all day until the 5.15pm buzzer when the belt gets turned off leaving it strangely quiet. We discard overalls and turbans and trickle out past the security guard, now Therasa's husband. He randomly checks womens' shopper-type bags in case they've pinched any produce but just winks at me and her. He has nothing to fear. You go off cake after a while. Therasa and I are going to have an evening out this week which he doesn't mind about even though they've only been married a few weeks. He's nice and doesn't tell her what she should do or criticise her friends!

I arrive back to a sour bottle of milk in a hot airless room. The bucket of cold water substitute milk fridge hasn't worked, but I have some powdered tasteless stuff. Outside, far off thunder unsettles the birds so they squawk then quieten between rumbles, but I'm not going anywhere tonight so it doesn't matter.

THURSDAY 22ND AUG

My dad's offered to get me an application form for factory hands at Kellogg's. The pay is better and they really look after their staff. At Christmas they get a bonus, a hamper, a turkey and a party for the workers' children! The thing is, my workmates are so loyal and such good fun and it might not be the same, but it was so hot and uncomfortable today. A bakery must be the worst place to work in a hot spell but would cornflake production be any cooler?

Machinery radiates additional heat. The supervisor has switched on extra fans but I'm damp with perspiration. Underarm deodorant; did I apply enough this morning? A current TV advert features a loudly whispering workmate indicating someone has 'B.O', lips pulled down in disgust at the unfortunate perspirer. That could be me – the B.O one! I could be shunned or whispered about. I ask for cover for a toilet break so I can splash water under my arms, then have to figure out how to dry them. I manoeuvre the roller towel but it's the wrong height for armpits so I flap my arms like a chicken. My mouth feels dry. A Pepsi machine drink entails going to my locker for coins and I've been gone long enough to get told off. I slurp water from cupped hands and return.

FRIDAY 23RD AUG

We've had Chris as our supervisor since Ivy's been ill. He doesn't complain if we sing or get giddy. I sent the application form to the Kellogg's factory which is paying much better. Chris said he would give me a good reference.

I had the sense to take water to work in a lemonade bottle today. I missed stamping some cakes thinking about Colin's mental state. They sneakily sailed past and Chris noticed. 'It's a simple job – concentrate,' he said half joking. Sometimes I can't.

Manual stamping is about as boring as it gets but gives you chance to think. I stamp little paper discs on circular cakes gliding down the belt. Stamp, stamp, stamp. My eyes glaze over as I worry about Colin who thinks invisible friends are telling him to find me a bigger flat, who thinks every man is lusting after me, who thinks he's being spied on, but still I love, despite.

Dirty Mary hilariously lowers the tone and raises the mood of the afternoon. We sing very ribald versions of songs at the top of our voices. Someone's getting married and we plot silly tricks to play on her.

SATURDAY 24TH AUG

Mum has been discharged from hospital today. She still has to take streptomycin tablets which she hates! They're huge and look like the sherbert 'flying saucers' I used to buy as a child. She says they taste disgusting and she may have to take them for months.

Chris, our temporary supervisor, let me go early so I could be there and clocked me out at the usual time which was so good of him. He's nicer than Ivy who scowls at us all the time. Colin came with me and I introduced him to Mum. He'd bought us both flowers. Utterly charming she thought. Well yes, he can be.

Mum's only been home a couple of hours and already she looks tired. She's been dying to meet him since I told her about him. They wouldn't let him on the ward at the hospital so she'd only seen him through the window overlooking the road but she'd noted how good looking he was. She gets up to greet us.

'No, please don't get up Mrs Dale,' he insists. 'You must rest as much as you can,' he says caringly. She still gets up because she thinks it's good manners and doesn't want to be seen as an invalid.

'Mum, this is Colin, Colin, Mum.' He holds out his hand takes hers, then holds it there gently in both hands for a couple of seconds. 'Won't be a mo,' my dad calls from the kitchen. He's rustling up refreshments but can't wait to see the car.

'I'm so pleased to meet you at last Mrs Dale', says Colin politely. 'I've heard a lot about you and it's so good to see you're making such good recovery. Lizzie's been worried about you.'

'Thank you Colin,' says Mum weighing up his neat appearance and natural looking smile. 'And I'm so grateful for the help you gave her bringing her to the hospital. She wouldn't have been able to visit half as much without your help. Oh… and aren't these beautiful!' she says accepting the bouquet he hands her. I clutch its twin. We stand there like a couple of bridesmaids then settle on the settee, Mum looking approvingly at this charming individual. Dad brings in tea and biscuits and soon, him and Colin are talking car language, with a promised demonstration of its power and speed.

'He's a nice fellow but isn't he a bit old for you?' he says later.

Cheek. He's the same number of years older than Mum.

MONDAY 26TH AUG

Went to see *Gun Fire at the OK Corral* at the Gaumont with Therasa. Mum used to do the books there so when the box office lady recognised me, she let us in free after asking about Mum. She probably isn't supposed to. Then we went for last orders at The Lloyds and met two of my old classmates. One called Brian walked us home because everyone is scared because of the missing girl, Pauline Reed. Colin was waiting for me outside the gate. I hadn't expected him. He embarrassed me being so unfriendly to Brian.

'Oh hello.' I'm surprised to see him. 'What are you doing here? Oh. This is Brian from my old school.' I indicate and turn to Colin. 'Brian's walked me home. He walked Therasa home first,' I add, sensing a need to explain myself. Brian detects a cool atmosphere and takes his leave.

'Where have you been?' Colin demands. 'I rang the house and they said you'd gone out. I waited for you and you come back with… that man!'

'He walked us home, Therasa first, then me. It was very good of him and you weren't a bit friendly.' I'm annoyed at his bad manners. 'And we went to see a film if that's alright!'

'Well what time did the film end? It's taken a long time to come home hasn't it? What were you doing until this time. I was worried about you?'

'We were in The Lloyds having a drink. I don't get time to talk to Therasa at work. We had things to talk about. What's wrong with that! Can't I see a friend without you turning up and spoiling it. I was in a good mood before and it's gone… with your …nasty suspicions. Go home if you want to be like that!' He's taken aback at the vehemence.

'It's only because I care about you.' His tone has changed. 'What if you'd disappeared like that girl in Gorton? My friends think she won't come back.'

'Friends?' I sigh. I don't need to ask which ones.

'Never mind. You'll say I'm imagining them. You don't understand how real they are and what sense they talk.'

I don't want to hear about them! I don't know how long I can tolerate their intrusion. I want to shout 'Shut up about them! They aren't real,' but I resist. I must be patient.

'Look it's because I love you …and I don't like seeing you with someone else – in case you're going off me. I want you to myself. Look I've brought you something too.'

He produces a photograph of us taken by a visiting photographer in a restaurant. We're mounted in a lovely silver frame and look so happy. I admire it. It calms me and recovers my mood.

WEDNESDAY 28 AUG

Watched TV with Doris again. This coloured man called Martin Luther King made a really moving speech and everyone was excited. Doris said it was all about the Civil Rights Movement in America which I'd heard about but hadn't realised the coloured people there were so badly treated. They have to use different buses and schools – and even different public toilets! That's awful. At least we don't do that here.

I've not seen Brenda lately or Janet. I miss my friends so much. That's what happens to us girls. A default acceptance allows us to neglect each other once a man comes along: as if our friendships have less value and can be postponed. We understand, we say, but after a time – they've moved on, entwined in their new relationships and we've lost them.

Because of Doris, I'm now aware of The Civil Rights Movement in America. It's making waves which I'm sure will reverberate for decades to come but issues closer to home are beginning to preoccupy me. I'm finding it more difficult lately to cope with Colin's moods and obsessions.

FRIDAY 30 AUG

Colin wants to control everything I do. He's too possessive and I'm seeing far too much of him. I want to spend some time with my mum and my friends. It's been a whirlwind romance and we've gone too quickly. I just need a short break for a while. I'm going to talk to him but I'm dreading it! I think he will react badly.

We're in my room as I get ready to go out. I decide to face up to him and be as frank and calm as possible.

'Colin, I have to talk to you about something,' I begin. 'Something's been bothering me for some time. You know my

ROOM TO GROW

mum hasn't been well? And I don't visit her enough. I should go and see her more often, for a while. That means we need some time apart to give me time. Just for a while. I've been seeing so much of you lately.' There, I've said it.

'You can visit your mum whenever you like. You know that. It shouldn't affect us should it?'

How can I explain this without upsetting him?

'It's not just that, I need some time to myself as well, to see my friends and… be on my own sometimes. Not permanently – just a few weeks, maybe we could just see each other at weekends for a while.'

'But, but you love me don't you? Don't you? DON'T YOU?' His voice rises with each repitition.

'Yes…well I thought I did, and I do, but I was lonely then. I wanted a boyfriend like everyone else and then you came along and it was lovely. But now I'm feeling …more independent. As if I need to think about other things besides just us…You're still important to me though.'

'Oh, I see. So you just used me so you could conform! So you could have a boyfriend! Well you enjoyed the meals out in restaurants didn't you, and the drives out in the car? And the things I bought you. And you let me have sex with you. You liked that too didn't you! So now you think you can drop me like that! Well you've got another think coming!'

He glares at me and I can feel his intensity. I've got to cool this.

'Colin, I'm not going to drop you! I only want a break for a while, for some evenings with friends. I didn't know it would go this far, that I wouldn't be able to see anyone else, not even my friends, or that my mum was going to be ill. It's all happened so quickly.'

COLIN

'You're just like Brenda aren't you. Out for a good time. Fooling about with that Bobby behind my back ...and using me!' He grabs my clothes and pulls me to him. I'm afraid of the strange look in his eyes and I'm not sure what he'll do.

'No, No. You're wrong,' I plead. 'Bob's only a friend. And yes, yes, of course I enjoyed everything. You've been very generous and I've had some lovely times. But you keep me to yourself all the time and make me feel trapped. I need time for others. Please Colin, can't we just leave it for a while...or just see each other at weekends. I don't want to end everything for ever. We can take it up again later.'

He keeps tight hold of the front of my clothes so my breath goes up into his face. So intimate but so uncomfortable.

'Later? What do you mean later? Later? You can't just keep me on a string. Who do you think you are dealing with? A fool? I won't stand for it!' He shakes me hard and I begin to panic.

'Get off me Colin, get off me! Stop shaking me! Let go! I'll scream ...and Mrs Bryson will come ...and Brenda and Bob!' I'm half shouting, half pleading.

He stops. He's thinking. Bullying a woman could ruin his gentlemanly image, respectable citizen, protector of the weaker sex. Moments pass, then he releases my clothes and transforms into the caring Colin, the one that I fell for, the one buried inside the possessive tyrant. It's resurfacing but I don't know for how long or even if it's genuine.

'Oh ...I'm so sorry Lizzie. I don't know what came over me. I shouldn't have shaken you like that. I'm upset. I don't want to lose you. You mean such a lot to me.' He continues begging for forgiveness as I quieten and recover composure. It's been more difficult than I'd bargained for.

'We should get engaged. It would secure things – then we wouldn't have all this arguing. "It will settle things if we have a definite future together. Come on darling. Lets go out right now. I'll buy you a beautiful ring.'

'Not now. Not now. It's not the right time and it's getting late,' I plead. But I don't want a ring; I don't want to be engaged, we may not even have a future, but then I remember how good he's been to me; driving me regularly to see Mum in hospital, taking me places I wouldn't be able to go on my own, making my life much more comfortable and loving me more than anyone else has. I think he is ill and needs me. But I suspect he's capable of being violent.

SATURDAY 31ST AUG

Went food shopping with Brenda in the morning and saw Bob in Fine Fare. They want assistants but Brenda thinks it's demeaning to work in a store. Just because she works in an office – she's a shorthand typist not a princess! Then we went for coffee in the jukebox café and I asked her things. Things I needed to know I'd deliberately not mentioned before, especially about the pills I'd found. I was shocked when she told me.

'So, yes,' I say. 'I found the pills by accident and wondered what they were for? Was he taking them when he was seeing you?'

'Don't you know?' she sounds surprised. 'Don't tell me he didn't tell you! After all this time and he's not said! He's supposed to take them every single day to control his symptons – his mood, you know, to calm him down and suppress the aggression and those things I warned you about. You didn't listen to me

COLIN

though. He's not being straight with you Lizzie.'

But I'm listening to her now. I've been too sceptical about her. She may be prone to exaggeration but she's not doing it now. I should have asked months ago but didn't want to admit that voices or unusual behaviour were anything to worry about and I've always thought other peoples' medication is no-one's business, but because I care about him, it's about time he was honest. It's much more important than I thought and I'll ask him outright. I deserve to know.

Later in the afternoon a huge bouquet of flowers arrived at the house for me. I've never had such a huge bunch before. So gorgeous; roses, carnations and lilies all done up in cellophane and pink ribbons. He can be so romantic but so unpredictable. Brenda took them from the Interflora delivery man at the door. She didn't seem impressed.

'Lizzie.' There's a knock on my door. 'Something's just come for you. Come and see.'

She doesn't bring it up or say what it is. It's not my birthday or anything and I'm not expecting anything. I open my door.

'Thanks Brenda – what is it?'

'Go down and see. They're by the telephone. They'll be from Colin. Typical,' she says with an almost weary voice. Then she's gone. I run down the stairs and find the extravagant bouquet with a sweet little note.

'I'm so sorry sweetheart. I'll make it up to you. Forgive me.'

Such beautiful flowers, but this is too easy and doesn't make up for the fact that he assaulted me the other day!

SUNDAY 1ST SEP

I refused to see him, even after the flowers and ignored his calls.

'Tell him I've gone out,' I told anyone who answered the payphone. It was a lovely day so I went out for a walk but had this odd sensation he was around. Am I imagining things? Am I catching this from Colin! Thinking someone's spying! It's what he says about Ellis! But I know him. He's very capable of following and hiding and I wouldn't put it past him at all. Look how he used to lurk behind the hedge before I knew him.

He has a history so I'm not being over sensitive. I keep walking and my instincts are correct. Look behind across the road – he's there, a long way behind, but there's a man's shape moving steadily along. I craftily wait around a corner until he catches up, then he can't deny he'd been behind me. But he's quick with his response.

'Oh at last. I'd been trying to catch you up for ages. You walk so fast!' Does he think I'm stupid or blind? I make it clear I know he's been following me – but he's more concerned with winning me over with love talk, apologising for his dreadful behaviour and promising to reform. But I'm having none of it. It's time for frank talking. I need to know about the pills.

'Colin stop,' I begin. 'Don't say any more. There's something I need to know – so stop talking and listen. Are you alright?'

'Of course I am. What do you mean, "am I alright?"'

'I mean about those pills. The ones you didn't want me to see – but I did. What are they for? You need to tell me about them… and why did you hide them?'

'Oh...' He sighs and pauses. 'I didn't want you to know about them.'

'Yes, obviously.'

'I was trying to protect you – that's all. It didn't seem necessary to say... well if you must know...' he pauses.

'Yes I must. We've been so close, and you owe it to me to be honest. I want honest answers so tell me the truth. I don't care what it is but please don't lie to me.'

'Yes I know. I'm really sorry. It's because I didn't want to worry you. They're to control...to control, what you called my creativity and inner voices. There, that's what you want to hear isn't it?'

'Why do they need controlling? Is that why you lose your temper? Is it an illness? Tell me.'

'My doctor thinks so...It's a long story. Are you sure you really want to know?'

'Of course I do. It's really important!'

'They were prescribed for me when I saw a psychiatrist. Yes, a psychiatrist. Don't be shocked. Loads of people see them. More than you think. But I don't always take them because I don't need them. I wouldn't even have gone to that quack ...if Ellis hadn't pressed me. He kept on at me. For my own good, he said. He said I'd lose my job if I didn't. He says I'm getting worse and it's affecting my work... but he's an idiot. He's trying to find reasons to fire me so he watches me, or gets others to. They have walkie-talkies. I can sometimes hear them through my television set. It must be on the same frequency so I hear them talking – about me – what they're going to do to make things bad for me. It's been going on for some time Lizzie – and you know some of it already but now you know about the pills too.'

Colin is probably more sick than I could have ever imagined. I know now that he is not over imaginative or artistically sensitive or anything else I've wanted to believe about him hearing voices. He is ill. That's why he thinks he is being spied on and sees symbols in things. I can understand him worrying about losing his job… but people following him with walkie –talkies that interfere with TV signals? That's not creative. That's not normal.

But, he is a friend in need isn't he. He's having big problems and it wouldn't be fair to drop him now as he doesn't seem to have anyone else to help him. Where is his family? Or tangible friends? I don't know how people are supposed to handle situations like this – or even if I can. Do I even still love him? It's a changed kind of love now if I do.

'Colin,' I begin gently. 'If the doctor said you should take the medication – you really should you know. Some things don't work at first. Take them for a while – regularly – please. They can't do any harm if they don't do good.'

He nods in agreement. He'll do it for me he says, but he's somewhere else.

TUESDAY 3RD SEP

I need to take in what I've learned and what to do. And my job. What am I going to do about that? I've got an interview at Kellogg's but I'm turning it down because of the shifts. One starts at six o'clock in the morning! Imagine that! Then there's

COLIN

an evening shift until ten o'clock which blots out any social life. There just aren't many options for girls with no qualifications or special talents.

Half a crown more at the gas-cooker parts factory? Worth it? Or the jam factory? Shop work? Filing clerk? Print works round the corner? Jobs are two a penny but no better than the one I've got moneywise. Maybe I should find a good husband; that's what most girls are looking for. One thing's certain now, I don't want it to be him, but I'm no fairweather friend and he needs me.

I always feel better having written about these things. It is my 'listener' while I sort of talk to myself and sort out my thoughts. Is having a listener like having an invisible friend? No, because I know it's me.

WEDNESDAY 4TH SEP

I've been thinking about what Bob said. He's got me more interested in the news and less girly things and said anyone can get O Levels, even me! So, I'm going to the local Further Education College to inquire about evening classes, just like he said. It's only an enquiry isn't it? I am a bit uneasy about telling Colin though. He'll react and say it's a waste of time and may get angry if I insist. Maybe I should just do it while he's not here. I could change my mind and nobody's going to drag me to lessons if I do. I need to take this risk and stop dithering.

THURS 5TH SEP

I've done it! I enrolled at College today for two evenings a week. I'm only doing three O'Levels as I need time to do the homework.

The College administration officer doing my enrolment application looks at me above half-lensed spectacles.

'So you want to do three subjects?' I'm suddenly not sure, or if I'd be capable of any at all. I wish I'd asked Bob.

'I think so. Do you think that will be enough …I could do more next year.'

'Depends what you want to do with them. How old are you?'

'Eighteen. I was eighteen in June.'

'Well that's good. You won't have to pay this year. I'd do them while you can if I were you.'

Pay for them? It hadn't occurred to me. I thought it was like school, free for everyone forever. I quickly go through the form filling and hand it in.

'Right that's all done,' he says handing me a subject timetable. 'You start next week.'

I want to hug him I'm so pleased with myself, but I'm seeing Colin tomorrow. That's the hard bit.

FRIDAY 6TH SEP

I knew it. He didn't like this bit of independent action one bit! Bob was pleased though. But he doesn't understand Colin – and thinks it's so simple.

COLIN

'Just tell him,' he said. 'It's up to you if you want to go. Don't let him talk you out of it – say you have already decided and it's not up for discussion.' I wish it was so straightforward.

'You've done what?' Colin looks incredulous as if I'd joined a Band of Hope or the Red Brigade.

'I've enrolled at College to do O Levels; three of them,' I repeat.

'I did advise you against this Lizzie, but you've chosen to go against me. I doubt you'll be able to see it through. Enroling is one thing. Wait until you get difficult assignments, when you've been working all day at the bakery and want to go out.'

'Yes, I have thought about that and I'll try my best. That's all I can do.'

'And we wouldn't be able to see each other as much would we? What about that?'

'No, there would be two or three evenings when I'd have to attend or do the work but we can manage that. We could still have all weekend together.'

'And what about the expense – the extra bus fares?'

'I have a bike remember?'

'Oh that old thing. It would let you down and it's not safe is it?'

'Yes it is different because it has a fixed wheel, but I'm used to it now. I never fall off now.'

'It's got no lights either.'

'There are places that sell lights you know!'

'Hmm. I don't think you'd cope with studying so ...why waste time? You're just not cut out for it. Education is wasted on girls anyway – they just get married so what's the point?" And what if we got married? You wouldn't need O Levels then would you?'

I'm stunned. Married? Who's talking about marriage?

ROOM TO GROW

'Colin – we've only been together five months – that's not long really. We may not be together forever you know. I'm only eighteen.'

'We will,' he states. 'Because I'd kill myself if you didn't want me anymore. But I'd kill you first.'

He's so matter of fact he can't possibly be serious. It's something people say on impulse isn't it? Or is it? I'm not going to rise to the bait though.

SAT 7TH SEP

Saturday nights are never lonely now. I'm in a settled routine. Shopping in the morning or meet a friend in the café, glossed over so he can't find fault with anyone. Then off to Colin's where he makes me lunch and I stay the night after we go out. I always return to my bedsitter on Sunday evenings to do little jobs.

SUNDAY 8TH SEP

Evening: Washed some clothes, sewed a button on a skirt and went through a book list for my subjects. Showed Bob who was impressed.

'You're going to do it aren't you?' he says. 'Good for you.'

MONDAY 9TH SEP

My first evening at College. So exciting and already I've made a sort of friend – as nervous as me but we're both going to persevere. The curriculum for English, Maths and History is so scarey and there seems so much to learn! Will I be able to do it? I have a short English assignment for next week to establish what I can do! I wasn't sure what the tutor wanted so I asked.

'Call me Pat,' she says. Don't worry too much about this first one. You'll learn from it. Descriptive writing just means describing something which can be very ordinary. You could be anywhere, walking through the park observing children playing, shopping or at work.'

I'm relieved. Flowers and nightingales are not me. The evenings are still light but I'll need bike lights soon.

TUESDAY 10TH SEP

Bought some bike lights and fitted them on. Enjoyed the history class. It was about the Industrial Revolution and I have an assignment to do about Manchester but not due in for ages. My bike lights work really well and it saves me money to cycle. Bus fares went up this week.

WEDNESDAY 11TH SEP

He's been more like the man I love this week so I'm more relaxed. College wasn't mentioned and he said he was taking the medication which seems to be working. I told him about the girl I'd got to know at college and my college work and he seemed interested and not resentful. I'm going to stand by him as long as there's no more temper outbursts or attempts to stop me seeing people. I'm not going to have much time to see them anyway. I've started the first assignment.

I'm enjoying the good life again. He's bought records I like for the car and talks about the London trip we're going on. I'm given the cameo brooch I'd admired in a shop and Mum gets flowers on her birthday.

'Oh isn't he wonderful,' she says.

We go to see *Carmen Jones* at the Odeon cinema in town and choose one of the trailers for next time. People behind us seemed to have brought a picnic and others smoked throughout the film including Colin but don't complain as I feel he's getting better. He'll beat his illness, I know he will, and all will be fine. I could have a good life with him.

FRIDAY 13TH SEP

Such a panic today. Due at College at six thirty for my maths class but my bike had gone! I had to get a bus but I'd looked everywhere and asked the other tenants so it made me late. I was so embarrassed walking into the class and everyone looking at me.

Olive said she thought she saw a man in dark clothes riding it down the road on her way home yesterday. Then she forgot about it. I'm upset about it. I should have bought a padlock but I never thought anyone would want it.

'What time was it you saw him? I ask her.

COLIN

'It must have been about six o'clock. Yes, I'd been shopping when I saw this bloke on a black bike, but it was getting a bit dark, so I may be wrong about the colour. But it looked like yours.'

A momentary flash of intuition! No, it couldn't have been. My heart sinks. Surely an impulse theft by some local youth, but there's a nagging doubt. I walk dejectedly to the bus-stop. Bus fares were not included in the week's budgeting.

SATURDAY 14TH SEP

Jacky escaped today! Doris forgot he was out of his cage and opened the window. He made a fast bid for freedom straight into a beech tree. She was so upset. Brenda and I tried to help her catch him until we all had stiff necks watching him up there cheeping merrily, enjoying himself, no intention of coming down.

It began in the early evening as I was off to post a birthday card to Marian when I collided with Doris on the stairs carrying Jacky's cage. She was clearly upset.

'Are you Ok Doris?' I ask wondering why she's carrying the birdcage.

'No. Oh, can you help me please Lizzie. It's Jacky! I opened the window…I forgot…and he's flown away. Oh I'm so stupid. I'm going out to the garden to see if he's there. He might come back if he sees his cage.'

'Of course I will.' I join her into the garden. Olive is there emptying rubbish. We can hear Jacky before we see him. A sweet trilling followed by budgie gibberish and then, plain as can be.

'Who's a silly bugger then? Hello Jacky! Jacky's a pretty boy, Hello Jacky, chirrup, chirrup, chirrup.'

He's perched unattainably high, and not at all tempted by Doris calling his name and waving his cage about. Half an hour later it's dark and we know it's not going to work. Mr Bryson has come out to watch.

'I'd give up if I were you. The wild birds will kill him. He won't last long.'

Doris bursts into fresh tears. We take her inside with the empty cage.

I'm reluctant to leave her when Colin arrives even though he's booked us in at the Midland Hotel for dinner and I'm looking forward to it. He comes up to find me. I've brought chocolates to share with her and put the radio news on to distract her. He's concerned the chocolate might spoil my appetite and doesn't understand at all why she's been so upset.

'A budgie? A bird! She's upset because a bird's flown away? I can get her another one for five bob,' he says, as if she's not there. What colour would she like?'

'Shush – listen what's happening in China. It's awful.' I'm trying to distract her but I'm also interested in this as so many people are involved. There's been a miniscule chink through which some brave soul has managed to acquire a modicom of extremely forbidden news. Anything other than official propaganda invites severe punishment so it's a miracle. Millions of Chinese are dying every day in the name of their batty communist leader Mao Tse Tung's revolutionary plan to kick start their sustenance economy to unrealistic heights. There's hardly any food and they're skin and bone. It's 'The Great Leap Forward!' Great leap to starvation more like.

'We're lucky to have regular food supplies in this country,' I comment.

'Hmm. You weren't around in the war were you. I remember rationing and dried eggs.'

He sounds like my parents. We say goodbye to unhappy Doris leaving her with an empty cage and a half box of Milk Tray.

'We could stay at the Midland one weekend,' he offers on the way. 'It's a smart hotel and famous people stay here. Would you like that?'

'That's a lovely idea,' I say. 'What a treat that would be.' He's really back to his old self. I'm enjoying things again.

SUNDAY 15TH SEP

Jacky is dead. I found his stiff little body on the path. His feathers are a pretty green and he has black spots round his neck like a necklace. I went in and found a little box I'd had bath salts in and laid him in it. Then I took it to Doris. We both cried.

'I'm so, so sorry Doris,' I weep as I hand her the box. She looks inside it, embraces me and sobs into my shoulder. We're clamped in a wet embrace when Mrs Bryson looks in at the open door. She'd seen me pick the bird up in the garden.

'Oh dear. Did you find him, love?' she says. 'Let me see.' Doris opens the box for her. 'Oh he was such a pretty bird wasn't he. We'll make a nice coffin for him and then we can bury him in the garden if you like. Shall we?'

Doris nods a tearful approval to Mrs Bryson who leaves returning with a piece of royal blue velvet to line the box and a length of red ribbon. Mr Bryson hovers behind looking cynical.

'Earnest, go and make a nice little wooden cross for him,' she orders. He mutters something under his breath. 'Go on!' she remonstrates firmly. 'Don't just stand there. Go and make a cross. We're going to give him a Christian burial.' He slouches off.

Later we stand in a repectful row along a patch of weeds, Doris holding the box. It's fastened with a red ribbon bow like a lover's Valentine gift.

'Well get on with it Earnest, dig the hole for it. No, not there! That's where the snowdrops come up – here,' she indicates the spot. He presses the spade into the ground with a resentful expression.

Next door's dog has wandered in and stands sniffing the air. It's a sort of many times crossed-bred. It's not friendly and bares its teeth if you speak to it. It's brown and white with a squashed face and watches with interest as clods of earth are extracted and a shallow pool appears.

'Right that's deep enough now,' she asserts. 'Now I'll say a little prayer for him before he goes into the earth. Dear God,' she says. 'This little bird, one of your innocent creatures, is on its way to you. Take him into your loving care… and may he rest in peace. Amen.'

I imagine Jacky fluttering up to his birdie heaven. I'm not convinced God is interested in dead budgies but it's unexpectedly poignant. I've never attended a funeral, but if this is sad, how on earth would I cope with my mother's!

COLIN

MONDAY 16TH SEP

I've had some good luck although I haven't got the bike back. Helen, the girl I got talking to at college, lives just round the corner from here and her mum will pick me up on the corner in her brand new Austin Mini on College evenings. It's the smallest car I've ever seen except for a Bubble Car. She loves any excuse to drive so she won't accept any payment. She passed her test only last week so it's a novelty. My English essay is due in but I'm self conscious about it because I haven't done anything like that since leaving school.

The blue mini arrives. It's drizzling so I've stuffed my writing essay up my jacket to keep it dry. I must buy a file, pencil case, a suitable bag and some jeans so I look like a proper student. I've seen the Manchester University students on Oxford Road; about the same age as me and they wear jeans, and shoes like I used to wear for P.E at school. They are in the top two percent of ability and attend this prestigious red brick university but look relaxed as if studying is something that fits in around their social life. I envy them. It's 'freshers' week soon and they'll do some serious partying. They also have free grants – probably not much less than my wages over the year and have weeks off in between terms to enjoy themselves. What a life!

I'm early for college. I place the essay on Pat's desk. It's strange to use a teacher's first name; at school it was always Mrs this or Mr that, but here it's more like having a friend. My handwriting isn't that neat and is decidedly loopy but it's easy to read so I'm not worrying about it. As long as the content is OK. My descriptive writing essay is about going to work in the urban rush hour.

TUESDAY 17TH SEP

I had a nasty surprise today in the garden. Jacky's little grave had been dug up. The Christian cross Mr B had made was lying flat amongst piles of earth and the cardboard box chewed and mangled with no sign of the bird except for a few bright green feathers. That dog must have eaten Jacky! I told Mrs B who said choice words about her neighbours.

'God knows why they kept that bloody mangey mongrel,' says Mrs B. 'A stray they found – vicious mut! It chases bikes and bit a chunk out of the postman. They let it out to do its business here, and it's sniffing round the bins and growls if you shoo it. Pass me that bucket. I'll teach it.

She fills a metal bucket from the outdoor tap. It's brim full and slopping over the side ready to be chucked should it appear, but she can hardly carry it.

'Use that hosepipe instead,' I suggest. She unwinds it ready for use.

'It's on maximum force,' she says gleefully as she adjusts it. 'I'll teach it!' We push piles of damp earth back down the hole and stick the cross back upright.

'There. She'll never know,' she says. 'We don't want her upset again.'

WEDNESDAY 18TH SEP

I'm getting excited about our London trip on Friday. I've washed and ironed some clothes and sorted my wash-bag. Someone said they provide soap and shampoo at hotels but I've packed some anyway. I keep changing my mind about what to take as Colin will be immaculate as usual and I'm determined to look my best. I'd hate them to think, 'who's that scruffy looking waif he's scraped up from the gutter?'

I put in another sweater. No, too hot... takes up too much room, and do I actually need this night dress? I don't usually wear anything in bed. I reject it for a dressing gown in case of fire. I don't want to assemble anywhere naked. A clean white blouse to go with the two piece suit? Yes ... well, no. Anything spilt will show and I'm a sloppy drinker. Better take a stain camouflager so I go for one with small coffee coloured shapes. What about other unforeseen accidents; heel breaking off shoe, bra straps snapping, ladders in stockings. I cram in emergency replacements until the bag is bulging fit to burst then sit on it and drag its reluctant zip shut. By tomorrow I'll have changed it all again.

THURSDAY 19TH SEP

I'm pleased my assignment is out of the way. Now I can concentrate on getting ready for London tomorrow. I'm getting so excited. I'm going straight after work tomorrow which means I'll have to take my grips bag and wear smart clothes to work. Tonight I've bathed, washed my hair and shaved my underarms so thoroughly they'll be on fire when I apply deodorant.

It's hardly necessary to be prestine clean for a two-hundred mile car-ride preceded by a day's sweating in a cake factory: our room will have an en–suite bathroom which I intend to make good use of as soon as we arrive – but I'll smell utterly gorgeous at work! As I come bathrobed from the bathroom Brenda appears needing salt for something she's cooking so I shake some in a bit of paper and screw it in a wrap for her.

The cooking smell permeates the landing and stairs and wafts into my room.

'I'll save some for you,' she offers but I'm too preoccupied with my beautification. She knows about the planned weekend but she's come to terms with us and keeps negative thoughts to herself although I suspect there are plenty.

'Oh God I've forgotten about my nails,' I exclaim looking at patchy former nail colour. 'I haven't got any nail varnish remover.'

'Don't panic. I've got some. I'm doing a casserole for someone. I'll get it in the oven then come down and do your nails for you. What colour do you fancy? Deep Pink, Punchy Peach, Bold Red, Pearly Pink– I've got loads of them.'

'Thanks Brenda,' I say, relieved of the trauma and glad of a calming influence. She turns up with a varnish array and we coo over the pretty colours. It's good to have girl friends sometimes, even if their boyfriends are more important to them.

FRIDAY 20TH SEP

The journey took longer than I thought. Too tired to write about today.

COLIN

SATURDAY 21ST SEP

Morning: We arrived last night and signed in as Mr and Mrs McKay. He wore a new suit, a dazzlingly white shirt and a fashionably narrow tie. I'm writing this in our super hotel room with it's own bathroom and a fridge containing drinks and ice cubes. Colin's company paid for the hotel. I've never stayed in one before. He had to go to a meeting this morning so I went out alone and wandered up Pall Mall to Buckingham Palace. The guards looked like large stiff toys and didn't blink an eye. Then I took a tube to Oxford Circus – only because I'd heard of it and wanted to use a tube train. Northeners strike up conversations on public transport but these people don't meet your eye.

Afternoon: After lunch in the hotel we went to see Agatha Christie's *The Mousetrap*. I wore a matching skirt and jacket and pointed high heels.

SUN 22 SEPT

Breakfast: Smoked salmon with scrambled eggs, croissants and as much coffee as you wanted, then a walk in Hyde Park where people can get up and speak to crowds. It was a beautiful sunny day and felt good to be alive. We had a meal later in a café nearby. It was the best weekend I've ever had!

Contentment envelopes me like a mist and I'm pleased with myself for being such a good influence. I'm changing this man to how I want him. The medication is effective and he knows he must take it. Now it will be like it was before. All will be well. As we walked past the Hotel Reception desk he suddenly asked:

'Did you notice how she looked and picked up the phone as we passed'

'The receptionist? Not really. Should I have done?'

'Guess who'd she be ringing?'

Let me guess, she's in league with Ellis but I don't say it. I don't want to encourage him. It's been so good.

MONDAY 23 SEP

College today. I don't understand the maths assignment I was given but Bob did of course and helped me. I didn't tell Colin that because I know what he'd say! I love learning now. Even when it's difficult I feel sort of content and satisfied when I've done it.

WEDNESDAY 25TH SEP

Colin has to go away on business soon so it's given me the break to finish my Maths assignment. Janet is having a break from Andy. He's the one who instigated it so he can't complain if we have a night out like old times. As expected Colin tried to block it but I'm still going to do it.

'So what will you do with yourself at the weekend,' he asks casually as if it didn't really matter. He's awaiting my reply though. I can tell when he has that look – a sort of sideways glance.

'I'm going to the Odeon to see *Cleopatra* with Marian one evening, and out with Janet on others.

'Janet. Hmm. One of the King's Arms crowd. You know what I think of that lot. Immature and rowdy, showing off, always in pubs.'

'Well she's one of my oldest friends – and we won't be going in a pub. I'm bored with pubs.'

'She'll probably behave like that wherever she goes. Why don't you have any respectable friends?'

'Colin! She is respectable. What do you mean? What has she ever done that's not respectable?'

'Your birthday?' he sneers. 'Remember? She organised that rumpus didn't she? And kept giving you drinks until you didn't know what you were doing?'

'So? That was up to me if I drank too much, not Janet.' I'd better be careful. Not too assertive, not too like Brenda. Keep calm.

'And those awful tight clothes she wears. Yeah, very respectable.'

'There's nothing wrong with her clothes. Look, she's my friend and there's no harm seeing her. I can't just sit at home waiting for you.'

'You're not being fair.' he says. He looks upset and hurt. 'I'm only thinking of you and your reputation. And I'm already stressed about him watching me without this from you. Look,' he points to the window.

I look through the window. 'I don't see anyone.' He looks at me exasperated.

'Well no. He disappears like he usually does. She does too. Every time I want someone to see them they do this. They're like ghosts. It's frustrating and it's making me feel unwell.'

I don't argue. I don't want him feeling unwell. What kind of unwell? Is it something I should be afraid of? Do I have to lie if I go out with Janet while he's away? I don't see why I should.

FRIDAY 27TH SEP

Janet and I did go out and had a brilliant time! We saw The Hollies at the Twisted Wheel on Brazonose St in Manchester and did lots of dancing (and drinking!). We got offered 'purple hearts' – a drug which peps you up for half a crown a pill.

'We're pepped up enough thank you,' we said, but the bloke tried to pursuade us,

'They're harmless,' he said, 'only like strong coffee.'

'We'll stick to strong coffee then,' we said.

We liked the Twisted Wheel. It promoted fledgling bands and unknown artists and had the extra attraction of the all night café on Princess Street. We'd spent all our taxi money so we squashed into a red GPO telephone box, rang Janet's dad who'd gone to bed, and reversed the charges. He wasn't pleased.

'For God's sake – couldn't you have rung earlier!'

SATURDAY 28TH SEP

Poor Bob had terrible toothache and when Brenda and I tried to look after him the Dragon called me a trollop! That means a

COLIN

prostitute the cheeky sod! I almost slapped her but glad I didn't. But we're being given notice tomorrow so it's not funny! I don't know where I'd go.

It's 1963, but the Dragon sees herself as a self-appointed moral regulator of her tenants' behaviour. Just after midnight I went into Bobby's room in my nightdress to administer aspirins, as the poor lad was writhing in agony with an impacted wisdom tooth that had decided now was the time to break out. Brenda, similarly clad, had taken him a tiny bottle of whisky that looked as if it belonged to toytown or a dolls house. We put on 'Radio Luxembourg' to cheer him up and were sitting on the bed with him feeding him aspirins and sips of whisky when there was a banging on the door.

An unmistakable loud voice booms out.

'Hello. I know you're in there… Lizzie.' I don't respond. She tries again. 'I know you're in there. Whatever you're up to – turn that noise down! People are trying to sleep.' She knocks at the door again.

Brenda gets up and turns down the radio. 'Ok Mrs Bryson. Sorry.'

'Oh. You're in there too! I might have known. What are you both doing in that lad's room at this time of night?'

We look at each other and suppress giggles. Does she think it is a ménage à trois?

'Nothing Mrs Bryson…What do you want?' I reply.

'Open the door. I want a word with you both. I've told you before about making a noise at night.'

'Making a noise! We're just talking,' retorts Brenda indignantly, 'and Bob has very bad toothache.'

'Well you should be in your own rooms this time of night. It's nearly one o'clock – and blaring music! Do you want to wake everyone?"

Bob unexpectedly joins in.

'If the electric wasn't set so high we wouldn't spend so long in each other's rooms! It's daylight robbery what you charge,' he declares, toothache overriding his usual good nature. Brenda and I exchange knowing looks. We'd never told Bob our winter secret. Maybe we should have. He must have been cold.

'Don't tell me how to run my business. And get that girl out! I've seen her running round before half naked, showing all she's got. In front of my husband too!'

What a breathtaking accusation! Did she mean me or Brenda? And who'd want to tempt him!

'I've had the police round here before. Do you want to ruin me! They already think I'm running a brothel! I've got a key y'know. Come out now or I'll come and get you both out myself!'

'You'd better do no such thing!' I retort, angrily at this gross interference. Who does she think she is! Mother of morality? Chaperone of the chaste?

'Don't backchat me young lady, if you behave like a trollop, I'll treat you like one!'

Trollop! Right that's it!

'Don't call me a trollop!' I shout as I rush to the door and open it. She grabs me and yanks me out by my nightdress.

'Get off me you sanctimonious cow!' I'm so close I'm almost spitting in her face. 'You're a – loud – mouthed – stupid –

woman,' I say, separating words for effect. She looks shocked. I'm surprised myself.

'You'll give my house a bad name you little hussy. You'd do it with anyone wouldn't you!' she shouts.

'What! Well no-one would want to do it with you would they!'

Intelligent responses aren't forthcoming and mindless insults slide off the tongue easily.

She's still got hold of my night dress and shakes me again.

'How dare you speak to me like that. I've had enough of girls like you!'

'Girls like me! Girls like me! What do you know about girls like me you …you…fat snooper?' I shake free from her grasp as her alarmed husband makes an ineffectual appearance.

'Hilda, Hilda, leave it, leave it, come downstairs,' he begs looking terrified.

'Leave it? It's them two who's going to leave it – in one week's time!' She doesn't include Bob curled up in agony. No, us. Brazen hussies, exploiting a poor man's weakness and she'll end our tenancies in the morning. This is worrying as there's little tenant protection and neither of us have any money for a deposit on anywhere else.

She turns and marches away muttering: no shame, no respect, no decency. Bob has an operation in his mouth leaving him unable to speak and to live on tins of Campbell's soup for days. Maybe I could paint the tins and make a fortune, like Andy Warhol did last year.

SUNDAY 29TH SEP

I didn't get evicted. I apologised profusely and so did Brenda. The Dragon blusters a lot, shouts and threatens, but rarely carries anything out and after digesting the apologies she admitted that we weren't bad tenants compared to some.

'And better the devil you know,' she added. We were quiet, polite and grateful for not being made homeless. She's had a stream of bothersome tenants.

'That's why I'm so fussy about what happens here,' she explains. 'I've had such bad luck. The worst was that poor little scrap who was selling herself for that horrible man. That caused a lot of trouble for us y'know. I said I would never have young girls here again. The police thought we had something to do with it too; really embarrassing, all over the papers and everything.' She thinks I don't know. I don't tell her everyone does for miles around.

'And then people leaving owing me rent, like that burglar they haven't caught, and then the attempted suicide when we had to get the ambulance out. Then two years ago the bloke selling drugs here. Police here over that too!' I listen fascinated. Creative writing ideas for my English O Level appear.

'So you can see why I'm not going to stand for any funny business or bad behaviour here,' she continues. 'I don't want no police here, I don't want no social workers, I don't want no journalists. I just want a nice little business with no trouble.'

I nod to say I understand but cheap rents don't attract ideal tenants and she can't really increase rents with the state of the house.

COLIN

MONDAY 30TH SEP

Colin has brought me a pair of lovely, soft, kid leather gloves back from his work trip. I didn't tell him about the Brenda and Bob fiasco as he'd probably side with Mrs B! But I made the mistake about the Twisted Wheel. I'd enjoyed it so much I wanted to share it. I have to keep so much from him I sometimes can't remember what I should or shouldn't say. At first it was Brenda he objected to, now it's Janet, or anyone I'm friendly with. No way will I tell him about Jenny! He has been better lately but it didn't last.

The evening begins so nicely. We're snuggled up on his sofa listening to music and I'm admiring my present. He checks if Ellis is outside spying and returns to the sofa. It's my chance to speak out, firmly but nicely. Don't upset him.

'There's no-one there outside. I don't want you to keep worrying about being spied on, and checking the window and everything. And those voices. They aren't real, it's all in your head and it won't do you any good. I thought you were getting over this and I was so pleased... but you're doing it again.'

He ignores me and softens the lights.

'Did you miss me?' he asks. I'll try again later I think. Be patient.

'Of course I missed you. I always miss you when you're away ...but it was nice to go out with Janet again – even though I thought about you a lot.'

He frowns at the mention of Janet but says nothing. I tell him about The Hollies, the beaty music, the atmosphere, the all-night café and he nods and listens.

ROOM TO GROW

'And some guy tried to sell us Purple Hearts.' He's suddenly animated. Mistake. The lens is on me and it's going to come zooming in.

'WHAT! They're offering drugs now at that seedy joint! I knew you'd get up to no good with that girl! You think its Ok to go to a dive like that – where drug addicts go? Have you no sense? Don't ever let me hear you've been to that awful place again! In fact next time I go away – you'd better come with me.' His voice has risen and he looks really angry. I shrink away.

'I didn't say we'd bought any,' I protest. 'We refused for heaven's sake. We didn't want them!'

'And you danced all evening? Who with? Did you know them? How many fellas did you dance with? How many did you lead on gyrating around and drinking – and her in her sluttish clothes.'

I'm speechless with indignation. Janet may not be a tasteful dresser. She's put on weight and her clothes have got tight but they are not sluttish.

'She's not a slut!' I'm angry now.

'How did you get home? Who took you home?' He's the Gestapo. He'll want to invade Poland next.

'I don't need to be "taken" anywhere. We took ourselves home!'

Why ever did I tell him? So stupid of me – but why should I have to be deceitful? We part on bad terms and I don't want any more flowers.

COLIN

TUESDAY 1ST OCT

He rang. Someone told him I was in so I had to speak to him. He was sorry of course and he was coming round with something for me. I forgave him as usual but I haven't forgotten what he said about Janet. Some days he seems quite back to normal. But every time I think he's improving – it starts again!

Like tonight. He's bought me a modern cookery book with coloured pictures of complicated dishes. Is this a hint? Everything needs a 'Kenwood Chef' and each page has a smiling woman piping icing onto things or smirking with a perfect soufflé. She's not like Fanny Cradock. The heat would probably ruin her fancy hair do and singe her silly apron and there's yards long lists of ingredients, some of which I've never even heard of.

'My friends have been telling me I must teach you to cook,' he informs me. He doesn't mean real friends. He hasn't any has he. He turns the shiny page. A whole salmon baked with fennel lies covered in lemon slices.

'I thought we weren't going to talk about them,' I say calmly looking at the pouting fish.

'My friends? No, I said I'd only tell you the nice things they say. Not the bad things. Anyway they tell me cooking is good for relationships. It's an act of love – like when I do it for you.'

'Well I don't even want to hear about the nice things they say, but thanks for the book. I'll look at it.' Posh cooking? I'd rather not bother but maybe an easy recipe, just to please him.

235

ROOM TO GROW

Surely there can't be unusual signs, symbols or imagined voices involved in cooking!

WEDNESDAY 2ND OCT

I'm fairly sure he can't be taking the medication he was prescribed. Not all the time. I looked round his kitchen when I was making coffee and found pills in a kitchen drawer – more or less the same number as before. It's probably why his delusions are getting worse.

'Ellis followed me when I went shopping yesterday,' he states. 'He was so obvious – just standing there. I'd make a much better spy than him. So I went into the bank – but I think he can see into my account if he's anywhere near – he has this power, so I changed my mind and came out. That's why I've no money. Have you got any?'

'I've got some for tonight.' I sigh. It's tiresome having to humour him but I don't know any other way. He gets so upset these days if I doubt him or argue. I hand him a ten shilling note. It's all I have until Friday.

'It's OK. I'll give it you back. I just need to get to the bank in secret because Ellis wants to see how much I've got. He thinks I'm fiddling the company accounts and I'm going to run off with the money. That's why he's watching. God told me I should open an account somewhere else but Lucy, that's the nasty one, says I should kill him.'

I thought he was only telling me nice things! I'm alarmed. It's the second reference he's made to killing someone. Last time it was me!

COLIN

THURSDAY 3RD OCT

Killing and dying threats. Don't we all do this? Like, 'I'll kill her if she does that again!' or, 'I'll just die if I don't ...' It's just an easy way of expressing annoyance or hope, flipping effortlessly off the tongue without verbal planning. And Colin was only repeating nasty but non-existent Lucy. He wasn't saying he was going to kill Ellis. So just calm down. But those earlier threats?

FRIDAY 4TH OCT

I tried to reason with Colin about not taking his medication. I tried to do it nicely without accusing or admitting I'd looked around his kitchen but it just made him react and deny it. He repaid my ten shillings although I didn't want to take it. He said he thought he'd seen Ellis again on the street in a different area where he'd managed to open another account.

'What do you mean you thought you'd seen him?' I ask, careful not to question the logic too much. 'If you went to a different bank, how would he know you'd be there? That's unlikely isn't it?'

'I don't know. I knew he was around though. When I looked round he'd gone – disappeared.'

'Colin, I know you don't like taking them but we agreed ...so tell me...those tablets. Have you been taking them? Regularly, like you said you would? Like you promised? It's just that some days you imagine things more... So I'm wondering if that's when you haven't taken them.' There, I've said it. He stares at me.

'I have been,' he says, 'though I don't think they do any good. And don't say I'm imagining things. I genuinely hear things that others can't. Some people can do this and I'm one of them. Remember when we talked about telepathy and dreams, and you didn't think that was strange? It's very much like that.'

'Maybe you could go back to that doctor and explain,' I suggest tactfully. 'He might change them to something better. He might understand and be able to help in some way... so you don't feel so ...so threatened, maybe just to listen...or some other sort of treatment?'

'Are you kidding Lizzie? Some other treatment! I've already been through all this. Yes, they told me about other treatment alright. Do you know what they had in mind? Do you know what they do?'

'No, I don't. Tell me then.'

'They hold you down on a table and electrocute you! Electrocute your brain! Fry it! Hold you down by force with your arms and legs thrashing about!' His eyes are wide with emphasis. 'Then you wake up like a zombie – and of course you won't trouble anyone then, so that's Ok for them. Imagine that. A zombie for the rest of your life! No, I am not going back there. I do not want electroconvulsive therapy!'

He's bristling with indignation. Be careful. I hadn't heard of this treatment before but it sounds awful and I don't blame him not wanting it. I don't believe he's been taking the pills though.

COLIN

SATURDAY 5TH OCT

Did some cooking today using the cookery book he'd bought me as a nice gesture. I produced a meal of sorts but I don't think I'll ever be a good cook – but do you need to be? There's things you can keep in the freezing part of the fridge like fish fingers, beefburgers, Arctic roll and frozen vegetables – and lots of tinned food you can just reheat.

We're unpacking the shopping, two steaks and salad stuff. 'Why don't you cook today,' he asks. 'You could find a steak recipe in that nice book I bought you. Or just grill it. Meat that good cooks itself – in minutes.' I can't really refuse. He's done it for me so often.

So first I make a salad. Easy. Any fool can do it and I artfully cut zig zags around tomatoes and arrange cucumber slices around the edges of a pyrex dish. I look for an easy recipe to show I can follow one and have put his gift to use. 'Sirloin steak with Pepper Sauce.' That can't be too complicated. 'Now make a roux for the sauce,' instructs the recipe.

'Colin,' I call from the kitchen. 'What's a roux?'

'Oh you just have to stir some flour into melted fat – then you can add liquid to make a sauce.'

Umm sounds easy enough.

He's now decided he's forgotten the ice-cream dessert, and while he's out he may as well buy bananas and a newspaper. Good, so I can experiment on my own with pepper sauce. I turn the grill to heat up for later. Now for the roux. The flour blends in with some butter nicely but I don't stir the liquid in quickly enough in small amounts so congealed lumps appear. Squashing them with a wooden spatula produces smaller congealed lumps. I pour the slimy mess into some newspaper. It seeps out so I stuff the lot into a paper carrier bag and take it down to the dustbin and hide it under some rubbish. Back upstairs to a cupboard where I've seen a packet of instant gravy. I seize it.

'Add boiling water and stir.' Yes I can do that. It makes brown, tasteless but lumpfree gravy. I haphazardly tip in a large quantity of blackpepper and peppercorns and hope it passes as pepper sauce. The steaks are clever and cook themselves.

'That was really nice,' he says later. 'Especially the pepper sauce. I'll make a cook of you yet.'

It's been a good day today. Perhaps he's thought about taking the regular medication. Perhaps he's realised there's a lot at stake if he doesn't.

SUNDAY 6TH OCT

I'm so disappointed. Jenny is leaving Manchester with Joyce soon. There goes the one friend who puts me before men and is good company. They're moving in December, after Christmas. I can visit any time I like, but it won't be the same. I don't see her much, but only two miles away if I want to.

I'm meeting Jenny in the Seymour about eight. He doesn't know of course. My face falls at her news about going to live in London.

'Is it definite then?' I ask, hoping it's not so I can keep her. 'I'll really miss our evenings out and our chats. Why do you have to go? What's so good about living in London?'

'It's not just about living there. It's a business opportunity for Joyce. She's going to open an escort agency and I'll be running it with her. Much better than what we're doing here.'

'What's an escort agency?' It sounds respectably above board – like an employment agency, or one hiring cleaners or equipment.

'Oh, well, it's sort of ...you know...if a bloke wants a pretty – or engaging sort of woman for the evening... say for a company do or a party or something, maybe he's not married – or even if he is...then we'll have women on our books he can hire for the occasion. Or he can wine and dine one for her entertaining company, or just visit her at home or a hotel.' I smile at the gloss over phraseology, nothing overtly stated, nothing ruled out, a make of it what you will sort of thing.

'So it's a ...versatile sort of service. All needs catered for?'

'Ah,' she says with a twinkle in her eye. 'There'll be a range of charges depending on what they require, but it's a higher class sort of business and, we don't need to provide living accommodation... not for everyone.'

'What about the girls living with you at present?'

'They won't all come. There'll just be about three of us in a large house – but with others on our books. We've even got a small office on the ground floor with filing cabinets and things and our own business cards.'

'Are they a new thing?'

'Goodness no. Only in name. Plenty around, always has been – but it sounds more business-like doesn't it? And plenty of demand for it too. Joyce has a good business head and did her research, so ...she's selling this place and starting one down there.'

ROOM TO GROW

'I suppose it's all sewn up then. I won't see you very often will I?' I say resignedly.

'Maybe not often… but you are my friend Lizzie, and always welcome to visit us – and stay with us for… as long as you like. Come, soon, after the new year when we're settled.' That's nineteen sixty-four. Where will I be then? Stuck with Colin? Living in a scruffy bedsit and working in a cake factory? I hope not.

MONDAY 7TH OCT

I watched Doris's TV tonight. The news is full of the Profumo affair. I don't care about politics but this is really good! I didn't think prostitutes could be pretty but Christine Keeler is gorgeous. There's another man called Steven Ward. I think he's part of it too. Vietnam is news too. I'm going to ask Bob about it. He is amazing. He can banter, gossip and talk pop music, but is also serious. He doesn't try and show off his knowledge, but he's a 'know all' in the nicest sort of way. The war in Vietnam is beginning but I don't actually know where Vietnam is, let alone who the Vietcong are.

'What are communists?' I ask. He patiently explains.

'They believe in a different system,' he says. 'They're people who believe that everything should be shared. Like money. Everyone who does their share of work should share the profits. Have you heard of Karl Marx?' I haven't. He's tried to educate me but I'm often too occupied with my complicated love life to care. But I'm agog at the Profumo / Christine Keeler affair. Keeler is the alleged mistress of a Russion spy and therefore a threat to

COLIN

national security when she sleeps with government officials but I don't care about this and want only the salacious bits. The juicy scandal is now of immense proportion. I'm lapping it up avidly from Doris's fourteen -nch black and white TV.

He did what? And with Mandy Rice Davies too! At the same time do you think? My mind boggles. The tabloids are having a field day. Profumo's downfall? He lied to the House of Commons and nearly brought down the government, so that was him gone. Poor Harold Macmillan retired on health grounds shortly after, but I didn't really care about him.

TUESDAY 8TH OCT

I've had the police round! They wanted to see if I knew anything about Colin's mental state. He'd been found acting very strangely, hiding in Ellis's garden then peering through his window. A neighbour called the police who took him away and questioned him. He told them Ellis was paying somone to kill him, so he was trying to see who it was! The same baseless tales of delusional persecution.

I am going to contact Mr Ellis at the office to see what's been happening and to see if we can help Colin between us. I just hope he hasn't sacked him yet.

I look up the number in the telephone directory and dial. I don't think Colin is in the office today. I hope not! What would I say

ROOM TO GROW

if he answered the phone! A female voice answers with the usual
salutations.

'May I speak to Mr Ellis please?'

'Who is it please?'

I'm nervous. I have to be careful in case he's there, next to
her!

'I'm a client of his,' I say, hoping not to sound mysterious, or
that more detailed identification is required.

'Hold on a minute… Mr Ellis,' she calls; 'Client for you.' He
picks up a phone.

'Hello. Who am I speaking to?' he asks. How do I explain
this?

'Er…Mr Ellis. You won't know me, but is it possible to speak
in confidence with you?' I ask. 'I'm Elizabeth Dale and I need to
talk to you about Colin …but I don't want him to know. Is he
in the office?'

I need to get this bit in very quickly or it could be tricky.

'No. He's not… but who did you say you were? How can I
help you?'

'I'm Elizabeth… his girlfriend, and I've heard there's been
some trouble. It must be very difficult for you …but I want to
know if I can help him. Or you even.'

'I see – but what can I do for you?'

'It's just… I don't know how to deal with this …weird
situation. I need to understand what's set it off. I'm not even
sure if I'm going to stay with him – but it might be helpful if
I knew the background of this problem. Is there anything you
could tell me?'

There's a lengthy pause. He's unprepared and not sure what
to say. Will he even discuss it with me?

244

'Elizabeth…I can't talk about his now. I'm in the middle of something. Yes, it's been difficult but my advice to you is to leave him – cut your losses…It's very complex and I doubt whether you will be able to handle it on your own. That sounds harsh but that will probably be the best for you in the end – but it's up to you of course.'

'Yes, yes, I understand, but I can't do that now – not so suddenly. It's impossible at the moment. I need to keep everything calm while I manage it.'

'Yes, I know what you mean. Look, I can't speak now, but I suppose we could meet somewhere…Can you get to the office tomorrow morning? He won't be here tomorrow.'

'Yes, I can do that,' I offer. It's rash of me. I'll have to take time off work but I don't tell him that.

'What about mid morning, say ten-thirty?' he asks.

'Yes, that's fine. Thank you very much Mr Ellis. That's very good of you. Ten-thirty then.'

WEDNESDAY 9TH OCT

I met Mr Ellis today. I was nervous. I won't get paid for the time off but it was worth it for what I found out. He is not the furtive plotting figure Colin makes out but has actually tried to help him and I think he's on his last chance, it may be even too late.

I arrive on time and directed to an unoccupied office where I nervously wait. An office girl offers me coffee which I gladly accept. It will give me something to do with my hands. I have

ROOM TO GROW

a little side table for the delicate-looking china cup and saucer probably kept for important clients and there's a huge road map on the wall spiked with drawing pins like a war chart. A book case with indentical looking, gold titled books are displayed in neat rows as if they are never read.

A cream-coloured telephone on the desk suddenly rings and startles me into slopping coffee down my blouse. I'm dabbing at it with a tissue as Mr Ellis walks in past me, smiles a greeting, picks up the phone and has a brief conversation with someone before turning to face me. He's fat and smiley like a favourite uncle and offers a chubby hand.

'George Ellis. Sorry about that. I was expecting that call earlier. So… you're Elizabeth… You're much younger than I thought,' he observes. 'But you have to be careful what you say to ladies about their age, so I hope I've said the right thing.'

He smiles at me. His mildly joking manner puts me at my ease and I start to relax. 'Well now, what can I tell you about what's been happening with your er …boyfriend. He's been here several years now and, well… he's been one of our most successful employees. Did you know that?'

'Not really, he doesn't really speak about work except… he seems to think you want to get rid of him …I know most of what he says is nonsense; like you're following him or trying to see into his bank account and things. It sounds ridiculous… but he's convinced.'

'Yes, I know he is – he's becoming quite ill isn't he, and believe me I've tried to help him. It was me who managed to get him to a psychiatrist – paid for by the company by the way, but he refuses to go along with regular medication. So what can I do? I had

COLIN

high hopes it would work…would control the symptoms so he could carry on, but it seems not.'

'Yes, I know he's not taking the medication.'

'That's where the idea I was going to sack him has come from – because I was. I told him if he didn't take it he would have to leave the company because on some occasions his behaviour has been well, frankly bizarre, for want of a better word. You know, we can't have some of our important clients being told voices are telling him what to do.' I nod in agreement.

'Of course not, Mr Ellis, I do understand…and I'm doing my best to make him aware how important the medication is they've given him…but he doesn't always listen,' I explain. 'I have tried to get him to take it – but I never know whether he's telling the truth.' I sigh. 'I've tried so hard to be understanding about it.'

'Well, I've booked him on a business trip in Glasgow next week including a very important meeting which I haven't been able to find a replacement for. He is representing our company so I hope he won't let us down.'

He clearly has some hope for Colin. It's not all hopeless if only he will just see sense.

'I'm so glad you're giving him a chance Mr Ellis. I just hope he doesn't spoil things.'

'I must stress that it's his very last chance believe me. I've laid it on, that if there's just one single report of unusual behaviour, no matter how trivial, he won't have a job here anymore. That will be the end, and that's a shame because he has been one of our most efficient assessors and achieved some excellent results but this… this …thing…this illness is getting worse.'

'I know. I've watched it go from odd ideas to some really strange warped reality.'

'Yes, and I've tried to be very fair. So that's the situation Elizabeth. I think it's best you know the full story and I wish you the best of luck.'

'Thank you,' I say. 'I think I'm clearer now…about the background…about the fear of dismissal. It makes a bit more sense…although there are …other things. But you've been very helpful. I need to think about it – but thank you very much Mr Ellis.'

THURSDAY 10TH OCT

I daren't tell him I've seen Mr Ellis. It was behind his back, but I needed to know what's behind it all. I'm desparately trying to understand it. Today, the very day after this visit, Colin brought me a job application from his company for a receptionist/clerical worker/telephonist! I had a struggle to get it off him. He was going to fill it in and take it back!

'Apply for it,' he says thrusting it at me before I can see what it is. 'It would mean we could be together – every day, all the time,' he says. 'You could do that job. Better than working in a bakery in all that heat you were complaining about. I get a bit embarrassed when I tell people you work in a factory.' Oh really. I can't think who he would tell. I've never met his family or friends – and embarrass him? Who's the embarrassing one now!

'But Colin,' I protest. 'I haven't had any of that experience. I've never worked on a switchboard for starters.'

'It's only a little one. It's not like working at the GPO or anything. You're only eighteen and you're intelligent, so you could be easily trained... and you have a nice demeanor for a receptionist,' he adds smiling at me. It's a lovely smile. I've not seen that smile as much lately and I miss it.

'Yes, but think about it. What would your boss think about your girlfriend working there? What if I turned out useless? It would be difficult for him ...knowing we were together.'

'Oh, we wouldn't tell him we knew each other. We could pretend to meet at work. And there's no way you wouldn't do a good job. Look, let me help you. I'll fill it in for you.'

He begins entering my details. He'll sign it for me if he gets chance – get it off him!

'No!' I snatch the pen from his hand. 'I'm going to look for my own jobs – and I'm not ashamed at working in a factory. It's good honest work with good honest people.'

He raises his eyes to the ceiling and mutters something. I'm surprised at the snobbery. He wasn't like this when I first knew him. He wasn't like a lot of things then. I take the form and rip it up.

FRIDAY 11TH OCT

I have to write something for college and it's due in soon – a discussion essay. I have to balance two sides of an argument using such phrases as: 'on the other hand' and 'others would say'. I'm doing the Nuclear Bomb because I discussed it with Bob before Aldermaston and can remember the arguments.

Studying is getting a bit easier but I still have to rewrite and change things. I chew biros and nails and become ever more critical about what I've written – rubbish mainly. The bin fills up with abandoned attempts. I swear and run out of paper and patience. I'm an imperfect perfectionist, a drafter of drafts, a stayer upper until midnight in an attempt to produce something acceptable and I don't give up. Pat, my tutor, writes encouraging comments and useful suggestions in the margins which I greedily absorb and put into practise as soon as I can. What's more I am enjoying it.

SATURDAY 12TH OCT

Colin goes on that business trip on Monday; the one Mr Ellis told me about, but I'm not supposed to know so I looked surprised. He tried to make me go with him but I made excuses about essays and work. I've now seen how nasty and insistent on getting his own way he can be, then change like Jekyll and Hyde. It starts low key.

'Come on Lizzie. Just get some things together. It'll mostly be like a holiday. A few days in Glasgow and Ellis is paying! We can go out places after my meetings and I won't get so anxious about you going out while I'm not there.'

'I don't think it's a good idea,' I say. 'I have homework to do.'

'That could wait. Such a waste of time when we could be together. And it won't get you anywhere. Do you really prefer doing that to being with me?'

'No, but what about work? They might not like me taking time off. I could lose my job.'

'You're always saying you're fed up with it – so what would it matter? You could move in with me while you found another. So what's to worry about?'

COLIN

'I'm not ready to move in with you. I'm just not ready for it. We've been through all that before, a few weeks ago, remember. Not yet.'

'Not yet. Not yet,' he mimics. 'You can never make your mind up about anything can you? Even about his trip! In fact I'll make it up for you. I won't be messed about by you. Give me that bag. I'll pack your things if you won't!'

He snatches the grip bag I've half-heartedly picked up and yanks open my underwear drawer. He throws in the matching knicker and bra set he's recently bought me, a sweater, a skirt, a night dress and he's muttering away and talking to his voices in that strange tone he uses with them. I don't know what to do. I'm beginning to panic.

'Colin, no, no, no, I can't go with you. I want to see my mum this week. We nearly lost her…I want to be around to see her.' I'm choked at the memory and break down in sobs. She thinks he's a gentleman, but he's double-sided. Charm the birds from the trees one minute – nasty as a viper the next! He can switch convincingly with silver-tongued practice.

'I'm going to tell her what you're doing to me. What will she think of you then? She won't think you're so marvelous then will she?' I sob. 'She thinks you're so good, but you're a …a…bully.'

'That's just playground language,' he asserts. 'Grow up!'

I sink onto the bed and weep into the pillow.

Amazingly he stops, throws down the bag and sits next to me. He's thinking about his image. He needs to conceal his dark side. Who might I tell? He tries to blame his so-called friends.

'Oh Lizzie, I'm so sorry,' he says. 'I have upset you haven't I? I am so sorry. It was those voices, first the nice one and that was OK. Then *she* goes and butts in and I've told you what she's like haven't I? She's trying to stir it up. Trying to make me hate you. She's always trying to. She's the very devil I tell you. That's what set me off like that,'

At the mention of the voices I recover and glare at him.

'Don't look at me like that Lizzie; you know I can hear her, and I swear I'm not making it up; then Godfrey... he said not to listen to her and not to force you, so I'll only listen to him in future. But please don't get upset again and tell someone I've been mean to you because of her, the evil bitch,' he spits with venom, then gently, 'put my mind at rest; just until I get back. Then I'll make it up to you. I promise.'

I try to look comforted but I'm thankful for a few days' break from him.

SUNDAY 13TH OCT

I know life was dull, penny-pinching and lonely before he came along, but his illness is getting me down and I'm going to have to get away from him. He's mentioned killing me, himself, and his boss so far and I'm not sure how seriously to take it. The 'vicious' female voice is frightening too. I've no one to talk to about it or to advise me.

Brenda understands, but she did warn me and I feel foolish that I didn't listen to her. Also, I don't want to keep bothering her and create 'needy friend' fatigue. And Bob. How could I explain my extraordinary love life and keep his respect? I'm eighteen now, still not legally an adult, but hope I'm strong enough to sort it out!

COLIN

MONDAY 14TH OCT

Drama today! The front flat was on fire! Olive and Stan have had to move out and I will too. Most of their room was blackened and the whole house could have burned down! The firemen put it out very quickly but after they went through all the rooms and the cellar they were not happy. There was a long discussion with the Brysons who looked very resentful. And I will never, ever buy a chip pan!

'Can you smell something?' asks Brenda as I open my door to her curious face. I take a deep sniff but overpowering hair laquer blocks anything else.

'Something's burning,' she says. 'Coming from the front flat.'

'Maybe Olive and Stan are cooking something smelly,' I suggest.

Actually the house is on fire. Not all of it. Just the flat along the corridor. The one we need to get past to get out.

'Fire!' shouts the Dragon who's appeared. 'Get out, get out!'

At first we can't make out what she's saying. She's been known to shout before so we don't bother. But she did say 'fire' didn't she? We stand there confused as if we don't understand the word.

Smoke curls from the doorway. The dragon is waving her arms about and shouting. Stan, useless as ever, throws a bowl of water over the flaming chip pan and makes it worse. It's already caught the curtains so they both flee and thunder down the stairs. Someone has had the sense to call the fire brigade, but meanwhile, I need to get out and I'm in my underwear. I grab

ROOM TO GROW

dressing gown and slippers and dash downstairs followed by Brenda passing the Dragon who has foolishly not closed the door on the fire and is hoarse with shouting.

'What about Bobby!' shrieks Brenda and tries to go back. We like him and don't want him incinerated. The Dragon seizes her clothes and drags her backwards. Fortunately, he's out. Everyone now huddles outside as a fire engine and competent firemen arrive, take charge and quickly put out the fire as in a film happening to other people. A trainee fireman takes a shine to Brenda, as do most men, which is bound to lead to another of her amorous encounters and involve me in some way. He's called Tony. Malek is now on the boyfriend scrap heap.

Later, the Brysons are prosecuted for not complying with fire regulations, and made to replace the useless fire escape. There are no fire doors and there's a nightmare conglomeration of electrical wiring down the cellar, bodged up and repaired with fraying black tape and immediately condemned by the Fire Brigade. Most tenants, including me, have to find temporary alternative accommodation whilst this is put right.

TUESDAY 15TH OCT

I called round at Janet's today to tell her about the fire. She said I could move in with her while everything's being put right but she'll ask her mum first. I'll tell them at 'home' tonight. I don't want to add pressure at home while Mum is still recovering so I'll not stay there. Bob and Brenda are each going to stay with friends and I'm not sure about Frank. Stan and Olive's flat is

COLIN

blackened but everywhere else seems Ok but the house must be made safe.

I have to dash 'home' after visiting Janet to circumvent any alarmist news bearers who may worry them but my mum and dad are blissfully unaware of the fire.

'I'm fine, I'm going to stay at Janet's for a while,' I say with optimistic assumption her mum is going to agree.

'Well, as long as you are alright,' is the general reaction. 'That's the important thing.'

William's eyes light with excitement. He can hardly wait. 'Is the house all burnt up now?' Everything's an absolute with him.

'No, just a bit blackened.'

'Did a big fire engine come with bells and ladders? Did a fireman climb right up the house?'

'Yes, just like in your storybook,' I say.

'Oh Lizzie! I wish I'd been there!'

'Shall I set this house on fire so you can see a fire engine?' Everyone laughs except him until it dawns: adults joke sometimes.

THURSDAY 17TH OCT

Hooray. Janet's mum says I can stay. I'll have to share a bed with Janet but she is my best friend and it will be great. I'll move in quickly so I'm settled when Colin gets back. Then I won't have to move in with him. He'll not like it though. I'll say, 'Well there was a fire and you weren't here – so I had to go somewhere.'

FRIDAY 18TH OCT

Great staying here and so glad I could. I'm dreading telling him though.

SATURDAY 19TH OCT.

Still worrying about his response. I have a feeling that there will be an outburst; an explosion of anger and jealousy that I've gone to Janet rather than him. How could I? He wasn't even there, but he probably won't listen. I'll have to get it over with when he's back tomorrow.

SUNDAY 20TH OCT (LATE SUNDAY, EARLY HOURS OF MONDAY)

I'm writing with shaking fingers after tonight's serious incident. I have to write it all down to remember it to make a statement to the police. It's early morning and I'm safe now in Janet's bedroom but he badly assaulted me tonight – at his flat. I have a black eye, bruised face, bruised ribs, ringing ears and, and pains in my shoulder. My head hurts from the blows and I still feel sick.

As I feared, he got furious I was staying with Janet, not him, after the fire, but I didn't expect this and I was afraid for my life! I managed to escape but thought I'd never get away and was terrified he'd do something worse. The police found me and took me to Casualty. Janet was shocked. She's sleeping now but I can't. This was the worst experience, in my life.

He was very sweet at first. He'd been drinking, pleasantly enough, and wanted me to stay at his flat, but I refused which altered his mood. So he drove me, swaying around the road a bit, to his flat regardless. We sat on his sofa as I explained why I couldn't stay the night.

'The reason I can't is I've told Janet and her dad I'd be back. I don't want to mess them about and…I have a letter to finish and get in the post …and I won't have time tomorrow if I'm working – and, well, I usually go back on Sunday nights don't I? I have little jobs to do. It's my routine…so I can make time to see you in the week.'

'So you can go to college you mean.'

'I can fit both in if I do it this way.'

'Have another drink,' he says swinging a topless bottle of gin around so it dribbles down the side.

'No thanks. I've had enough. It makes me feel sick if I have too much.'

'Makes me feel sick. Oh dear,' he mocks. 'I thought you liked gin now you're a big girl… Are you no fun anymore?'

'I'm sorry. It's just that I don't want to be sick on your nice settee. Can't I just have a glass of water for now?'

'Only with a gin in it… or two.' He laughs, but is he joking? 'Lucy thinks you're using me. You only stay with me because I give you a nice time and now you're going off me – trying to end it so I'll be on my own again. That's why you chose Janet.'

'You said you weren't going to listen to the bad things they say.'

ROOM TO GROW

'Yes, I know, but she's usually right. She thinks I put up with too much. I shouldn't let you get all your own way all the time. You do don't you? Always get your own way – like a spoilt brat!'

I try and reason with him.

'No Colin. That's not true. I'm trying hard to understand what you need, to see the good side of you. I don't want to see the side that's causing these problems. I want you like you were when I met you. I don't want to make you unhappy.'

'Yeah, so you moved in with Janet when you know how upset I'd be. When you could have moved in with me. Prefer her don't you. Yeah, that's really good of you. Made me feel really wanted!'

He sploshes gin into my glass so it's half full, followed by orange juice spilling and cascading over the side. His co-ordination has gone and he sounds bitter and reckless.

'Yeah really nice,' he repeats. Then he's muttering to himself; 'Rejecting me for a girl friend! I should really teach you a lesson. What do you take me for? Eh? EH? Answer me, ANSWER ME DAMN YOU!…I'll teach you to mess me about. You're going to have that drink first though, like it or not!'

His hand shakes as he tips in more gin which spills even more. He grabs my hair, pulls back my head and tries to pour the liquid into my mouth. I splutter it out down my chin and onto my clothes. I'm beginning to be frightened. What is he going to do? He's bigger and stronger than me. I'd lose if I tried to fight back and could get hurt. Should I run? No, my bag's over there and I may need money for a taxi. I won't be able to get across the room to get it …and I need to find a key as I'm sure he's locked the outer door. No, no, I'll have to stay. I must keep calm and not anger him more.

COLIN

Seconds pass and he releases the grip on my hair. Keep calm. Don't argue, don't plead.

'I need to go to the loo,' I say calmly, although I'm trembling with fear.

I get up slowly as in a casual trip to the bathroom and take some steps. I'm taking my glass so I can tip the gin away but he's suddenly behind me. I feel the air change before I hear him. 'Where are you going with that?' he demands. 'I said drink it. Drink it damn you.'

He grabs the glass and tries to force it to my lips again. I splutter and cry out. He throws it against a wall where it shatters. My back is against the door as he fields the first blow. Slap! A back-handed one across the face follows, a punch, then a full-blooded punch to the face then one to the ribs and one to the stomach. It takes my breath away but I'm too frightened to feel pain. I sink to the floor grateful he wasn't holding the glass!

'Come on,' he slurs. 'Get up.' He yanks me to my feet, blood pouring from my nose.

'You're staying here tonight. We're going to bed. We – are – going – to – bed,' he adds syllabically, dragging me by the arm.

I'm too fear stricken to resist. He grabs my clothes and shoves me through to the bedroom where I stumble onto the bed. I'm conscious of blood staining the quilt, the pillows, his shirt as he lands on top of me and begins to yank at my clothes. I daren't fight back. It will make him angrier and it's futile anyway.

But it doesn't go to plan. Alcohol and sex are not good bedfellows and he sinks into a drunken stupor muttering incomprehensible endearments and garbled nonsense to do with his 'friends' before falling asleep as if nothing has happened.

I'm sore, bruised and terrified but in brain overdrive. There's another key in the kitchen drawer. I must rise silently, take small light steps, bit by bit and get it. I raise myself and sit statue still on the bed. I can hear the quiet, rhythmic tick of a carriage clock, then some pipes rumbling. I'm willing them to stop in case they wake him and he stirs and grunts. I wait silently, heart thumping until he settles again. His breathing is slowing so I can now, very gradually, lower my legs off the bed, then cautiously stand. Has he noticed the pressure change of the mattress, my absent warmth and breath? Where are my shoes? I don't know but I have the sense to put on my nearby slippers as I can't run in bare feet. I don't know if I'm still bleeding but that's not a concern now.

I creep silently, incrementally, to the kitchen, listening at every step, move, freeze, check, move again. He might wake if I rush or bump into something. There's just enough light to see my coat on the way to the door. Grab it. I can hardly go naked onto the streets. I slip it on but can't do the buttons properly because my hands are shaking. I tiptoe to the drawer in the kitchen and open it slowly and silently. Faint street light through the kitchen window aids my search but the key is hidden by table mats and for a moment I'm defeated, frozen to the spot. Then, there it is, that tiny thing, the most important thing in the world to me at this moment, the answer to my prayer. I want to kiss it in relief.

Listen again. Don't ruin it now. There are faint snoring sounds. It's now or never, and my hands are shaking so much I can hardly pick up the precious little piece of metal for fear he'll hear the sound as I pick it up. I carry it towards the door, put it into the lock and turn it conscious of a slight click – oh God, did he hear that? And it's open. I'm out – out on the landing – out on the stairs bounding down them, out of the front door, down the path, out of the gate, onto the street never looking back; running, running, running.

I must run to Janet's. It's two miles away but I mustn't stop. If I hear a car I'll dodge into a garden and hide. I'm fuelled by adrenalin my legs moving like pistons but beginning to feel strange then, oh no! Oh God! A car! It must be his car coming this way! It's shining its headlights! He's seen me! I turn down an alley dark with trees and scratchy shrubbery. I'll hide. If he's seen me he'll think I've run ahead down the alley. I must keep very, very still until he passes. Footsteps, then nearer footsteps, rustling sounds, torchlight, torchlight in my face!

'Hello there Miss. Are you alright?' I fall into the arms of a policeman.

He leads me staggering to the police car and helps me in. There's another policeman in the car who assesses my injuries; bloody and unsightly but not serious he thinks. My nose could be broken but they'll patch me up at the hospital. They will take me in the police car as its such a short way. Straight to Casualty we go, me trying to answer questions as I dab my painful face with tissues. Do I know my attacker? They don't seem surprised that I do.

'Are you going to press charges against him?' one of them asks.

I don't want to think about this now. He's in enough trouble anyway and I don't want him getting locked up on account of me – even though he deserves it. I'm uncomfortable and I might vomit in their smart police car if I don't concentrate and keep still. If he'd just stay away from me. That's all I can think of. I could get over it in time and move away out of his reach.

'No, I don't think I will,' I answer eventually. 'He's my boyfriend you see,' I explain – as if this justifies the attack. 'I don't want to cause trouble for him…because, he's not well …He's ill…he's having some mental problems. It's not really his fault – it's an illness which he can't help. If you could just talk to him – tell him not to contact me, I'll not take it any further. I'll drop it if he leaves me alone.'

They give each other a knowing look. Why do they try and defend these abusive men? She'll be calling us again no doubt. They always do.

'Well, take some time to think about it. You can change your mind if you do. He really needs dealing with you know. We'll send an officer to see you tomorrow when you're feeling better.'

I hope he doesn't. Face a reminder of the worst night of my life? No thanks!

It's Sunday, past the weekend peak for the brawling brainless but two of them are spread over each other and three seats. They'd tried to have a punch-up and sustained injuries because they were too drunk to remain vertical. Best of mates now they make loud slurry comments they think are funny.

'Name, address, religion?' I'm asked at a reception desk. 'Next of kin? Is it your mother?' I'm asked when I hesitate too long.

'Yes, but I do not want my mother contacted.' Fortunately she won't need to be as I'm staying alive, but I need to contact Janet.

I'm taken into a cubicle out of turn but the drunks don't care. A nurse cleans my injuries, wipes off the dried blood which has matted into my hair and asks if there is someone to contact to collect me. There's a phone there and I weep my story into the handset. Janet's dad comes in his new Cortina to collect me. He's horrified at my puffed up face and he's all for confronting Colin in the morning.

'He needs sorting out that one!'

'Please don't!' I beg. I don't even want to think about it.

'Well I hope you're going to take this up with the police,' he says.

I tell him I'll think about it but no, I don't want Colin arrested and I'd be too scared of what he might do. The unpredictability is frightening.

'Let's get you back and make you comfortable,' he says kindly.

MONDAY 21ST OCT

I'm taking a couple of days off to recover and hope my face improves. Janet's family have been so good. I want to talk to Bob but he's staying with friends and I wouldn't want them to see my face. I know where Brenda is though, and I might try and see her. I tried 'Panstick' make up but it was too sore to rub it in. Colin doesn't know Janet's address but I'll still be wary going out. Janet's dad is going to meet me from work for a while when I go back.

TUESDAY 22ND OCT

Should have gone into college this evening but I'll have to miss it for a while. I phoned my tutors and will work at my History assignment. It's not going to stop me studying. I didn't leave Janet's house all day but I can't do this every day. I need to go to work. I need the money.

'I've had a bit of an accident,' I lie to my tutor. Well it was a sort of accident. I didn't go and smash my face up on purpose. I'm embarrassed she might think I'm hooked to some out of work, punch-happy drunk, and it's too complicated to explain. I'd have to start at the beginning and retell the story of how I longed for a love life and it all went wrong. I haven't the emotional energy, and why should she have to listen anyway.

She was understanding and I needn't have worried.

'Oh dear, Lizzie!' she says sweetly. 'Whatever happened?'

I don't want her to be nice to me, it might make me cry. I tell her I'd fallen off my bike and I'll be fine in a few days or so.

WEDNESDAY 23RD OCT

Went in to work. Everyone was horrified at my puffy bruised face and one swollen and blackened eye. Chris was wonderful. He said he would arrange for me to be paid for the two days off. Therasa, Marian and Mary were enraged! They'd tear Colin to pieces like a pack of hyenas if they could. Mary's eighteen stone could do him serious damage!

COLIN

'Your boyfriend did that!' We're in the work's canteen. They gather round like mother hens. Therasa's incredulous.

'The bastard!' Marian is also shocked. She knows about police interviews and hospitals; about evidence and pressing charges on someone you love. She's a victim herself of mistaken loyalty herself to a bloke who regularly smashes up her face and house.

'Don't be such a fool,' say friends; 'but I love him,' she says. 'I'm giving him one more chance. He'll change now. I know he will.' Yes, he'll change alright we think. He'll get worse.

I'm surrounded by protective workmates by day and Janet's dad meets me at 5.30 in the evenings so that's Ok. Then Janet thought she saw Colin in a shop doorway near where I get off the bus which was disturbing. Why would he be there? It's not his area. Was he waiting for me? She checks there every evening now on her way home. She's good at it too. She's a spier of spies, stalker of stalkers, spotter of watchers – and I'll get a report from her every evening.

FRIDAY 25TH OCT

I'm in a routine. He doesn't know where Janet lives or how I'm getting back from work so that's good. I haven't been out yet. This weekend is going to be dull; staying in watching TV at Janet's while she goes out with Andy. I rang Jenny. I wanted to see her before she goes to London, but she's there at the moment with Joyce seeing an estate agent and solicitor and won't be back until Thursday.

Get a grip, I tell myself. Colin can't be everywhere all the time and I'm definitely going to go out, tomorrow. It's not just fear of physical hurt, it's his ability to manipulate and persuade and I'm already beginning to feel sorry for him. How can that be?

SATURDAY 26TH OCT

I plucked up courage to go shopping on my own today. All the time looking behind to make sure he wasn't there. It's not like him to give up easily and accept that he's lost and move on. He might be watching without me knowing.

Not knowing. That's the worst part of it. What will he do now?

MONDAY 28TH OCT

My face is like a rainbow now! Colourful. The swelling has gone down a lot but Panstick doesn't really cover the bruising. Janet's dad met me outside work but he won't be able to do this for ever. He has his own family to look after without an extra burden like me. I'm going to have to manage on my own. I've had a message from the Brysons inviting me to see my newly decorated room at the weekend. I'll ask Janet to come so I don't have to go out alone.

'We'll both come if you like Lizzie. You'll feel safer with Andy there.'

'Can't we just go alone? Just me and you – like old times?' I want my friend to myself. I want the familiarity and warmth

COLIN

of an established friendship. Just this once when I need it. She reluctantly agrees.

WEDNESDAY 30TH OCT

Same routine. Janet's dad meets me from work and I stay in and watch TV with Janet's mum while Janet goes out with Andy. I can't go job hunting. Who'd want to employ someone who looked as if they'd been in a fight! But I've looked out for rooms or flats as it doesn't entail meeting anyone at the moment.

I've looked in the local paper, the newsagents and inside the University entrance on their advert board. There are student 'house share' situations but I haven't the confidence to apply with my technicolour face. Even though it's fading, I get some odd looks on the campus. There are some ads for female flat—mates – maybe in some future time.

I stroll into the student refectory and buy myself a cheap sandwich and a coffee. The hot meals look appetising, not expensive either. No one seems to question my entitlement to this subsidised food so I might come here for meals sometimes!

THURSDAY 31ST OCT

Jenny's back. We met after work. She was furious when she saw what Colin had done. She noticed immediately even though

I'm kidding myself it's not that bad now. I told the story again and she thinks I ought to get far away from him, like move to London.

'He's obviously bonkers!' she says. 'Whatever made you hook up with such lunatic!' She's not mincing her words; no polite terms like 'mentally ill', disturbed, unwell or other niceties. It's strong, plain language for strong plain feelings. She hugs me and makes me want to cry. I thought these emotions had dissipated but, raw like a new flesh wound they, hurt if touched.

'You must get away from this man. It's no use staying round here. You'll be reminded of him all the time and besides he sounds past helping. Make a clean break. Come with us to London.'

'How can I do that? I won't have a job or anywhere to live.'

'We'll need a sort of housekeeper... and someone to make appointments and things. You could work for us Lizzie – until you find something better. You could sleep in the room behind the office for now. Go on. Think about it. It might work out and you'd be with women who'd look out for you.'

I'm thinking. I'm going to see my old room tomorrow. Maybe I don't intend to stay there long but not sure about her suggestion. What if Joyce doesn't want me there – or they wanted their room back. I won't know anyone else in London and, indirectly, I would be living off the proceeds of immoral earnings! It would get me away from him though but it's the devil and the deep blue sea thing. She's not pushing it though. It's up to me but make your mind up.

COLIN

FRIDAY 1ST NOV

Went to the house to see my room after work with Janet. The locks had been changed so we had to ring the bell and wait glancing around. We even checked next door's front garden hedge and gateway.

My room is very plain but looks cleaner and lighter. The new fire escape is installed but there are things to finish so I won't be moving back this week. Mrs B was astonished at my face. 'Whatever have you been doing?' she asks the minute she sees me. I tell her I hadn't been doing anything. I was the one being done to. She guesses immediately. She'd worked out the Colin – Brenda – me – thing ages ago.

'Him again! And he's the one Brenda was keeping away from isn't he!' she exclaims. 'First we had to look out for her – and now it's you we'll have to protect! Whatever made you get involved with that nasty piece of work. He'd better not come here again!'

I don't explain. It's too complicated. He's complicated, and I just want to see my room which I'm told will be finished next week. I go upstairs past startlingly white walls to my room, white, the same. Oh, and new curtains. They have huge arty orange and yellow flowers on them – certainly eye catching but a bit much? No, it's just such a contrast; I like them, they're fun. I'm so busy admiring the gaudy colourful fabric I forget my gaudy colourful face.

Frank pops his head round my door and stares. He's come to look at his newly painted room too. White. Everything in cheap white emulsion.

'Lizzie! What's happened to you? Who did that to you? Come on…Tell me who did it. Maybe I can help you sort it out?'

What does he mean? I wearily explain yet again.

'Listen, I know you probably don't want it right now, but I could have a quiet word with this guy. I could teach him a thing or two….not to hit little girls!'

Little girls! He thinks I'm a little girl. Maybe I am. I feel like one at the moment but I don't want him to hurt Colin. I think of Frank's GBH history. It's really strange. I'm afraid of Colin but I still want to protect him.

SATURDAY NOV 2ND

Janet has gone out with Andy. They asked me if I wanted to come but I said no because I don't want too many favours from anyone. I need to keep some in reserve. Everyone has been so good to me I don't want to be seen as a burden, someone you have to be kind to all the time and be taken places. I stayed in and watched telly.

The TV is on but I'm catching up with my journal and contemplating some college work. For English I have to write about a noteworthy experience; with lively details about how it made me feel, how I responded etc! How ironic is that! I could use that awful night as dramatic fiction. I'd probably get a good grade for lively detail, but why relive something that makes me feel bad. Instead I choose a tame 'Leaving home' title and add made up bits. It doesn't have to be true. It's just a writing exercise I'm told.

COLIN

SUNDAY 3RD NOV

I'm writing in the early hours as I cannot sleep. Janet is asleep and I don't want to disturb her so I sit very still. I'll finish this page which I can just about see by the little night-light she keeps on. I heard noises before but there was nobody there when I looked out. Why do things seem much worse at night?

It's a sleepless two in the morning. Only five hours and I'll have to be up. Then four. Count downs are not very helpful for getting to sleep. Never try to sleep, someone said. It pleases itself when it comes and is not under conscious will. You have to take it unawares, pretend you're not even trying and think of something nice like lying on a beach in the sun. Then when it thinks you're not trying it sneaks up on you. Janet has stopped snoring at last, the silence enhancing my hearing and I'm tuning in to a faint rustling noise.

What is it? Is it outside? Someone padding about in the garden? Him? He doesn't know her address – or does he? Perhaps someone has told him and he thinks he can get me. To do what? Persuade me to take him back? Or drag me away and punish me? Janet's house is quite secure so there's nothing to worry about. Or is there? Did the dog just give a half-hearted bark? I creep out of bed and peer out of the window holding the curtain very slightly to the side. I don't want to look like a frightened face at the window. I stare out but see no one. I go back to bed to count down the few remaining hours.

MONDAY 4TH NOV

Janet's dad is on a different shift now so couldn't meet me from work so I'm using the bus again.

Mrs B rang me at Janet's to say she'd seen Colin about five o'clock when she'd gone for the paper. He hadn't been there when I got off the bus though. She said he'd looked scruffy and unshaven. Not like him at all!

Colin scruffy and unshaven? Surely not? I've never once seen him scruffy and you could set your watch by his shaving routine; seven-thirty in the morning then six o'clock for a tidy up. Almost regimental. I recognise he's ill now and getting worse, but this is not creativity, or some imaginative muse. It's serious but despite what he's done to me, I'm sympathetic. Part of me wants to console him and make things better, but this can flip in seconds like that 'Peter and Mary' vase perceptual puzzle. Is it a black vase, or two white people facing each other? Am I in fear or love? Is he dangerous or tragic?

Recalling that horrible incident he is dangerous but I also remember the way he was: caring, successful, tastefully dressed, handsome, smart Colin who changed my life with experiences I didn't know existed and taught me about love. But I've been hurt, physically and mentally and that can make you ill and I can't afford to be. I know how Marian feels now and I called her a fool. But she gave in to love without regard to herself and I'm not going to do that.

COLIN

TUESDAY 5TH NOV

Went to a bonfire on waste ground with Janet and Andy. The local lads had been collecting for weeks – wood piled high, old furniture and all sorts dumped on it so it lasted all evening. The best evening for ages – until I saw Colin on the other side of the fire which ruined the night.

So, six-thirty and we're off to this bonfire. Janet's terrier trembles at the bangs, whizzes and flashes and cowers under the table. We leave him with Janet's mum who consoles him with tit bits and strokes his head.

'Have you got some fireworks?' asks Janet's dad. What? Does he mean us? Of course not. They're for children, ignore him, but a bonfire, well that's different; adults can go to bonfires. They can light fireworks safely and tell naughty boys off who try to throw them.

Janet, Andy and I are a threesome, me clinging to Andy's other arm. I'm out for the first time in ages. The fire is already lit, the 'guy' awaits his fate in a wheelbarrow, his trilby hat cocked over his face. Andy had seen him and his creators earlier outside Fine Fare with 'Peny for the Guy' pinned onto his chest.

Smoke's billowing, sparks are flying, it's alight. A digusting looking mattress smoulders and bursts into flames in a snowstorm of stuffing and toxic fumes but it's great fun. We shriek at the bangers, whoo at the rockets and accept hand-held sparklers offered despite our earlier disdain. There's jaw clamping treacle toffee and I offer round the traditional 'Parkin' cake I'd watched hurtling down a conveyer belt for the past fortnight.

ROOM TO GROW

Someone's giving out toffee apples, another is placing potatoes on a metal tray at the edge of the fire, when I see him through smoke and sparks on the other side of the bonfire. He's there. It's him? No it's not? He's reappeared… oh …he's gone now!

In seconds I'm breathing too heavily and quaking. It becomes a violent shaking. My jellified legs are about to refuse my weight so I slowly sink to the ground, light-headed and dizzy. A panic attack I'm told later. Two concerned faces appear before me

'Ooh, are you alright love?' asks one face to my pale one. 'Where's the nearest telephone box?' she asks the other. 'In case we need an ambulance.' Janet appears from somewhere, squats down next to me and holds my hand. 'She's with me,' she says. 'I think it's probably nervous exhaustion.' Nerves getting exhausted? I've never heard of that one but I'm too anxious to care and huddle down.

'I'll take her home. She's had a bad time lately. It might be a breakdown.'

A 'breakdown? Cars and horses have breakdowns, but better than saying you're cracking up going loony, or having what the Victorians called 'hysteria', strictly a female complaint. Shut up, Janet. I don't want a breakdown if it makes you do this in public. I don't want to be visible. I want them to go away.

'I'm Ok.' I say. The shaking is subsiding as I become calmer and I'm helped to my feet and lean against a wall brushing myself down, Janet looking on anxiously. Andy goes to investigate the nebulous sighting. He walks all round the fire and back glancing around in all directions bumping into excited children

COLIN

and ignoring rip-raps and bangers landing at his feet – but no sighting. This drama has punctured the mood and we begin making our way back in subdued spirits, fireworks going off in all directions. Booth Hall Children's Hospital will be busy tonight. Children and seasonal gunpowder are not a good mix.

WEDNESDAY 6ᵀᴴ NOV

Got the *Manchester Evening News* for jobs. 'Assistants wanted for busy supermarket' reads an advert. I may apply but it will include Saturdays and I like my Saturdays off. 'Hoffman presser' required at a well-known dry cleaners in Urmston. What is a hoffman presser and what do they do?

I ask a workmate. She tells me, miming the actions.

'It's like a huge ironing board with a lid that comes down and presses a garment. It puffs out steam when you press a foot lever,' she explains. So it's basically a huge steam iron. As I frequently burn myself with even a small one I wonder if it's a good idea. I apply regardless. Have confidence in yourself said Eileen (Janet's mum) when I told her. The job's not rocket science and you wrote a good letter.

THURSDAY 7ᵀᴴ NOV

I'm awaiting a possible interview but they've probably not even received it yet. Watched TV. Janet and Andy got back about eleven as I was about to go to bed. They'd seen him and blurt out the news.

ROOM TO GROW

'He was there!' says Andy. 'Hanging round outside The King's Arms – looking for you I'm sure …but he avoided us… just walked off and didn't even let on. Stupid man. As if you'd be daft enough to still go there now.'

'He looked awful,' adds Janet, 'as if he'd been gardening or painting or something, and his hair – looked as if he hadn't combed it for a week.'

'I hope he didn't follow you home. That's all I need, him knowing where I'm staying.'

'Lizzie, we're not idiots!' says Andy. 'We know what he's like so we went a different way, then pretended to walk up Mike's drive so he'd think you was staying there. You're still Ok here. Relax. We're all looking out for you.' I feel the same as I did before, safe for now.

FRIDAY 8TH NOV

Work: The fun here cheers me up. The men behave like naughty children but they make me laugh which I need. I'm glad they've abandoned their latest form of amusement though – I wouldn't like to see them lose their jobs.

Their prank crosses the boundary of fun and consists of causing a letter of complaint to be sent to the company about one of the products. Inedible objects are placed into the cake mixture or packaging, eliciting written complaints which are prominently pinned to the notice board supposedly to shame, but causing hilarity! They vie with each other for the most disgusted customer letter. These and other things find their way into products: cigarette ends, matches, a dead spider, tiny toys from cornflake packs and the most outrageous – a pair of false teeth!

Eventually they came to their corporate sense before they were caught. Most teasing, banter and horseplay continues though, which brightens the days and makes time pass more quickly. I almost wish I hadn't applied for that job. I'm sure I won't find characters like this again.

SATURDAY 9TH NOV

Got the job at the dry cleaners! The manager doesn't care I've only done shop or factory work and can I start on Monday please. But I can't, as I need to give notice at the factory so I start a week on Monday. My bus happens to stop at the same place so it looks as if I'm coming from the bakery. I don't want him to know where I am working. It's not much better pay or prospects but it's a step out of shadowy scrutiny.

SUNDAY 10TH NOV

I've been staying with Janet for weeks now but she's a nightmare to live with! She snores and grinds her teeth in the night and gets bad-tempered in the morning. She won't let me smoke in her room either, but at least I'm safe here, although tomorrow I move back to the bedsitter. I'm looking forward to it yet anxious. He said he'd kill me if ever I left him which I didn't take it seriously then, but in his worsened state who knows.

But it will be good to see Bob again, and Brenda who's been staying with a married friend and sharing a bedroom with an insomniac child. She's desparate for a good night's sleep and some privacy so she'll be glad to return.

MONDAY 11TH NOV

I'm all at sixes and sevens with some clothes and college notes at Janet's and some at 'home'. There are now glaringly white, bare walls which will look better with my posters, if I ever find them again. Everything is jerky and disorganised. It's only temporary as I must look for somewhere else; a new room with a complete new identity, like a child murderer coming out of prison. I'll be careful until then. I know him, hider behind hedges, watcher and follower. But am I becoming delusional too? Is my own sanity disintegrating?

TUESDAY 12 NOV

I've told Jenny I've decided definitely not to take up her housekeeper offer in London. I'm not confident it would work out. Then what would I do stuck in a strange city! She was fine about it. I've a new job to go to, and I'll be fine.

I meet her briefly after work to tell her.
'So sorry,' I say feeling I've rejected her help.
    'It's Ok Lizzie. You don't need to apologise. I was worried about you that's all…and you have to decide about things

COLIN

yourself. I'm going just after Christmas, so maybe we can get together before that. You'll come and stay for a while after Christmas won't you?' she asks giving me a hug. I'm relieved she doesn't think I'm ungrateful for her offer. So typical. So generous. I'll miss her so much.

WEDNESDAY 13TH NOV

Olive and Stan have found a bigger flat as their baby is due so they aren't coming back. A man has taken their front bedsitter room with its own little kitchen and all white walls. Bob isn't back yet. Frank has taken on the role of my defender – although I didn't ask him to.

'Remember Lizzie,' he says, 'If he's ever there outside call – get to the door quickly and shout for me or Mrs Bryson. She said she'll watch out for him too. If he gets to be a nuisance I'll deal with him.'

Deal with him? What does he mean? No blood please, and don't get yourself into trouble again because of me. I don't want him to hurt Colin who has been a big part of my life these last few months, lover and friend. But Frank's presence is a comfort, especially after those shadowy presences. Was this reality? Did I imagine them? I'm beginning to doubt my own perceptions.

FRIDAY 15TH NOV

Work: Last day of this job. I'm quite sad really. They bought me a present and a big card which everyone had signed and pinned raffle tickets to my coat!

Evening: Brenda's back looking different. She's been on a diet and her hair's blonder. She had news about Colin and gave me an update on her love life. She saw the bruises straightaway even though they're fading and I told her everything.

'Lizzie! Your face!' she exclaims immediately. 'He did it didn't he, the evil bastard!' She doesn't say 'I told you so,' even if she's thinking it, but sits with concerned or scowling expressions at sordid details. She emits a stream of unrepeatable swear words.

'He should be locked up,' she finally declares.

'I've missed you so much,' I tell her. 'Only you could really understand what it's like.'

'Well he's been sacked you know.'

'How do you know that?' I'm not that surprised, just a bit taken aback that she knows before me.

'Well, you know the woman I stayed with, Doreen? She used to do some typing in the office there. Yes, well she's still in touch with the secretary who said he'd accused Ellis of sending him messages through the television set!' She pauses, eyebrows raised, and twirls her digit finger to her head.

'He's completely cracked isn't he? He'd been getting worse – everyone had noticed and poor Mr Ellis was sick of him. So he sacked him there and then, no notice, just his salary in advance to get rid of him.'

We exhaust the topic over coffee and the bashed up cake I regularly bring home and turn to her other news.

'So Malek? Not back together?' I knew she'd met Tony –

but she's not always a one-guy girl so nothing would surprise me.

'Oh no... that ended ages ago – and I'd met Tony after the fire, as you know. Besides, Malek's parents ...well they were Ok at first, but they changed. It was a mutual parting though. We were bored with each other anyway. Tony's wonderful though.'

Her face lights up at his name. She likes a man in uniform and extolls his virtues: he's a brave fireman, so strong, so handsome, so generous, so funny, he treats her so nicely. Perfect really.

'And what about the woman you stayed with, Doreen?'

'Oh she liked him too. She thought he was really...'

'No, I mean what about her? How did it work out – with all those kids? I didn't think you were that keen on children.'

'There were only three of them, two boys and a girl. But they were all under six, so I'm not kidding Lizzie, it was a nightmare. One of them barely slept and screamed the place down at night. Another one found my make-up, squashed it all out, tried to eat my lipstick and flushed my hair band down the loo, and the other, well she was alright, but I had to share a room with her so that ruined my love life! But – Doreen was a good friend putting me up at short notice. So I just silently screamed.'

We exchange anecdotes and news, admire each other's newly decorated rooms and part company. Alone I think about Colin. What will he do now? I don't know if he has any savings. What will he do for income? What about his rent, his car, his bills? Why should I care?

SATURDAY 16ᴴ NOV

Bob's back today. We hugged each other. He's been with a friend in Stretford called Ron. I didn't ask what kind of a friend but he's happy. He was horrified about what happened to me and we talked and talked until after midnight – quietly, no Dragon attracting music.

Like Brenda, he noticed the fading bruising right away. It's jaundiced yellow with an occasional faint blue patch and faded scratch marks making an interesting pattern. You could sell it to Liberty Prints for dress material design. 'You've had a bad time,' he remarks, not wanting to name him but guessing right away.

'Yes,' I reply wearily. I'm sick of retelling this story but I must share it with him. So I tell him, stopping at one point to wipe a tear at the recall of a particular detail and he listens and listens.

'And I thought you weren't coming back,' I say through tears. 'So that made it worse because that would be two of you lost.' The thought of it brings on a fresh weeping attack and he offers me a chunky loo roll as a tear soaker.

'Yes, well they kept the room for me on the promise I would return,' he tells me as I recover. 'They want to keep us you know. We're good tenants compared with what they've had before! But tell me, what's happening with Colin now? Are you in touch with him? Has he tried to contact you since?'

I tell him about the silent phone calls, my evasion tactics, and how people are looking out for me, my new job, my plan to find a new bedsitter and quietly disappear to start a new life. He listens.

'Yes, I think you're making the right decisions Lizzie. You've changed, I can see. You need to leave here. You've had room to grow. Room to grow in this room. You need to move on.

SUNDAY 17TH NOV

There's been some silent calls again. I've told everyone my suspicions. I'm pretty sure when he loses a relationship, the calls begin like with Brenda, even though he denied it. It happens randomly. Whoever goes to answer gets silence or crackly noises. No one wants to ignore it in case it's a call for theml. Brenda's fireman, Tony, sometimes rings and someone for Bob, so no one's willing to ignore it. My fellow tenants tut and mutter at fruitless journeys up and down stairs to the payphone. He's a time-wasting nuisance.

'A bloody annoying nutter,' says the new tenant. 'I'm going to tell him what I think next time. He doesn't know the complex history, only the inconvenience. I must get to know him. I think he is a soap salesman.

MONDAY 18TH NOV

New job started. It's quite tiring and more physical than I expected but I've plenty of energy so it will be good for me.

I follow the example of my workmate trainer. It's like a keep fit routine every two minutes: arrange garment flat on board, pull down large heavy top, press foot and expel steam, wait, press foot on vacuum pedal to suck away steam, lift, remove, hang garment up, start again. Repetitive – but sort of satisfying like when you iron a shirt and it hangs it nice and crisp on a hanger. Dealing with people in the shop sounds better but they want to train me for this job first. I make friends with another presser who has a handsome brother in the navy I'll meet one day.

TUESDAY 19TH NOV

The silent caller wasn't today. A polite sounding voice asked for me but I just heard a crackling, faint far away noise. Really weird. I put the phone down straight away, but later, when I tried to ring Janet it was still connected. No one else could use it for ages!

It's an annoying, attention-seeking ploy: stay connected blocking the line so no one can use it. We wouldn't be able to contact emergency services so this could be serious. 'Just ignore it,' others say but, as social communication gets more difficult, patience frays.

WEDNESDAY 20TH NOV

Unexpected call from George Ellis today. (He's asked me to call him George.) The police had visited wanting to know more about Colin. A serious complaint has been made about him. 'Is he ever violent'? they wanted to know. Or, 'has he ever threatened to be?' He was shocked when I told him he'd not only threatened but had been to me a few weeks back. He tries to tell me about sacking him but my own news is bursting through.

'Yes, yes, someone's told me that, but George, I need to tell you something first. I've left him. For good I mean – some weeks ago. He beat me up quite badly and ...well ... I'm afraid he could seriously hurt me another time if I took him back. I can't risk it.' A moments's silence. 'Whatever happened? Are you alright Lizzie?'

'Yes, yes, I'm Ok now. He became nasty after something didn't go his way. My face was a mess for ages and I was shaken up. I now think he's trying to get at me...to punish me or frighten me or something. I need to move away.'

'Oh ... heavens ... What can I say? This is getting worse and worse. I'm so sorry that's happened to you Lizzie ...but yes you must... and I will help you if I can. But let me tell you what I was calling about.'

'Yes, I know, you sacked him, and I don't blame you. He'll be even more convinced about his sacking theory now won't he!'

'It was getting ridiculous, but – that's not all why I'm calling. It's about the other night.'

The other night? What else can there be? Not more bad news!

'He was almost carted off to the police station because of his aggressive behaviour.'

'So what happened?'

'Well ...first he'd been seen muttering to himself – in the garden of the flats where he lives: saying strange things to a woman there... which frightened her. Then he accused another tenant of breaking into his flat and interfering with his television.'

'Interfering with it? Why would anyone do that?'

'It's one of his balmy ideas isn't it – people talking to him through the television. Then, when another tenant joined in to defend the first one, he threatened to push them both down the stairs!'

'So they called the police?'

'No, they complained to the landlord who didn't really want to know but came the next day. When he confronted Colin – he just repeated nonsensical accusations and demanded the landlord give him all the spare keys to the flats. When he quite rightly refused, Colin got nasty…and threatened to injure him. So he very wisely walked away and called the police.'

'So what did the police do?' Did they arrest him?'

'No, because he hadn't actually harmed anyone … although they could have got him for threatening behaviour…I suppose, or disturbing the peace or something. Anyway they decided just to calm things down and spoke to him in his flat. That's why they've asked me about him. I've had to call them before. They know about his mental condition.'

'So what's going to happen?'

'Nothing at the moment – but they said if he's becoming violent, he could be hospitalised next time – if it looks serious.'

'So what would they do with him? Which hospital?'

'Well… like I said – he may end up being taken somewhere like Prestwich Mental Hospital.'

'Prestwich!' I say, aghast at the thought. 'We used to call it the "loony bin" when we were kids! You were well and truly bonkers if you went there!'

'That was a left-over from when it was the county asylum,' George explains. 'There's more modern thinking about mental health now. He probably wouldn't be a permanent in-patient if he did go in. They'll try and stabilise him with medication. But I thought I'd let you know so you could take extra care while he's being so unpredictable.'

Take extra care! Can I take any more care. Do I have to stay indoors for ever! I thank him and return to my room to digest the disturbing news.

THURSDAY 21ST NOV

I kept thinking about yesterday's news. Poor Colin. I can't believe things have got so bad. I'll keep in touch with George who seems very well informed about new thinking about mental health. I wonder how he knows all this? I must remember to ask him next time we speak.

FRIDAY 22ND NOV

It's a terrible, terrible day! It reduces yesterday's news to pinhead proportions. President Kennedy has been assassinated! I cannot believe it. Everyone will forever remember what they were doing on this awful day. America is stunned and everyone is in shock.

It was earlier this evening (lunchtime for them) as he toured through Dallas in an open car. He was shot and very badly injured. People were praying he'd survive, but one hour later he was dead! I heard about it suddenly in the evening.

ROOM TO GROW

It's almost eight o'clock. I'm washing my hair in the sink when I'm called.

'Lizzie, Lizzie,' he knocks urgently. 'Come quickly. Open the door... Lizzie. Are you in?'

I know it's Bob, but what's the rush? I'm in a shampoo lather so I silently curse.

'There's some important news. Come to the door.'

I wrap a towel round my head and open the door looking like a Turk.

'President Kennedy is dead! He's been shot!'

'What? Who's dead? President Kennedy? He can't be! Shot did you say? No! ...When?'

'Come on up. I'm watching on Doris's TV. All normal programmes are suspended,' he says breathlessly and dashes off again.

I need a moment for it to register as escapee shampoo suds trickle past the towel and down my neck. He's got it wrong. Surely? No he wouldn't! I dash to the sink. No time to heat water in the kettle, cold rinse, replace turban, off upstairs where I find serious-faced Bobby, Brenda and Doris glued to the fourteen-inch screen. Doris is crying. A TV witness is gabbling and pointing to a window in a building where the shots had come from. They have caught a man they think fired the shots but there's chaos and police everywhere. It's shattering news.

Commentaries and interviews go on all evening; photographs taken only hours earlier are shown with a smiling President and his beautiful wife, Jackie, watched by adoring admirers soon to be switched out of their daily lives. All this comes via the new transatlantic TV satellite service launched just over a year ago

288

COLIN

called 'Telstar'. The whole world shares this news within an hour of the event with streams of images bouncing off the satellite and received within seconds. We say goodnight in subdued tones; brain full but craving answers, dog tired but not sleepy, so upset that this could happen to such a much-loved President. I won't be able to sleep tonight thinking about it. This terrible day is nearly over. America still has hours to go.

SATURDAY 23ᴿᴰ NOV

The papers are full of photographs; some heartrending. The injured President is seen slumped over his wife who cradles his head in her lap and we see photos of his two pretty children. The world is still reeling. We know more about the killer now. He is Lee Harvey Oswald an ex U.S Marine who recently defected to Russia, but no one knows why he would kill John F. Kennedy who was a popular President with a lovely wife. It is a terrible tragedy. Russia and the United States are sort of enemies – they nearly had a nuclear war last year – but to kill the President! But the US police and FBI think Oswald was a lone killer so we shouldn't blame the Russian State. Some people are doing just that and all sorts of theories are flying round and no-one knows what to think.

America grieves and everyone is caught up in the raw emotion. US politicians look grave and ordinary people openly weep. This cataclysmic event will go down in history. The new President: Lyndon B. Johnson was sworn in within an hour. He's not as attractive as JFK and I've never heard of him, but could anyone ever be like President Kennedy? I don't think so. For once I don't care if I'm not out on a Saturday night and I'm content to be watching TV with Doris, even though she cries every time the footage come on. I'm beginning to have tragedy fatigue though.

SUNDAY 24 NOV

This is incredible. You wouldn't believe it! Another man called Jack Ruby has shot and killed Lee Harvey Oswald – whilst he was in the hands of police! So now we'll never really know why LHO killed JFK and that is very frustrating indeed. Everyone is aghast and angry. So am I. I've never been interested or cared about a President or any other political figure but this one is different.

Rumours upon rumours, rumours about rumours, rumours denying rumours, circulate around the world. But the U.S press and other agencies assure us this was yet another lone killer on a mission and not some devilish international plot. People just love a conspiracy, to speculate on intriguing stories and sinister intent as opposed to listening to what reliable sources are saying; that Jack Ruby and Lee Harvey Oswald were simply unhinged individuals bearing irrational grudges.

MONDAY 25TH NOV

My new job as a hoffman presser is Ok, but there are not many others here. I miss my old workmates and the work is even more repetitive. Not much I can do about it for now. I'll look for something else, but it might not look good if I change jobs so soon

Within two weeks I'd applied for another job. My last English O Level assignment was to write a formal letter stating clearly its purpose and using appropriately formal language and conventions etc: a letter to an MP, editor, job application etc. I did a job application, sent a copy to Marshall and Snelgrove, an upmarket city department store who wanted cashiers, and got an interview!

TUESDAY 26TH NOVEMBER.

I'm enjoying college and I get a lift there and back with Helen so feel safe. I have to write about water power at the very beginning of the Industrial Revolution like water wheels and tanning and dying industries. The tutor is so good. He shows slides and photographs of places. Some of them I know. How come my school history teacher couldn't make it interesting like this?

WEDNESDAY 27TH NOV

The same badly disguised voice asked for me again. I watch as Bob picks up the phone. He can't hear. It's crackly and hissy.

'It's like Marconi's first message over the Atlantic,' he says holding it away from his ear.

'Marconi?' I query? 'Who's he? Is that useful for my History assignment?' I'm noting historical facts these days but chronology is wonky.

'He was…' Bob begins, but Frank has appeared expecting a call and is looking cheesed off.

'Is it that twat again?' he asks. 'Let me speak to him next time.'

THURSDAY 28 NOV

He was outside here tonight. Cigarette smoke wafted from behind next door's hedge as I stepped out of the door then quickly back in again. Don't smokers know their cigarettes smell! I'm self-righteous and disgusted now I've given up. But he's not as good at spying as he thinks he is. Was he hoping to accost me going out? Well too bad. I'm not going now.

Only him trying to make contact is unnerving. Unknown intention threatens my confidence and presents me with something I can't control. When I can't control something it frazzles my brain which can't deal with my body properly so I get the trembles. Am I ill too? Can sanity be wobbly? I fear for mine.

FRIDAY 29TH NOVEMBER

I knew it would happen. If it wasn't for escaping through the delivery entrance to Fine Fare I might have come face to face with 'him' in the store. He must have followed me from the bus stop on my way home from work. I looked round to see a shadowy figure turn into a garden and disappear as if he lived there. Was it him? It was like Bonfire Night all over again. I headed towards Bob's supermarket.

All jellified legs and breathlessness I rushed into the store. Bob was in an aisle building tins of fruit into an artistic display. I stopped quickly nearly causing a tinned avalance.

'Hey slow down,' he says surprised to see me. He notes my anxiety. 'What's happened?'

I blurt it out supporting myself on a pillar in case of collapse. He takes my arm and leads me to the tired old ladies' chair kept at the back of the store.

'Stay here. I'll see if I can see him – and maybe I can talk to him.'

'Oh be careful Bob. Please …don't, he can be unfriendly if he's not taken his medication and what if he wants to argue … so I'd rather you …'

But he's already gone. He returns looking puzzled.

'He's OK. He said he's sorry to have worried you. He only wanted to do his shopping and didn't know you were in here. Look, over there. He's gone round the vegetable counter picking up some carrots. He looks a bit untidy but he seems calm. Are you quite sure he was following you?'

So, so cunning and plausible. Bob probably thinks I'm imagining it now.

'Yes, I am sure,' I answer feebly. 'He kept well back but I know it was him. It was… I'll swear it. I saw him way behind me then he dodged into a garden. I know it was him …Bob? Can I stay here with you – until you finish, so we can leave together?'

ROOM TO GROW

'Yeah but...' he's thinking. 'I'm here for another couple of hours. Why don't you slip out the back – through the delivery door. He'll think you're still in the store – and I can keep him talking if you like. He was fine with me, honestly.'

I don't want to be a nuisance and strain this friendship. A work mate is looking at him. I'm being a pest – disturbing him, drawing attention to him. I'll do what he says. He holds the door open and wishes me luck as I sneak out and bolt, arriving red and fraught to meet Frank on his way out. I tell him what's happened – but immediately regret it because he's even more angry now.

SATURDAY 30TH NOV

Another another nuisance call. He's more time on his hands now he's not working. He'll find crafty ways of bothering me without revealing his intentions, just letting it drip, bit by bit. This time Frank actually threatened him so I'm hoping that will work.

Frank answers the phone. This time a badly disguised voice asks for me.

'Hello. Sorry to bother you,' he begins ever so politely,'could you get Lizzie for me. It's a friend from work'. But Frank is not fooled.

'Look mate, we all know who you are, you bloody lunatic. Don't ring here again. No one here wants to speak to you because you're a bloody head banger, and stop hanging round and bothering Lizzie or you'll have me to answer to – and you wouldn't want that, believe me!'

COLIN

I can't hear a reponse if there is one, but Frank is getting into his stride.

'Come anywhere near here again, mate, and I'll kick your fucking head in. Is that clear? In fact I'm coming for you anyway because I'm just pissed off with these phone calls!' He slams down the phone with vehemence.

'He might get the message,' he says. 'Let's hope so or I'll really have to make him understand. Know what I mean?'

I do, but I do hope he doesn't have to as I'm not comfortable with it. I wouldn't want to be on the wrong side of Frank. He'd be a formidable enemy!

SUNDAY 1ST DEC

Brenda had a problem to share today. She probably needs more professional advice and I'll go with her to the doctor if it doesn't get sorted out soon. She is still 'going out' with her firemen. She often stays in with him too and I've met him more than once creeping out in the morning to avoid Mrs B's nosey parkering. She is in love with a permanent starry–eyed look and rushes to the payphone when it rings.

But that changed a bit this week. She looked worried and is very quiet if our paths cross.

'Are you Ok?' I ask her today.

'No …I think I'm pregnant.'

'Oh no!' I say. I think she's going to cry so I put my arm around her. 'Are you sure?' I ask.

'Yes, well no, but I think so.'

ROOM TO GROW

'So, have you …is this with Tony?' I ask. She nods and sniffs.

'Yes of course. I've timed it and it must have happened those weeks when I was staying with Doreen… I didn't have anywhere private. I was sleeping in with her little girl so there was nowhere to go…so we did it in the park.'

'What in this weather! Wasn't the grass wet?'

'Yes. Everything was, so we did it standing up. We did it a few times. I thought there was less risk of getting get pregnant like that but…I'm not sure now.'

'Oh well,' I say remembering peer group conversations at school. 'It is possible you can get pregnant if you do it standing up. But if you think about it logically – it's all about gravity. Everything just slides down – so it probably couldn't reach the target,' I say authoritatively. She looks doubtful but relieved at this ill-informed piece of nonsense.

'But I do have the first signs. What do you think Liz? – What should I do?'

'Just wait a while and see if anything happens. Then worry about it.'

'I don't want to be an "unmarried mother", she says. I understand this, it's the stigma. It's whispered, or said out of the sides of people's mouths; 'unmarried mother.'

Some anti-natal clinics and maternity wards refuse to say 'Miss' thinking they're being tactful. I accompanied my old school friend, Joan Grant, to one months ago. We waited for her turn to be examined.

'Next please – Mrs Grant,' they called. But Joan had modern ideas.

COLIN

'It's MISS!' she snarled at them cradling her bump. The nurses were perplexed.

Brenda waits and worries for another week.

'Do you feel sick in the morning?' I ask.

'In the morning? I feel sick every time I think about it!'

We talk about gin and hot baths. Gin is expensive but worth the price if it works. We pool resources and buy a half bottle of Gordon's gin. Princess Margaret and the Queen Mother drink it so it must be good.

'Do you have to drink the gin as you're actually having the hot bath?' she asks half seriously.

'No, but it's double security like belt and braces. It might work better. Who knows.'

So we decide the dual approach. Hot water for the bath works on a geyser that works on a meter fed with coins, so we get armed with shillings which blows our paltry heating budgets. We plan for a time when the shared bathroom won't be too busy – after 8.00pm.

As we head there at eight o'clock the new tenant passes us heading straight for the bathroom.

'Erm… excuse me. Are going in there?' I ask. He looks at me quizzically.

'Yes, why do you want to know?'

'Sorry… I meant will you be long?'

He is puzzled by the questioning and thinks I'm dying to use the loo.

'I doubt it. Do you need to go first or something?'

'No. No we can wait. But don't go running the hot water off.

Brenda wants a bath soon,' I tell him. We both stand and watch him go in. He gives us a strange look.

Brenda gets into a very hot bath. Within minutes her face is puce but I insist she doesn't draw any more cold water and go to prepare the gin. I pour a generous measure and taste it. It's horrible without tonic or something sweet. Orange juice maybe. Then I remember a leftover tangerine in my lunchbox. I fetch it and squeeze a couple of its segments into the tumbler. Still awful. I put the glass and the rest of the tangerine on a tray and carry it like a cocktail waitress to the bathroom.

As I'm doing this Mrs B comes up the stairs for mundane busybodying and sees me take the tray into the bathroom. She looks questionly at me but I say breezily, 'Brenda wanted a glass of water,' and hope she believes me in spite of the fact that fresh water is available in a bathroom and doesn't require a friend with a glass on a tray.

MONDAY 2ND DEC

No more silent calls or any more signs of hiding or following. I think Frank has scared him off but not knowing if he is around is the worst. I'm an indecisive semi–recluse never knowing whether it's safe to nip out to the shops, visit my family or even open the curtains. Am I imagining some of this? I am becoming as suspicious as he was about George Ellis. I badly need to keep my sanity but it's slipping backwards and forwards and I can't trust it.

I decide to risk a visit to my family home. I haven't seen them since 'the incident'. I've been waiting weeks for a normal-looking face.

'Oh, who are you?' asks my dad peering at me. It's his idea of a joke if he hasn't seen anyone for a while. 'Where's the posh boyfriend with the car then?' he asks lightheartedly. Umm….how to tell them? Mum appears and after a pleasant inquiry about Colin I offer a bland explanation. It was mutual. We decided to end it, and it was ages ago anyway, but she suspects something I know. You're not telling us everything, she's thinking.

'Have you lost a bit of weight?' she enquires fishing a little.

'I don't know. Have I?' I pull my jacket closer to avoid scrutiny.

'Maybe you'll make it up.' she says. 'I hope so. He was so nice.'

TUESDAY 3RD DEC

The new tenant, now in Olive and Stan's flat, works for Procter and Gamble in Trafford Park. I've seen his car parked on the drive. He wears a smart suit and a tie. Brenda has already found out he's getting divorced. Typical of her! He gave her free samples of 'Head and Shoulders' shampoo. It's for dandruff but Brenda said it just sticks it to your head. I like Silvercrin. Maybe he'll have some of those too.

We call him Shampoo Man. He is still on good terms with his soon to be ex wife. She visits briefly sometimes, is very glamorous and drives a smart little sports car. The Dragon doesn't know who she is and thinks he's ordered a call girl. She watches the comings and goings with interest and frowns at the attractive woman Shampoo Man lets in. She detects her perfume like a sniffer dog and comes out to fiddle around with the post. Her curiosity peaks as the woman smiles charmingly, goes up the stairs, then, after some time comes down again, without a word, still smiling.

'Who is she?' Mrs B asks one day when Mrs Shampoo has teetered past in six-inch stilettos and seamed stockings leaving 'Chanel No 5' fragrancing the hall. I pretend not to know leaving it to her imagination. Having a Cusson's sales rep in the house is good as he leaves sweet-smelling soap samples, shampoos and body wash in the shared bathroom so it smells like a tart's boudoir. I can't resist these tempting toiletries and use a Silvercrin shampoo sachet, then feel guilty because it wasn't mine.

When I confess he says, 'Oh that's Ok. Use them. Anyone can. I get lots.'

WEDNESDAY 4TH DEC

No phone calls or sightings so I'm a bit more relaxed. Mum visits sometimes now she's getting better. She brings food parcels, egg cups and useful things. She encountered Mrs Bryson today who gave her a most charming smile and introduced herself. Mum took the cue readily as she likes a good chat. Bob and I were on the landing listening to them after she'd come in.

'…and I always try and keep my eye on 'er y'know…so many temptations these days aren't there? … so many funny people about … she's only young isn't she?' says Mrs Bryson pretending not to be a dragon.

'Yes, but she's strong-headed my daughter. You have to be firm with her and she doesn't always listen. I think she's looking after herself but…I think she's looking a bit thinner lately.'

'Yes, maybe. But you know I watch out for the young tenants. I think they need someone to tell them things sometimes. They think they're so grown up but sometimes they still need an adult.'

'I agree Mrs Byson.'

'Oh call me Hilda,' she says to my mum with a smile.

'And I'm Margery,' returns Mum. 'Nice to have met you.' Mother is seriously impressed.

'What a lovely woman,' she enthuses. 'I'm so glad you found a room here.' Next visit she's invited in for a cup of tea in the Brysons' lair.

Then, tea in 'The Lair', regularly. They put the world to rights whilst I slave over the two-jet cooker upstairs to show I'm capable of making something to eat. They're in league over my welfare now. Am I eating properly? Losing weight? Well I certainly can't afford meals out anymore so I probably am.

THURSDAY 5TH DEC

I was beginning to feel a little bit more relaxed now with the absence of any attempted contact but George rang today with news of 'him'. He had disappeared after being given notice to quit over that incident at his address two weeks ago and no-one knows where he is.

'Just be aware Lizzie. You know what he's like,' warns George. 'He doesn't let things go and may turn up if he hasn't got anywhere to go. Don't worry too much. Call the police if he arrives and causes any trouble. They know about him now.'

'How did you find out he'd gone?'

'Well, I know the policeman involved in that incident. He happens to be a neighbour and knows about his warped idea about me… so he tipped me off …so I'm passing it on.'

My heart sinks. I was doing so well; looking forward to starting my job at Marshall and Snelgrove on Monday and searching the ads for a flat or room. Please don't tell me anything's going to spoil it now.

FRIDAY 6TH DEC

George rang again. This time to say that Colin was in Prestwich Mental Hospital. I'm sorry for him but relieved; he'll be better cared for in there and I can have a break from being on the alert. We spoke for quite a while so it will have been expensive.

Frank anwers the phone.

'WHO IS THAT?' he bellows thinking it's Colin. 'Oh… sorry George.' He hands the phone over to me.

'Lizzie? George here. Who was that shouty bloke?'

'It's just Frank…a tenant. He thought it was Colin. He was trying to protect me…I've been having nuisance calls…from him. Frequently. Everyone here is sick of him.'

COLIN

'Well you won't be getting any for a while because he's in Prestwich Mental Hospital…Lizzie? Are you there? Are you OK?' I'm momentarily stunned.

'Yes, yes. I'm listening. Go on.'

'I just thought I'd let you know. They probably won't keep him for ever. Maybe just weeks if he improves. The new drugs they have are much better now so if the treatment starts to work successfully they'll let him out. Meanwhile…go out. Enjoy yourself a bit. Find yourself another boyfriend – a more straightforward one!'

'George?' I ask. 'I've been wondering.'

'Yes. What is it Lizzie?'

'How is it you know so much…about the new drugs …and the system changing and everything?'

'Umm.' He pauses. 'I don't usually tell people…but I may as well tell you…you see I have a brother with a similar condition. He's in Springfield Hospital in Crumpsall. Been there on and off for about four years so… I've picked up a lot and done some reading. Unlucky aren't I? A brother *and* an employee. Most folk go a lifetime without encountering one – and I've dealt with two!'

Have I touched something painful here? I'd hate any of my family to have this affliction.

'Sorry George… I didn't realise… you'd been so personally affected.'

'It's Ok… It's been a long time and I'm resigned to it now. Just one more thing though. I didn't want you to think all schizophrenics become violent. Most aren't. My brother isn't. Depends on how it affects their thinking – so don't lump them all together. They're all different.'

303

I'm soaking up the knowledge. This is all new to me. So there are people functioning harmlessly with this much stigmatised disease. George is still speaking.

'Colin's been unlucky that it's affected him like that – and getting progressively worse. That's why I tried to be tolerant of him… well, at first anyway, while he was still managable. I sort of understand the condition.'

I'm beginning to understand too, thanks to him. We say goodbye and he'll let me know if he hears anything further. He's been so helpful.

SATURDAY 7TH DEC

Oh my God. I have dropped Bob right in it! I cannot believe it. What have I done! My mother knows his mother and she'll tell her she's met him, and he's working at Fine Fare. This is awful. Why did I invite him in when she was here! I've ruined it for him.

I've casually dropped this bombshell. Bob has brought up some mail and I've invited him in and introduced him to my mum. A mistake.

'Bob, this is my mum. Mum, Bob, Bobby Renshaw, the one I told you works in the new supermarket on the main road.

'How do you do Mrs Dale.' He offers his hand. So polite and well brought up.

'Nice to meet you Bob. I've heard about the supermarket. They play Hawaiian music while you shop don't they, and have those nice blue nylon uniforms. How are you finding it there?'

'It's fine thank you – Fine – fare,' he smiles. She doesn't get

COLIN

the pun so he moves on. 'Yes, I'm enjoying it a lot. It's only been open a few weeks... but I do like it there.'

It's good to have some small talk and company so I open it up a bit. 'Bob used to live near Gran, Mum. On Everette Avenue.'

'Everette Avenue? Everette Avenue? And did you say your name was Renshaw?' Bobby nods. 'Renshaw! Oh what a small world! I know your mother, Ethel. We were in the local Civil Defence together, you know, when we thought there might be a third world war. We were great friends. Oh, how is she? I must get in touch again and say I've met you here. What a lovely coincidence,' she enthuses.

Bob's face falls. He's streaks ahead.

'Er... She's very busy these days ...with the church; she does an awful lot for the local church, and the Housewife's Register too.' He's looking at me anxiously. I can read his mind. He's desperately trying to change the subject pointing to the window.

'Just look at those dark clouds, I'm sure it's going to rain,' but Mum's not listening.

'Well I'm sure she'll find some time for an old friend. We sometimes went shopping together after the meetings. Yes, that's it. We could do some shopping at your new supermarket! She'd like that I know. Especially with you working there. Oh, I must contact her soon. I'll do it at the end of the week.'

I'm mortified – responsible for his imminent exposure. He'll be disowned, cast off, a misuser of parental finance, a deceiver, a source of embarrassing failure, and all because of me.

She leaves passing Mrs B who's pretending to be dusting but it's a sort of social ambush. What she's really after is a chat.

'Would you believe it,' Mum says, pausing for some small talk. 'That young man up there is the son of an old friend of mine. Isn't that a coincidence? Such a pleasant young man too. He works at that supermarket.'

'Yes, I believe so. I go there now. They have five brands of tea and a large meat counter to save you going to the butchers. So convenient.'

'Well, I've tried to be loyal to my local grocer, but it will save so much time won't it. I'll certainly do Christmas food shopping there. It's open later too. That makes it even more convenient.'

'Yes... Look, come on in if you're not in a hurry,' says Mrs B. 'I'll put the kettle on.'

Meanwhile, Bob and I discuss how we'll deal with my indiscretion.

SUNDAY 8TH DEC

I'm going to have to confide in Mum we've decided. It's the only way. I'll ask her not to say she's met Bob if she rings his mum. It's tricky. She may not want to be part of a conspiracy against her old friend but I hope she'll understand. I won't tell her the actual reason he left university, and that's another level of deceit, but what can I do? I need to protect Bob.

Some good comes out of it as it's prompted him to talk to his parents. He's knows they're bound to know one day, and he's going to see them next week. I just hope they don't 'black sheep' him. Another rejection won't do him any good at all.

PART THREE
New beginnings

MONDAY 9TH DEC

Started the new job today at Marshall and Snelgrove. It's really posh! Customers are from upmarket places like Wilmslow, Alderley Edge and Cheadle Hulme. Beautiful top fashion clothes and jewellery are for sale and the assistants dress smartly. The woman showing me the job used to go out with the radio DJ, Pete Murray.

I get the job despite never having handled money in my life. It's on St Annes Square and beats Kendal Milne for classiness. The job is easier than expected. It has a sort of vacuum tube system for cash and receipts. A customer's cash is inserted into a cylindrical container to be sucked up through tubes to a cashier in an upstairs office who puts in the correct change and a receipt and whizzes it back. Even with staff discounts it's more expensive than C&A, so I drool over the merchandise and rarely buy anything.

I'm not earning that much more. It's poorly paid 'women's' work, with few opportunities for advancement although working conditions are pleasant and the upmarket clientel and luxury goods give it a 'decent job' feel. Would a man do this job? How much more would they pay him I wonder. I don't see how my wage could support a family.

TUESDAY 10TH DEC

It's great to work so near to city shops. Went window shopping for family presents. So much choice but I have to watch my budget as I do not want to be broke for Xmas. I need to be able to contribute to drinks and things even though I rarely drink. I'd forgotten how expensive socialising is because Colin used to pay for all that. All the shops are lit up and it looks wonderful.

I'm enjoying working in this humming, throbbing city. It's alive with pre Christmas festivity; carol singers, Xmas trees with twinkly lights, shops decked out with tinsel and streamers and mountains of consumer goods irresistibly packaged and prominently stacked at unmissable eye level. It's hypnotic but demanding on eye and brain; all designed to mesmerise and encourage spending – but I'm loving it.

The biggest Christmas tree I've ever seen stands in Albert Square, lights already fully on. I stroll in and out of Debenhams, Littlewoods and Henry's surveying their merchandise, noting prices, planning future shopping. In Lewis's, Father Christmas is parting hard-earned cash from indulgent parents of children who form a fidgety queue for the pleasure of sitting on his festive knee. They get 'ho ho hoed' to and receive a cheap,

NEW BEGINNINGS

gender specific gift then have a look into his 'grotto' if they're lucky. Very small ones think they're having a nightmare or just look dumbstruck.

I have brain overload. It's visually exhausting and I've not eaten the sandwich I put together this morning so I eat it sitting on a bench in Piccadilly Gardens watching the busy world go by.

WEDNESDAY 11TH DEC

Mum's agreed not to 'shop' him. Phew! She'll send his mum a Christmas card and take it from there. Bob's parents now know about him leaving university. Something general to do with the course he'd said. They were surprisingly supportive once they'd got over the disappointment. He's been university prospecting for September 1964 and I've a feeling he may not come back after Christmas.

THUR 12TH DEC

A good day at work. Worked in the store for the first time. First I had 'training' on smiling, talking pleasantly, being helpful but not pushy and fronting up the display. All fairly obvious; as if you'd scowl and ignore people! I was selling handbags – very expensive ones. They're just things to put things in, so why spend so much on them, but it was enjoyable. Interaction with people instead of inanimate metal tubes and cash is more rewarding and I wouldn't mind a transfer. Had lunch in Piccadilly Gardens

ROOM TO GROW

down Market Street to watch buskers, pavement artists and beggars. Some colourful city characters here.

The dishevelled looking 'Footsore man' is one. He's old and smells and looks vulnerable. He's skilled at catching unwary suckers with his practised limp and is well known.

'Could you tell me the way to the Foot Hospital?' he'll innocently ask.

'Sure, just get the number 123 bus over there and when you get to Ancoats…'

'Oh I can't get the bus. I meant to walk. You see I haven't got the bus fare,' he says plaintively.

Coins are then found for this poor man with his painful affliction who bows in feigned gratitude then practically skips down the street.

FRIDAY 13TH DEC

As I feared, Bob is not coming back after Christmas. He's managed to get a place at another university in September miles away. He's been such a special friend and I'll miss him a lot. But I'm making other friends at college and I'm going to be studying more in January so I'll have plenty to occupy me. I've not felt as anxious lately – but still need a new address and I'm going to see a flat on Sunday. Bob went home this evening. I helped him pack his things. Clothes, posters, record player, records, and lots of books from his old course – all crammed into two suitcases and a large box leaving his room bare and echoey. He leaves me some mugs and a fountain pen as well as a jar of Nescafé, and hopes my Christmas will be Ok and that I'll be strong and safe. He'll be thinking of me on Christmas Day and I'll raise my sherry glass to him. I wish him success in his degree and tell him not to get distracted this time! Then, a car horn outside, his parents have arrived so we haul his belongings down the stairs and into their car. They assume I'm his girlfriend and smile warmly at me. We hug on the street and swear to keep in contact, then say goodbye – forever, with promises. I wave at the car until it's out of sight. We'll exchange Christmas cards for some years I expect, always intending to meet up – and maybe we will, but I know we're travelling on different life streams.

SATURDAY 14TH DEC

It's great to be able to do shopping in the city. Bought a new skirt today, dogs tooth check, twenty-nine and eleven from C&A. It's a bit long – or I'm a bit short, but before I do anything, are skirts longer or shorter now? It changes before you notice sometimes like the colour of the sky. Definitely shorter I think, I'll chop the hem.

I sit shortening the hem with neat oversewing stitches. I'm thinking of earlier times when Mum bought dresses too long for me and I'd feel like a droopy frump, as if I was wearing someone else's clothes, but she'd say:

'You need to leave room to grow.'

Well I'm grown now, but have another three years to official adulthood so I need to grow into that too.

'Leave room to grow.' I play with different meanings as I sew. Yes, I must leave room, leave this room, to grow, to grow away

SUNDAY 15TH DEC

I've been to see a flat. It is actually a small flat not a bedsitter. It has a small living room / kitchen and a small but separate bedroom. The landlord doesn't live on the premises so no nosey dragon to contend with. I can afford it though because it involves a small job I didn't expect to have!

'Well? What do you think of it?' asks my potential landlord indicating a sunlit room with modern furniture and zig zag patterned curtains, lime green and purple, bright and lively. I love it.

'It's really nice. It's more than I'm paying at present,' I add cautiously, 'but I could manage. It's so much better than my present place I think it would be would be worth paying a bit more.'

'Did you say you were a cashier? At Marshall and Snelgrove?' he suddenly asks.

'Yes. I haven't been there long yet, but I like it. I'm going to stay.'

'Hmm… So you can add up and handle money and things?'

'Well yes. I do it all day.'

'Would they give you a good reference if I asked them?'

'I think so. You could ask them. I mean, there's no reason why they wouldn't.'

'Do you think you could do some rent collection for me and keep records and things like that?'

'I don't know. I've never thought about it. I suppose I could. Why?'

'It's just that the last tenant used to do it for me, and I reduced her rent – so maybe that would suit you – and me of course; I've not found anyone else to do it. You'd have to have good references though,' he adds. I'm taken aback.

'Yes, of course …I understand, and I'm absolutely sure they'll give me one.'

It doesn't sound too complicated. But what about my studies, my O levels. Would it take up much time? I'm thinking of adding three more in January which actually started in September so there's a backlog to catch up with. He's reassuring about that.

'There's no pressure,' he says. 'The tenants won't give you any trouble – they're a decent bunch. You'd have to collect the rents each week, enter them in the rent books, bank it and keep the slips for me. It doesn't take long. You can do the very small amount of paper work monthly. Just simple records. My accountant does the tricky bits. Do it in your own time to suit you like the other lady did.'

Is this my lucky day! It sounds too good to be true. We negotiate a rent which works out no more than I'm paying for my present tatty bedsit and he'll ring for a reference to save time. I can't wait to give Mrs B my notice.

MONDAY 16TH DEC

This is my last English session this term. I can't believe it has gone so quickly. I used to think that you had to be clever to do O Levels. No, as long as you have time and inclination for the work

ROOM TO GROW

– anyone could do them. It's just remembering and regurgitating what they tell you. I have work to do over the holidays but I'm still going to celebrate Christmas.

Pat the tutor tells us that good writing counts a lot in English O Level work. To write well we must read a lot, not rubbish books; only mind-stretching ones which increase our vocabulary. She gives us a list. I've chosen *Jane Eyre* from it because Doris has it. She's read everything! We also ought to read some poetry, and try a Shakespeare play so I've looked at MacBeth, which they'd tried to teach us at school but I'd read 'Jackie' comics under the desk and only looked up at the gory bits. There's much more to it. The madness themes are familiar, especially MacBeth's delusions, then the poor mad woman in *Jane Eyre* kept in the attic incinerated in a house fire. I hope Mr Rochester had it insured. All a bit close to home.

TUESDAY 17TH DEC

Yes, the arrangement is on. I was able to give a fortnight's notice to leave the room that has been my home for eleven months. My future landlord was happy with whatever they said about me at work but Mrs B was not pleased about my leaving.

'In a fortnight!' she exclaims. 'You're giving a fortnight's notice – but it's almost Christmas. How can I advertise it now with everyone too busy to view and everything about to close soon?'

I don't know anything about tenant legalities but I've given her good notice and it's not my fault it's Christmas – and I can't afford to mess my new landlord about, so I stand my ground.

NEW BEGINNINGS

'I'm really sorry Mrs Bryson but I do have to leave. I've got somewhere secured and don't want to lose it… but do hope you'll find someone very soon.' I hand over rent up to the third of January which she grudgingly accepts.

'Where is it you're going?' she asks.

'Withington. It's a bigger room, well two, to be exact. You see I need to leave this room now. I've sort of outgrown it and I need something bigger.'

She tries again.

'Withington 'eh. A bit down market from 'ere isn't it. Are you sure you want to live there. The crime rate there is much higher you know. More burglaries, more muggings.'

'Yes I know, but I'll be fine. They're still rare.'

'You couldn't leave your bike out there or your window open. Can't I pursuade you to stay? It'll be hard to let your room and you'd be doing me a favour if you stayed. How much will you be paying for that?' She might be offering to reduce my rent, but I'm not interested. I tell her the situation. She sniffs and sighs.

'Well… I suppose I'd better put an ad in. I don't suppose you're going past the Post Office are you, love?'

WEDNESDAY 18TH DEC

I love to walk in my lunch hour in this busy city. My History tutor has really opened my eyes to it's rich history which I'd never appreciated before: its nooks and crannies, majestic Victorian buildings, rivers and canals. Each day there's things I'd missed as a mere shopper. I'm fascinated, like a foreign tourist. I walked along the bottom of Deansgate today and found Castlefield.

It's 1963 but history has not been kind to some of these areas. Castlefield is an old, run down, industrial landscape of crumbling warehouses, dirty polluted canals and huge overhead railway bridges. It doesn't even have the excuse of being a bombsite, it's leftover Victorian infrastructure, solidly built but becoming ugly in its demise. Coal is brought up from a filthy, delapidated coal wharf to street level from the Bridgewater Canal. Its days are numbered now, but coal from Worsley coal mines has been transported down this canal to this wharf for over two hundred years fuelling the factories and mills of the age. Some still arrives for remaining industries and for domestic purposes and you can walk along the old wharf, smelling the coal, black and gritty underfoot.

There was also a busy Roman settlement nearby and underneath layers of city weeds, lumps, bumps and bricks is the remains of a Roman fort which archaeologists plan to excavate. Perhaps some organisation will regenerate the whole area one day; worthwhile but would cost a fortune. Some future project maybe. But even all the bombsites haven't been cleared yet. I recently walked around one near the university; a prime city space begging for development; with an established gypsy encampment on it and little children playing barefoot on the rough ground. I'm not sure if they have access to National Assistance – or even if they want it, but it seems a hard life. That's in Chorlton on Medlock, often confused with Chorlton-cum-Hardy where I was brought up. I'm seeing more as life opens up. Who would have thought I'd be interested in History a year ago! My sanity doesn't feel so wobbly either.

THURSDAY 19TH DEC

Brenda is definitely 'in trouble'. The gin was a waste of time and money. She is ten weeks, vomiting each morning and off her food. She throws up at the thought of the curries she introduced me too, and she's peeing every hour!

She sighs after she's tells me about her predicament.

'I think I should have an abortion... but my parents are practising Catholics you know; so is our family doctor. I was once too – and I'm still not sure whether it's the right thing to do, morally I mean;,' she agonises. 'It's a baby isn't it? A living human being at the start of it's existence. How could I just kill it? Anyway I wouldn't know where to go.'

Neither would I. I've heard about illegal ones: unqualified people, unregulated practices; risky methods and equipment; women bleeding to death or succumbing to infections; young girls ruining their reproductive futures and instrument wielding quacks benefitting from their misfortune.

But I have seen a contact for abortion advice advertised in public toilets. It's a charity with a telephone number for unlucky girls alongside other helpful information like advice about venereal disease. I've seen it in telephone boxes too. I tell her about it. I'd never noted the telephone number as I'd never needed it so she'd have to look herself – and soon, which she's not happy about even though I say I'd go with her.

'What, walk round in the dark – just the two of us. They haven't found Pauline Read yet and I don't want to be the next one!'

ROOM TO GROW

'But two of us aren't likely to be attacked or kidnapped. He'd be chancing it a bit to tackle two of us!'

'Well what if there were two of *them*. I've heard someone say there was. I don't think it's a good idea after what's happened in Gorton.'

'But Gorton's miles away from here.'

'Lizzie – it's a bus ride, or twenty minutes in a car. No, I'm not going to do that.'

'Ask Tony to do it then,' I suggest.

'What! Ask him to trawl public toilets and telephone boxes for abortion advice! He's a man! I can't give him that responsibility,' she protests.

'Listen, did you put that baby in your own belly? No. So let him take some reponsibility

She looks at me doubtfully, but there's a chink in the armour now.

Later I meet Jenny and tell her. She's astonished.

'Why would she want to trail round toilets and telephone boxes? Terminations are legal now – on the National Health. She just needs to see her doctor. Didn't you know that?' I'm embarrassed that I don't. I learn later about a contraceptive pill being prescribed that will transform the lives of millions of women. I'm a bit behind sometimes.

FRIDAY 20TH DEC

Morning: Worked on the shop floor today as short-staffed there. Got to know another girl, Sheila, but she's leaving to work as a machinist at a rainwear place in Cheetham Hill. It's better money she says – but it's piecework, so unless you're a fast machinist, it might not be.

Evening: The bus was so late to leave this evening and I sat there on it waiting for ages. I watched a homeless person begging in the rain and wondered where they go in this sort of weather.

I'm on the top deck of a bus. It's been dark and raining for ages so I'm glad to be actually on it. It smells of stale smoke like all buses but it's warmer and dry. The bus has a driver but no conductor so sits, engine purring, waiting. I idly look out of the window: people making their way home, umbrellas raised, heads down, queueing for buses, moving, crossing paths with others. What's that though? Someone is just sitting there, on the hard floor of a doorway, a dark figure hood up and a blanket round his shoulders. He must have been out in the rain for a while because he looks wet. Is it a man? or a woman? It's a man.

He's said something to a passer by… He must be begging. Oh, but he's been ignored. They've looked away and walked on. He's hunkered down again waiting for the next one. Has he nowhere to live? Nowhere to keep warm? Someone like that asked me for money the other day. I gave him sixpence. 'Thank you. God bless you love', he said.

SATURDAY 21ST DEC

Half day today. Went shopping to Freeman, Hardy and Willis buying slippers for Christmas presents. Successful shopping cheered me up. But it ended with a nasty surprise like on Bonfire Night. I saw the homeless man again sitting on the pavement, and when I looked closer, then again to check… Yes. It was him, sitting there in the middle of the city in the same street as if he'd never moved from the day before.

But wait a moment. I'm looking from a different angle and there's something familiar. Just walk a bit further; now a little to the left, keep turning …yes, it is 'him!' No doubt about that profile. Oh God! A strange feeling begins in my belly. What on earth is he doing here? So scruffy and downtrodden. Has he slept there? Have his clothes dried out from last night? Has he eaten today? God! He's turning his head! Has he seen me? Fight or flight, says my no-logic brain and I'm wobbly. I recognise the panic and lean against a wall. I'm on my own! No Janet to scrape me up and explain to people so I stand still, frozen with anxiety.

I take some deep breaths and wait. That's better. It's lifting slowy, subsiding, as my breathing slows. It's alright, he hasn't seen me. It's OK. I can be normal again and I stand upright, take another deep breath, and walk away. He couldn't be looking for me, says sensible side of my brain. He doesn't know I work in the city and anyone who does is sworn to secrecy. He's there because of the footfall; the kindly contributions from generous folk and is totally unaware how coincidently close we are. Amazing close. Out of billions of possible co-ordinates – we are metres apart. Even he couldn't have designed it better.

Emotions alternatively flip. Relief he's not there for me, dismay that he's come to this, and pity for this bedraggled baggage of humanity I used to love. How this can happen in 1963 I wonder as I walk heavy-gutted to the bus stop? How can I enjoy Christmas now? I tell Brenda later, but she's not sympathetic. She has her own problems.

I need to talk with someone who understands the situation. George has given me his home number so I ring and hope he's in. His wife assumes I'm a colleague and gets him straight away.

'George?'

'Hello Lizzie. Is everything all right?'

'No. No, he's not in hospital. He can't be. I've seen him… in Piccadilly… begging. I'm not sure if he's homeless but I think he must be. He's been there for days. What should I do? I can't leave him there at Christmas!'

'Wait a minute. Are you quite sure it's him? I mean, they usually try to find them a room on discharge if they've nowhere to go. Mind you, housing is a problem in the city; there's never enough – but he may have had one – and blown it. I wouldn't be surprised. This is what happens when they're unstable.'

'So what will happen to him now?'

'I don't know, but it could go on and on and on. He may get help from the Council. Once out of the Mental hospital it's up to the Council – and the GP, who'll prescribe his drugs… if he'll take them of course, or it may turn into a never-ending circular thing, in and out, in and out. There's no easy answer.'

'Wouldn't it be better if he just stayed in hospital? I mean he'd be taken care of wouldn't he?'

'It all depends how bad he gets but there's something called the 1959 Mental Health Act, about moving towards closing down most mental institutions. They want it to be dealt with in

ROOM TO GROW

ordinary hospitals, or the community, but it'll be so expensive… it's going to take years and years before they can do that.'

'But surely his doctor will see he's bad enough to go into a hospital?'

'Well, he may do if he sees him. Yes, he may end up as an in-patient, but they'll probably try not to keep him. I just don't know. My advice to you is to leave well alone.'

'Sounds easy but I don't know if I can.'

'You'll be banging your head against a brick wall … and you're too young to have to worry about what should be the state's responsibility. Do you want to ruin your life running round trying to help – with no guarantee of success or your own safety?'

'No – I don't know what I want to do. I just wanted to see if I could do something, contact someone who could help him, anybody, anything.'

'It would tie you up in knots trying to deal with it Lizzie,… believe me. I've done it. I've seen it with my brother. You've got to forget about him – and keep yourself safe. If it's any consolation some charities provide Christmas meals for the homeless and find shelter for them. Look, I'll contact one of them, and the Council too – I know what to say and I have contacts. I'll do that so you can get on and enjoy Christmas!'

I thank him. It sort of absolves me. George is now a friend. He's older and more experienced with all this and I'm going to stand back like he advises. That will be my New Year resolution. Stand back. It's not my fault and I mustn't get into that anxious state and start doubting my own sanity again. I'm not responsible for this and I mustn't let it ruin Christmas, or affect my family and friends. But such a heartless decision to make; to leave my

324

lost love to his fate, especially at Christmas. And it sounds like closing mental institutions will need a long transitional period. What hope for Colin?

SUNDAY 22ND DEC

Last night: Seeing him did something to my mind and entered my dreams.

Weird dreams; situations magically changing but unquestionably real like this one. A fat Santa Claus tips children's gifts onto the pavement where Colin sits, then strides purposefully away towards a large sleigh – which was a bus just moments ago! Colin sifts through the gifts. He selects a toy trumpet and plays a mournful tune which wakes me with a start. For just a few seconds it's real. These are delusions. I didn't choose to hear that trumpet or see those images; they simply appeared without cues. Colin doesn't choose his either. How stange the mind is.

Later: Met Jenny tonight in the Seymour. I didn't tell her about seeing Colin or about talking to George. She wouldn't understand the conflicting emotions or the insoluble situation. She's decisive and hard. 'For God's sake Lizzie – get over it,' she'd say. 'Don't waste your pity. Get another one, preferably in his right mind!'

She's seen the horseowning councillor this week and has a suggestion.

'Listen Lizzie. I was thinking of you. You want to move don't you? That councillor. He'll have some influence over housing I'm sure. Do you want him to put you on the housing list – sort of high up? I'm well in with him you know. They're thinking of building some lovely 'deck access' flats in Hulme when they've demolished the area. But it won't be for ages though. Be great for you in the future, modern and right near the city. Streets in the sky they're calling them. *Streets in the sky* I think! Pies in the sky more like. We've war loans to pay!

'I doubt I'd be a priority, even with a nudge from him. There's thousands on the housing list. Besides I'm already fixed up. I move in January,' I say. Nice of her to think of me though. I'll miss her like I'll miss Bob.

She moves to London straight after Christmas. We've promised our friendship won't fizzle out with distance and I'll stay with her for a few days after the New Year when she's settled. That's two friends out of immediate hugging reach. But they have to move on. They need room to grow like I do.

MONDAY 23RD DEC

I've already started to pack up some things ready for January – only just over a week away. Brenda came down to see me this evening – so pale I thought she was about to throw up but people say you can look like that in the early weeks. We talked for ages. I'm not going far but our rooms have been only yards apart and I'm going to miss the nearness. Another one out of hugging reach. We talked for ages.

'Don't you want children Lizzie? she asks at some point.

'Not sure. If they can't talk, cry all the time and wet

themselves – probably not babies. After the age of four maybe…
but they don't arrive like that do they?… So don't ask me to
babysit will you!'

'You'd be a brilliant babysitter. We'll get you booked as soon
as it arrives,' she laughs.

TUES. 24TH/WED. 25TH DEC

Christmas Eve and early hours of Christmas Day. Just returned
with Janet, Andy, Brenda and Tony so these are just jottings
before bed. Evening at 'The Oaks' then party at Mike's. Parents
out. Great night. Didn't dwell on the Colin situation.

Mike's unwary parents find a bunch of teens/twenties and
a half-consumed drinks cabinet on their return from a
neighbour's party. They stand at the living room door looking
bewildered.

'Who are all these people?' asks his dad. 'I thought you were
just going to the Oaks for a quiet drink.'

'We were …and we did,' says Mike flushed with drink. 'But
that was with everyone in the whole pub. We wanted to celebrate
with …more special friends, you know, like you've just done.'

They can't argue with that, or fault our behaviour. Saintly
compared to my birthday party, but we're six months older and
wiser.

'You might have told us though,' he says eyeing an empty
Vodka bottle. He's a bit tipsy himself but genial and relaxed. 'Ok,
OK. you lot. It's Christmas and you've had a good time and not
disturbed anyone or made a mess … Happy Christmas everyone.

Cheers. Nice to see you all, hope you've enjoyed yourselves – but nice to see you all go home now,' he says jokingly.

We politely take our leave. I'm going 'home' tomorrow for Christmas Day and it's two o'clock in the morning. I'll need some sleep.

WEDNESDAY 25TH DEC

Lovely day at 'home'. Asked for and got money presents. Five pounds from parents and two from my grandma. Also perfume, talc, a powder compact and a hat and scarf set Mum had knitted. Theirs were easy. They all got slippers from one shop. Mr Dodds came for lunch and got some Boots shaving gear from the family.

It was like other Christmas Days, except for Mr Dodds, but I actually like the sherry, turkey lunch, Queen's speech routine as well as the presents. It's comfortingly predictable – as if the same people will be doing the same Christmassy things each year for ever. The Christmas tree had new lights flashing on and off like a bolisha beacon and the same motley collection of baubles and random Christmassy objects. The Christmas fairy/angel should be retired. She'd definitely passed her prime and looked tatty.

And Mr Dodds? Mum had 'picked up' the old man, through her cinema job and invited him for Christmas lunch so he wouldn't be on his own. She has a Christian's kind heart but isn't one. Mr Dodds is ancient. Seventy-nine, born in 1884. Imagine that! The bicycle had only just been invented and Vincent van Gogh had just cut off his ear.

We listen spellbound to this World War One soldier survivor who'd left school at eleven and lived in a two-up two-down, gaslit, rented terrace without bathroom or indoor toilet. He sips his sherry, his gnarled old hands trembling so you're sure he'll spill it, and speaks with the quavery voice of the old, but he can tell a good tale.

We're fascinated by sordid accounts of 'night soil' men coming in the night to empty the outdoor 'privies', the contents splattering down the side of the vehicle and the sharing of the weekly tin bath with his brothers. He's living history, a sort of portable museum. We turn on the TV at three o'clock for the Queen. He listens a while, nods a little, head drops to chest then sleeps through the speech.

THURSDAY 26TH DEC

Boxing day. I learned it's called Boxing Day because the upper classes used to give their servants their Christmas box on this day. A pay rise would have been a better gesture. Went to the Kings. Janet and Andy squabbled all evening. So romantic! Cheesy Christmassy songs were playing but after a few drinks everyone loved it.

FRI 27TH DEC1963

Christmas is over. Back to work. Walked again at lunchtime. I told myself I was going shopping but was drawn to the area

I'd seen 'him' in the other day – even though I knew it would disturb me. It's like having a sore in your mouth. You know you shouldn't but you run your tongue over it, even though it smarts. Why did I do it?

He's in the same place again, the same shabby blanket round his shoulders. He's sitting on a sleeping bag his face and arms leaning on raised knees. There's a cap with coins in it and an open rucksack by his side. Surely it's temporary. Couldn't he go in a café or find something more comfortable? Why the sleeping bag? I hope he doesn't sleep outside as well.

I'm tempted to run to him, snatch away that old blanket, hold him, tell him he's not alone; that I'll share his troubles and help with every ounce of strength I have. There's an invisible cord binding us. Once you've bonded with someone it doesn't break easily, even if you want it to.

I feel tears; a trickle at first, then my face beginning to grimace. It makes my head feel tight and I want to gasp. Please do not cry in a public place. I swallow and tighten my body. Hold it. Don't cry. People will look curiously at you. They'll be embarrassed, as if you're attention-seeking; crying in public like some unfortunate fool or abandoned child. I look at him; at his dislocation from human warmth, his false sense of reality, his diminished future. I'm feeling love, hurtful, pitying love and I am crying because he needs someone, and it can't be me.

But the objective, reasoning part of my brain is working. Don't be a fool. Don't waste your escape route now and ruin the plan. You can avoid that fear; that dread of being physically hurt, that inability to be in control if you're strong enough to just let it go. Let it go before you're sucked into an emotionally spiralling vortex. I take one last look, wipe my eyes and walk away.

SATURDAY 28TH DEC

It's the Christmas anti climax. 1964 is on it's way but now time to recover from rich food, drinking and late nights. My Christmas money was burning holes in my pocket, so I spent it in Littlewoods and C&A. sneaking through Lewis's and Littlewoods to Oldham Street to avoid the chance of seeing him in Piccadilly. Evening: College work. I must binge work for a day or two and have no more seasonal excuses.

SUNDAY 29 DEC

Brenda is getting married soon. I'd like to be a bridesmaid with a pastel-coloured dress and clutch of flowers but it's not that sort of wedding. She thinks her bump might be showing and wants a quiet do – family and close friends. Janet and Andy are getting engaged at last – that's another party looming. Neither things appeal to me now. They can creep up and happen to you but I'm choosing now. I want to be a teacher. Men are welcome if they can fit in but that's how it is. Brenda was dying to tell me about it though.

'We're getting married Lizzie! In February,' she squeals as we meet on the stairs. She's looking radiant. I'm pleased of course, but will it settle her down I wonder. Tony seems a nice guy, steady, reliable and quiet but I know she can't survive without an exciting love life and I just hope he's enough in domesticity. Her restlessness and roving eye could wreck it but I hope motherhood steadies her. We hug mid stair which nearly tips us off balance.

'I'm so glad for you.'

'It'll be you one day,' she assures me.

'Doesn't look like it,' I say cheerfully, but I don't mind being the single one now. What was the problem?

'Nineteen sixty-four will be your year Lizzie, I know it,' she says. 'And we want you to be a Matron of Honour at the wedding.'

I've never thought of myself as a matron: big buxom women like Hattie Jacques, harsh of tongue, and feared by nurses, are matrons, but I agree to the role.

'Oh thanks. I'd love to,' I say trying to imagine a matronly outfit. 'On condition you throw your flowers at me – like a bridesmaid – and I have a nice hat.'

TUESDAY 31ST DEC: AFTERNOON:

Tonight, a new programme called *Top of the Pops* begins on BBC TV, The Rolling Stones will be first to perform, then 'The Dave Clerk Five'. It's being televised in a building on Dickenson Road only about a mile from here and will be its regular venue with all the best bands and groups! Jimmy Saville, the Disc Jockey I listen to on Radio Luxembourg, will be presenting it. I like listening to his programme but he's very weird, makes strange yodelling noises and looks a bit like a clown. Definitely something strange about him.

NEW BEGINNINGS

TUES EVENING, 31ST DECEMBER TO EARLY WEDNESDAY MORNING, 1ST JANUARY 1964 :

Janet, Andy and I spent the last night of 1963 in bars on Brazonose Street and Princess Street in the city centre near Albert Square before congregating with hundreds of others on the square to let in the new year. We all kissed loads of people and lost Andy, last seen kissing a girl who'd almost swallowed him and seemed to have lost her shoes.

This decades-old Manchester tradition goes like this: drink lots of alcohol, gather on Albert Square, then wait for the town hall clock to strike twelve. At the last stroke, kiss friends and pretty much everyone else repeating the 'Happy New Year' mantra. Repeat in a year's time. All over in about fifteen minutes swapping enough germs to sustain colds, herpes and flu for weeks.

Then the rush for taxis, sometimes sharing with total strangers drunk going the same way, or think they are because they've forgotten which way they should be. Older folk sensibly count down minutes with Big Ben on the telly. I'll be like that one day.

LATER WEDNESDAY, MORNING OF JANUARY 1ST 1964.

I'm moving into my new flat tomorrow. New year, new flat, new life! Unhappy links to the past all severed. These are first and last notes for 1964. I'll use the time, effort and discipline on further education and I've enrolled for three more O Levels, even though the term began in September. It will bring me closer to a teaching career so a journal may have to wait. I'm tempted to keep very brief notes though in my new diary – just in case I change my mind because 1964 will be special. I can feel it in the air. War babies have boomed and grown and are making themselves heard. 'Times they are a Changing.' Yes they are. It will be the start of something and the world will be better for it.

This book is printed on paper from sustainable sources managed under the Forest Stewardship Council (FSC) scheme.

It has been printed in the UK to reduce transportation miles and their impact upon the environment.

For every new title that Matador publishes, we plant a tree to offset CO_2, partnering with the More Trees scheme.

For more about how Matador offsets its environmental impact, see www.troubador.co.uk/about/